# Players

## A Detectives Seagate and Miner Mystery

### Book 7

**MIKE MARKEL**

# Players

## A Detectives Seagate and Miner Mystery
## Book 7

ISBN-13: 978-1537298757
ISBN-10: 1537298755

# *Prologue*

She had been sitting on a small folding stool for almost an hour, and now her back was seizing up. That was one of the things she missed the most: a real chair. But a chair wouldn't fit. She struggled to her feet and, holding the tent pole for balance, bent at the waist to stretch her muscles. Last week, one of the guys helped her lash the tent to the shipping pallet on which it sat. Since then, she hadn't worried that the tent would blow over in the winds, which she had seen happen. As your world gets smaller, she thought, small things become bigger.

She couldn't make up her mind whether to do it. For the longest while, she stared at the aluminum foil cigarette wrapper inside the clear baggie. She reached a decision. Rummaging through the clothing and boxes of crackers and water jugs scattered around the tent, she found her jacket under an old blanket.

The rain had started some time ago, plopping on the roof and on the bags and lawn furniture and charcoal grills and the fifty-five gallon drum that served as a fire pit out near the center of the clearing. Drops had started to soak through the seams of her roof; soon they would begin to drop steadily onto her things.

She slid on her jacket and carefully sealed the plastic zipper on the baggie. The bulge inside the foil wrapper felt like three or four good-sized hits. Crouching, she made her way over to the flap. She emerged from the tent and zipped up the flap.

The guys who had been sitting in the lawn chairs around the drum had left a few minutes ago. The fire in the drum, already hissing in the drizzle, would last only a few more minutes.

Off to the right, the lights from the trailer park illuminated the sky. Three of the trailers shone brightly, their residents not bothering to hide the reflections of the grow lights off the foil-covered walls. Off to the left was blackness. She stepped off her pallet, her feet sinking slightly into the damp dirt.

The clearing was a rough circle about thirty yards in diameter. Lights bled from four of the seven tents and makeshift huts of wood, sheet metal, and tarps that ringed the clearing. She walked slowly and deliberately past the plastic buckets, old tires, toys, shopping carts, and bikes, past the hissing drum and the weather-worn redwood picnic table. The plastic bags hanging from branches on the spruce, pine, and junipers glistened in the rain. Wet laundry hung from a rope clothesline that spanned two thick branches outside a tent.

She approached Lake's tent, which was as small as hers. She didn't know how he maneuvered inside; he was a few inches over six feet tall. The rain had already darkened the stained, threadbare quilt stuffed between the roof of the blue nylon tent and the bowed aluminum poles that held it upright. His tent sat on the bare ground; soon the floor would be wet through.

She unzipped the flap, crouched, and entered the tent. She tried to breathe through her mouth until she became acclimated to the stench of the rancid foods, the soiled clothing, and his body odor.

"Hey," she said. A slender black man in his late twenties, he lay on the wadded-up blankets and foam padding that served as his bed. His head and feet distended the sides of his tent. His hair was uncut, with small grey tufts along the temples and in his beard. He wore a ragged gym-grey sweatshirt over a black T-shirt, navy sweatpants, and mismatched tube socks. He lifted his head slightly to see who had entered the tent. She lowered herself onto the overturned plastic bucket that served as a chair, then held up the baggie and smiled.

"What the fuck are you doing?" He raised up his trunk and leaned on an elbow. "I told you I don't have no money."

She shrugged. "Maybe I'm not asking you for no money."

He looked wary. "Yeah, well, that'd be the first time."

She started to lift herself off the plastic bucket. "If you don't want any, I'll find someone else."

He smiled. "No, no, baby, that's not what I'm saying." His tone was gentle. "That's not it, at all."

She returned his smile. "I didn't think so."

"You wanna close up the flap?"

She stood up halfway, grabbed the tent pole for balance, and duck-walked over to the flap to zip it up. When she turned back to him, he was sitting up, cross-legged. He had removed his sweatshirt. In his hand were a tiny spoon, a butane lighter, and a syringe. He pointed to the baggie. "You just get this?"

She frowned and shook her head. "Had it a while." She opened the baggie and removed the foil wrapper. She unfolded the wrapper and tapped the grey powder into the spoon, then leaned over and dribbled saliva onto it.

He lit the butane lighter and held the flame under the spoon. Almost instantly, it began to bubble and turn a darker grey. He loaded the drug into the syringe and slid the needle into the flap of skin between the index finger and middle finger of his left hand. His blood snaked into the syringe. Then, with a steady motion, he pushed the handle down. Within seconds, his eyes clouded, his eyelids drooped, and the syringe slipped out of his hand.

"This is good shit." His voice was low and slurred. He looked at her, confused that she was on her knees, next to him, staring at him. "Ain't you gonna do any, baby?"

"Maybe I will. Just a little."

He smiled. "That's it. Take a little pop, and we'll see if we can get something going. I ain't got any money right at the moment," he said, "but you know I'm good for it."

"I know that. I know you're good for it."

She picked up the syringe and held it up to the lantern hanging from a nail in the pole. There was still some hit mixed in with his blood. She pulled up the right leg of her sweatpants and raised the syringe to her calf. Pretending to shoot a little into the muscle, she closed her eyes and made a low moaning sound, as if she were feeling the warmth. She dropped the syringe and crawled over to him.

He had collapsed back onto the dirty foam pad. He rocked to one side, then the other, pulling his sweatpants down in small, slow movements. He wore no underwear.

She removed her jacket and pulled up her sweatshirt and her T-shirt, exposing her breasts. Then she lowered her trunk toward his face. But his eyes, half-closed, did not focus, and his head did not move.

Lowering her T-shirt and sweatshirt, she raised her trunk. She glanced at his groin and saw that his penis was flaccid. She put her ear to his mouth to listen for his breathing, straining to hear it over the tapping of the rain on the tent and the breeze rustling the leaves and the brush. He was already gone or soon would be.

Suddenly, fatigue swept over her. She lay down next to him, snuggling close to get onto the foam padding. Shivering in the cool night air, she tried to grasp some bedding to pull up over herself, but there wasn't enough. She didn't have the strength to move him even an inch to free up a tattered blanket. In seconds, she fell asleep, snuggled against his still-warm body.

Sometime later, she heard a distant voice outside the tent.

"Lake, we're going into town in the morning. You want to come?"

Trying to crawl back into consciousness, she saw a man's face shadowed against the tent flap. The zipper started to move, and the face came into view. "Sorry, man, didn't know you had company." The mouth twisted into a smile and then disappeared. The zipper on the flap closed.

Lake was motionless. She touched his cheek, which had already begun to cool. She picked up the syringe lying next to him on the quilt. She held it up to the lamp and thought for a moment. She pulled up the leg of her sweatpants, bent her knee, and raised the syringe to her calf. This time, she inserted the needle into the muscle and squeezed the handle, just a little. After a few seconds, the warmth began to spread through her body. As she lay back down, her fingers relaxed, and the syringe slipped out of her hand. She drifted off to a dreamless sleep, far away from the still body next to her. She did not feel the cold drops that had begun to drip onto her right hip from a pinhole in the roof of the putrid nylon tent.

# *Chapter 1*

It was 7:59 Monday morning when I hung my coat up on the rack in the corner of the detectives' bullpen. Phones rang, computers clicked, printers hummed, and people chatted about their weekends as they settled in to work. The smell of fresh coffee filled the air. I threaded my way through the maze of desks and filing cabinets and the bustle of uniforms and civilian assistants carrying files and envelopes. I approached my desk, which is arranged head-to-head with Ryan's. He was sitting in his chair, and one of the third-shift guys, Pelton, was sitting in mine.

During the bad old days, when I danced every night away with my lover Jack Daniel, I would roll into work around nine-thirty or ten because I knew that Chief Arnold, a corrupt, nasty troll, didn't arrive until closer to eleven. With his taste for strip clubs, he didn't find early mornings any easier than I did. Only after he fired me did I realize the main reason we hated each other so intensely: We were quite similar in important ways.

But now, during the less-bad new days, I dance with Jack only once or twice a year, after declining his persistent daily invitations. And I have a new boss, Chief Murtaugh, who arrives by six to lift weights for an hour and expects me to be at my desk at eight sharp.

*Expects* means two things: It's a job requirement, and I do it. For most people, showing up on time, sober and wearing clean, puke-free clothes, doesn't call for a celebration. Since it's still a fairly new experience for me, however, I think about it every day.

When I saw Pelton sitting in my chair, at my desk, my first thought was, Well, that's not my chair anymore, not my desk. But then I realized it would be the chief, not another detective, delivering the news. And the location would the chief's office. No, Pelton wasn't there to tell me to clear out my desk. More likely, he was there to drop a bag-of-shit case on me and Ryan.

"Good morning, guys." I made eye contact first with Ryan, then with Pelton.

Pelton rose out of my chair. He was about fifty, face getting a little puffy, body losing its angles. Tie undone, shirt blousing around his waist. But he was still in the game, still trying hard to be a good detective. "Hey, Karen." I caught a whiff of an apology in his tone.

I turned to Ryan. "How bad is it?"

Ryan put on a thoughtful expression. "Seven point five. Maybe eight."

Pelton spoke. "Homeless guy OD'ed."

"Wonderful. Downtown?"

Pelton looked uncomfortable as he shook his head. "Ten Mile Park. It just came in. Less than a half-hour ago."

I raised an eyebrow. "You know, I can look up when the call was logged. I'll know if you're lying."

Pelton gave me a sad smile, turned, and walked slowly toward the coat rack. His gait said his back hurt.

Ten Mile Park was about fifty acres of undeveloped scrub land off of Ten Mile Road. The city bought it about a dozen years ago at a fire-sale price. They hired some land-use people to study different plans, but the group concluded the land was too ugly and too far away from any housing developments to be worth putting money into. Then, when the recession hit and there wasn't any money to put into anything, the city changed its position to "Park? What park?"

Adjacent to Ten Mile Park, on the other side of Ten Mile

Road, sat Lyric Mobile Estate. Lyric was built thirty or forty years ago on county land just outside the Rawlings city jurisdiction. With low taxes and almost no services, it remained a squalid dump where the adults didn't work, the kids didn't go to school, and the feral cats duked it out with the rats and raccoons for the food scraps in black plastic bags outside the dilapidated trailers.

Actually, quite a few of the adults at Lyric did work. They grew, cut, cooked, and packaged the dope that the rural junkies bought before heading across Ten Mile Road to get wasted and pass out in Ten Mile Park.

I turned to Ryan. "Him dropping this case on us—this is exactly why all women think all men are assholes."

"Thank you. I was wondering about that." He nodded his appreciation. "You want to tell the chief we're going to take a ride?" He turned and started walking out of the detectives' bullpen toward the chief's office.

Because I didn't have a rich asshole to support me so I wouldn't have to drive a half hour to a homeless camp in a butt crack of a park to figure out exactly how some junkie killed himself, I followed Ryan out of the bullpen.

We walked past the incident room, the dispatch call center, and some administrative offices and storage rooms until we reached the little hallway that led to the chief's suite. Margaret, his gatekeeper, looked up from her computer and gave us an official smile and an official "Good morning" before picking up her phone to officially ask him if he was free. A second later she nodded to us.

Chief Robert Murtaugh looked up from his computer. "Good morning, Karen. Ryan." He gestured for us to sit in the chairs facing his desk. He was in his mid- to late-fifties, hair going grey, jaw still strong, no fat on him at all. He wore his daily uniform: dark two-button suit, pale blue shirt showing fold marks, and subdued tie. You could count on it, just as you could count on his precisely chosen words: direct, semi-formal, no-nonsense. The understanding was that, in exchange for us not wasting his time with small talk about football or fishing or some other crap, he would stop whatever he was doing and give us his full attention for however long we needed.

Because I took no interest in football or fishing, I considered it an excellent deal.

He glanced at his watch. "Caught a case already?"

"Yeah," I said. "Think we caught it from Pelton and Malone."

He gave me an understated smile. "Would you like to file a formal complaint?"

"A homeless guy in the camp at Ten Mile Park."

He nodded empathetically. I thought he was saying he was sorry. Then I decided he was saying he would have tried to drop it on the next shift, too. Then I realized he was saying both of those things. "We know it's homicide?"

Ryan shook his head. "We don't know anything, except that the first officer said he thought it was an OD. Probably accident or suicide."

"Need something from me?"

I shook my head. "Just telling you we're gonna head out there."

"Make it a great day."

This time I understood what he was saying. I put on a disappointed expression. "Sorry, I already have other plans."

We left the chief's office and headed back to the bullpen. As I was sliding into my coat, I said to Ryan, "Did Pelton tell you anything about the vic?"

"Black guy, my age."

"We'll need to inform Harold and Robin." Harold Breen was our medical examiner. Robin was our evidence tech.

"I already did. They'll be out there soon."

Over the two years we've partnered, Ryan and I had

established a good routine. He did most of the routine stuff without asking me. He was only thirty, but a mature thirty. He knew that unless the death is obviously natural causes—a ninety-year old sitting at the bingo table at the home clutches his chest, makes a croaking sound, then croaks—the medical examiner needed to rule it an accident, suicide, or homicide. And we needed to have the evidence tech there to start taking pictures and video and cataloging all the evidence in case it became a case.

I realized I did like Ryan and Chief Murtaugh. A dead homeless guy out in the woods, first thing Monday morning, before I even got some coffee? Not so much.

We got in our shiny Charger. When we phased in our new vehicles a few years ago, we decided to get black-and-white Dodge Chargers for our officers and dark grey Dodge Chargers for our detectives. Not that the grey Chargers fool anyone. They've got red, amber, and blue strobe lights mounted inside the cabin, near the rear window, with a big searchlight next to the driver-side rearview mirror. Plus, sticking up between the front seats, a laptop and the barrel of a Remington 870 shotgun.

I like the message the computer and the rifle send: First, we're going to find you, and then, if you try to run away, we'll shoot you. In the nineteen years I've been with Rawlings Police Department, I can't remember any of us grabbing the shotgun and spraying some shot, but I'm good with the bad guys knowing this isn't a video game. When we tell you to get down on your knees and put your hands behind your head—which we have to do surprisingly often—we don't want you to do anything else. We don't even want you to consider it.

Ryan and I headed west out of town on State Road 16, past the RV and no-credit-no-problem used-car dealers, payday-loan joints, gun shops, and the neon-window restaurants. Because Rawlings is a pretty small place, in normal traffic it takes only about five minutes to get to 1956.

Thirty minutes later, we reached the intersection with Ten Mile Road, which is ten miles from the main street in town. In Montana, we don't put a lot of effort into naming the streets.

We headed south on Ten Mile. Off to the right we passed Linder Lane, the rutted entrance to Lyric Mobile Estate. A little bit farther, we turned into Ten Mile Park and followed the two-lane toward the parking area, which was taped off. We parked along the shoulder of the entrance road, right behind the 1968 Beetle painted black and white. Not like a police car, like a cow.

Its owner, Robin, had already placed a bunch of numbered evidence markers on the dirt parking area. When she heard us approach, she looked up. "Hey, cops." She offered us a wide, toothy smile. Except for the paper booties over her ski boots, she could have been heading off to the slopes: red wool beret, a powder-blue ski jacket, and black leggings. "Sorry about taping off the lot. There're some new tire tracks from the rain last night I wanted to shoot."

"Yeah?"

She pointed to some tracks ten feet away. "I think that one's a dually pickup."

"Did the driver get out of the truck?" I said.

"I don't think so." Robin pushed a strand of her blue-tipped blond hair behind her ear. I counted six or seven new holes running up the cartilage, each filled with a tiny colored glass chip. She saw me looking and struck a pose. "What do you think?"

"I think, if you're happy, I'm happy." I turned back toward the taped-off parking area. "You got the path taped off, too?"

"Yeah, sorry. There could be some interesting shoe prints."

"How do we get to the camp?"

"Truman and I hacked a rough path off to the side there." She pointed. Truman must have been the first officer on scene. "The camp's less than a hundred yards." She looked at Ryan, who was wearing his MBA outfit: navy blue suit and black wool overcoat. She gestured to his shiny black wingtips. "Those were nice shoes."

Ryan smiled and reached into his pocket, pulled out a pair of booties, and slipped them on. We trudged along the path, pushing aside the branches and brambles as we walked, until we arrived at the encampment, our coats wet and our feet muddy.

This was one of those times I wish I had taken school more seriously.

# *Chapter 2*

The camp was a big circle filled with busted bikes, shopping carts, old tires, and other assorted junk. Bags hung from tree limbs, presumably to make it a little harder for the critters to grab stuff. Rope clotheslines criss-crossed the trees that formed the perimeter of the clearing. I counted seven tents and other shelters of timber, corrugated metal, and blue plastic tarps.

We walked toward Officer Truman, who was standing next to a picnic table, talking with four guys ranging in age from around twenty to more than sixty. They slouched, hands in pockets, feet shuffling back and forth on the wet dirt.

When they heard us squishing our way toward them, they looked up. Their expressions were a mixture of sadness and resignation. I couldn't tell if they knew the vic well or liked him, but this bunch of guys, who lived pretty close to the edge, seemed upset that someone had just fallen off.

Truman nodded and came over to meet us.

"What've you got?" I said.

"One of these guys, Walter Ramsey, called it in on his cell a little after seven this morning. Said he saw the vic, lying on his bed, pants down around his knees. Ramsey said he couldn't see the vic breathing, so he went into the tent, saw he was dead, came back out, phoned 911."

"So the crime scene's been compromised?"

"Yeah," Truman said. "If it's a crime scene."

"Did Ramsey say he thought it was an OD because he knew

the vic was a junkie, or did he see something?"

"Not sure. But he told me he didn't touch anything in the vic's tent."

"Has Robin gone over the tent yet?"

"No, she wanted to start out at the parking area before the tire tracks got messed up."

"Have you seen Harold Breen yet?"

"No, not yet."

"All right, Truman. Thanks. Which one's Walter Ramsey?"

He gestured with his chin. "Tan slicker, blue baseball hat."

Ryan and I walked over to him. "Mr. Ramsey, my name is Detective Seagate. This is my partner, Detective Miner."

Ramsey nodded. He was about fifty, wearing a plastic rain parka over a couple of sweatshirts, muddy dark cotton pants, and sneakers, soaked through, no socks. He needed a shave, a haircut, and two or three teeth on the bottom, near the front. The other guys stood there, hands in pockets, with downcast expressions.

"Can you tell me when you found the body?"

"Around seven, seven-thirty this morning."

"You went over to his tent?"

He nodded.

"Why was that?"

"Couple of us were gonna head into town, go to the Mission, get some breakfast. I went to see if he wanted to come with us."

"What was his name?"

"Lake."

"Lake? Is that a first name? Last name?"

Walter Ramsey shrugged.

"How long's he been living here?"

He thought for a second. "Two months, maybe three." He looked at the other three guys, who nodded.

"Was he a junkie?"

He was silent a moment. "We got a few rules here. Don't

steal; don't cheat. That's all. Lake kept to himself."

"You know if he had a girlfriend? A boyfriend?"

"Not that I know of."

"Is there a woman who sleeps with the guys, you know, for money?"

"Don't know of anyone like that."

"A guy?"

Walter Ramsey shook his head.

"You think of anyone he had a problem with? Anyone who'd want to hurt him?"

"He didn't steal, didn't cheat."

"Right," I said. "I got that." I turned to the other guys. "Can any of you help us figure out what happened to Lake?"

One of the three looked up and shook his head. Another said no. The third one didn't lift his gaze from the wet dirt.

Ryan said, "The people who live here—any of them women?"

Walter Ramsey said, "There's one woman here. Named Kendra."

I said to him, "You didn't think to tell me that?"

Walter Ramsey shrugged. "You didn't ask."

"Got a last name?"

They all shook their heads.

"She here now, in the camp?"

"No," Walter Ramsey said.

"You know where she is?"

He shook his head. "She comes and goes. She's not here every night."

"What do you know about her?"

"She don't steal—"

"And she don't cheat." I nodded. "Which tent is hers?"

Ramsey pointed to a grey camping tent, sitting on wooden shipping pallets.

I took out four cards and handed them to the men. "Thanks,

guys. You think of something, you let me know." They nodded and drifted away.

I started walking over to Kendra's tent. I stepped onto the wooden pallet and was about to open the flap when Ryan called my name. I turned and looked up.

"We can't touch it," he said.

"Come on. It's a tent, on city land."

"It's private property," Ryan said. "We need a warrant."

I shook my head, but he was right. I walked around to the side, where there was a screened window under a flap. "Can I look through the screen?"

He smiled. "I think we can do that."

I peered in. It was pitch black. "You got a flash?"

He handed me a small high-intensity flashlight, but I couldn't make out anything other than a camping cot, some scattered clothing, cardboard boxes, and a plastic folding stool.

When I walked over to give Ryan his flashlight back, he raised his eyebrows to ask me what I'd seen. I just shook my head. "You think the dead guy'd be okay with us looking at his shit?"

Ryan smiled. "I think it's more about the Constitution of the State of Montana."

"We have one of them?"

We walked over to the vic's tent. I unzipped the flap. "Since Walter's been inside—and Pelton and Malone—the floor's already been compromised."

Ryan nodded. We snapped on our gloves, crouched down, and entered the tiny tent.

"Whoa," I said. "It's a little ripe in here. That's not dead-guy smell, is it?"

"Little bit." Ryan had a handkerchief over his nose. "Mostly, unwashed-guy."

Ryan shined his flashlight on Lake's face. He was a black man, black hair and beard, untrimmed. He was lying on a dirty foam-

Players
19

rubber pad maybe four inches thick and covered with several soiled blankets and quilts. He wore a T-shirt, which had been pulled halfway up his chest. His sweatpants were pulled down to the middle of his thighs. I didn't see any underpants. By his side were a lighter, a small dope spoon, a syringe, an empty baggie, and a silver-foil cigarette wrapper used to package drugs.

Ryan poked around, looking for pockets that might contain a wallet or some ID. I started to feel around under the foam pad and in the clothing and other items on the tent floor.

I turned to Ryan. "Why are his pants down?"

He scratched at his chin. "Well, maybe he was preparing to have sex. Or he already had sex."

"Maybe he was yanking it?"

"Or he was yanking it." Ryan nodded. "Or he was looking for a new vein."

"Good morning, detectives." I turned. It was Harold Breen, our medical examiner, standing outside the tent, crouched over so he could look in.

Ryan and I greeted him. Harold was breathing heavily. At more than three-hundred pounds, he always breathed heavily. Usually, he was quite cheerful, but today, standing there in a wet parka with mud halfway up his brown polyester pants, he didn't seem at all happy.

He gestured to the victim. "The nerve of some people," he said. "Robin gone over this already?"

"No," I said.

"But we're pretty sure he's dead, right?"

"Yes, we are."

"Good, no way I could get in there and back out without knocking the thing over. As soon as Robin's done here, I'll bring him in and get him on the table. What do we think happened to him?"

"There's a drug kit next to his left hand," I said.

Harold nodded. "Seeing way too much of that these days." He paused. "You need me for anything?"

"No," I said. "You'll coordinate with Robin?"

"You bet."

Harold stepped back so Ryan and I could leave the smelly tent. We headed toward the path that Robin and Truman had made. Back at the parking area, we walked over to Robin, who was crouched down, shooting some photos with a serious-looking camera with a big lens.

"Harold's at the vic's tent," I said. "He told us he'd wait until you went over it."

"Anything in particular you want to know?"

"Everything. We couldn't find any ID on him. Start with trying to figure out who the hell he was. His kit is right next to him. What was he using? Did he want to kill himself? Did he just do too much? Was there someone else shooting up with him? One other thing: His pants are down. Was he screwing someone? Flying solo? Looking for a vein?"

"In other words, you don't know anything yet." She sniffed, then wrinkled her nose. "You two don't smell too good."

"We'll discuss that later, after you go over his tent."

"Oh."

"Yeah, oh," I said. "All we know is the guys called him Lake. The rest, you're gonna tell us, sometime this afternoon."

"The other guys at the camp didn't give you anything but a name?"

I shook my head. "Not sure they know his name. Doubt they'd tell us if they did."

# *Chapter 3*

I came back to my desk with a coffee and swapped out my wet shoes for a dry pair that I keep in a desk drawer. Ryan was already on his computer. "Find him yet?"

Ryan shook his head. "Tried *Lake* as a first name and a last one. Is that short for something?"

"Not that I can think of," I said. "Let me see if Robin found something in his tent." I picked up my desk phone and hit the four numbers. "Hey, Robin, who's our vic in the tent?"

"A guy who liked to stay off the grid."

"No ID, no papers?"

"Nothing."

"Well, shit," I said.

"You're very welcome," Robin said.

I hung up. "Let me see if Harold's got him up on the table yet." I phoned him, and he invited us to come on down. "Terrific." I thanked him.

Ryan and I went downstairs and walked past the shooting range and Robin's office. Ryan opened the wide, heavy door to Harold Breen's lab.

Before I could even see Lake on the steel table, I knew he was there. He had already funked up the whole lab, even with an HVAC system strong enough to reshuffle a deck of cards.

I turned to Ryan. "I'll stay here. You go talk to Harold." Lake wasn't mangled or anything, and Harold hadn't yet started to gut him or peel back his scalp; still, I wanted to let the dead rest in peace, preferably on the other side of the room.

As Ryan took up a position next to him, Harold turned and said to me, "Does Mr. Doe have a name yet?"

"We can't find him in our system or the obvious databases, and Robin couldn't find anything," I said. "If we can't identify him soon, we'll get serious and track it down."

Ryan and Harold were silent for a minute. Finally, Ryan said, "Did Robin figure out if he had sex?"

"She took some swabs. No semen or vaginal fluids on his penis."

"Was he looking for a vein?"

"I don't think so." The medical examiner looked up and ran a forearm across his forehead and his bald head to squeegee off some of the perspiration, even though it couldn't have been more than sixty-five degrees in the lab. "There's a fresh-looking track down here." Harold pointed to Lake's left hand.

"Can't imagine needing the drug so bad you're willing to inject it between your fingers," Ryan said.

Harold Breen sighed. "If this guy could reach a spot, he left tracks there. On his palms, behind his knees, on his feet and ankles, on his forehead."

"So he's been an addict a long while?"

"Years."

"Other than that," Ryan said, "anything jump out at you?"

"Nothing that explains how he died. He hadn't been to a dentist in a long while. One rotten tooth and one broken one. They must have hurt."

Ryan was frowning, looking at the vic's right leg. "Let me get in closer to the knee." Harold stepped aside as Ryan moved down a couple of feet. "Is that what I think it is?"

Harold leaned down. "Yeah, I think so. I'd have seen it on a scan, but good catch."

"What is it?" I said.

Ryan turned to me and offered a teasing smile. "Why don't you come on over and I'll show you?"

"Don't be a dick. Just tell me."

Ryan walked over to me, bent down, and pulled up his right pant leg. He pointed to a vertical scar, about four inches long, that started at the top of his kneecap and headed south. "You see these?" He pointed to two round scars flanking his kneecap, one to the left and one to the right of the long scar. "That's where they insert the instruments."

"The vic has the same scars?"

"That's right. He tore a ligament in his knee—the ACL. He had reconstructive surgery. Ten to one, he was an athlete."

"What sport?"

He gave me a sarcastic scowl. "A contact sport. Probably soccer, basketball, or football."

"Does the university have a men's soccer team?"

"No."

I turned to Harold. "How tall is he?"

"Seventy-four inches."

I looked at Ryan. "Tall enough for basketball?"

"Maybe."

"Which is it: basketball or football?"

"I'll guess football."

"Which position?"

Ryan gave me another look. "What do you say, Harold?"

Harold fanned out the fingers of his right hand and held it over the victim's hand. From across the room I could see the vic's fingers extending at least an inch beyond Harold's. "Wide receiver or tight end."

"Give me ten minutes." Ryan turned to leave. "I'll give you his name." He stopped and hurried back to the table, pulled his phone out of his inside jacket pocket, and took a picture of Lake's face.

"Thanks, Harold," I said. "I assume it's an OD, but tell me when you enter your prelim on the system, would you?"

"Sure."

I followed Ryan out of the lab and back up toward the detectives' bullpen. Ryan was already at his computer—he takes steps two at a time, three when he's excited.

"Who is he?"

He looked up at me and smiled. "Don't you have to get some coffee?"

"Come on, what's taking you?"

"His name was LaKadrian Williams. Put in some creamer and sugar and I'll have the rest of the story."

"LaKadrian. Okay, I'd use *Lake*, too."

Ryan was focused on his screen. I walked around behind him to see what he was looking at. It was some football site. I went back to my desk and sat down.

It was almost thirty seconds before Ryan spoke. "Lake was on a football scholarship at Central Montana State University for three years. He left the university seven years ago."

"He went pro?"

"Uh, no. I can't quite tell the circumstances, but he didn't go pro. I'm looking at some sites that handicap the draft picks. He was going to go in the second or third round, but that's where the story ends."

Ryan played football at Brigham Young. I didn't. "One question: What the hell did you just say?"

"What I said is that, when he was a junior at CMSU, the pro scouts were looking at him, and the people who handicap the process say he would have gotten a job on a professional team after he graduated. He would have made my salary."

"Your salary? That's all?"

"Yeah, every two weeks."

"But he didn't graduate."

"A lot of pros never graduated, but that's not the reason he didn't go pro."

"Okay, what is the reason?"

"I don't know. I'm just saying you don't have to graduate. You don't have to go to college at all. But something happened."

"The leg injury? Is that why you're a cop and not a pro football player?"

"No, I wasn't good enough even before I blew out my knee. But an ACL injury can end your career. When you go in for reconstructive surgery, they tell you the success rate is ninety, ninety-five percent. What they mean is, those are the odds you're going to walk again. What you hear is that those are the odds you're going to play at the same level as before."

"What are the chances of that?"

"About fifty percent. If you rush the rehab or blow it off, the odds go way down, and you can tear it again—and the second time you might not walk right again."

"Okay, you dig around a little and try to find out why he was living in a homeless camp instead of a mansion. I'll see if he's in the system."

It took me ten seconds to find him but two minutes to read it all; it was fairly lengthy. Ryan looked up when I started to speak. "LaKadrian Williams started shoplifting when he was a student."

"He got caught shoplifting on campus?"

I shrugged. "Maybe the bookstore or something. The food court."

"Anything else?"

"A few misdemeanor drug possessions. He moved up to distribution, which was a felony. There was one assault, while he was a student, against a guy named Cory McDermott, but McDermott never pressed charges."

"Does the arrest report say why?"

I shook my head.

"Let's see if we've got McDermott in the system." Ryan hit a few keys and waited a moment while it churned. He started to read. "Cory McDermott is a good customer."

"What's his specialty?"

"I'd say possession and distribution of controlled dangerous substances, including heroin, cocaine, and methamphetamines. He's been in and out of prison for the last eight years. Spends about six months in, then six months out."

"So Cory could be Lake's dealer."

"Sure." Ryan shrugged. "Or not."

"Do we have any contact information on Cory?"

"No known address. Let me try this phone." Ryan punched in a number and put it on Speaker, but the recorded message said the number had been disconnected.

"Cory and Lake are the same age, right?"

Ryan looked at the screen. "Lake was about a year older."

"You have access to the student system at Central Montana?"

He nodded, then hit some keys and watched the screen. "Cory McDermott was a student there for two years, starting the same year as Lake."

"Let me guess," I said. "Not a great student?"

Ryan studied the screen. "On academic probation as soon as he finished his first semester. Never even got a C. He hung around for two years. Then he was gone."

"That might not be the whole story."

"True, but that's all I can get off his transcript."

"Okay, we assume Lake died of an OD …"

"Assumed." Ryan nodded.

"And we know Cory's a dealer."

"We have no idea if Cory's been in contact with Lake in more than seven years. Or if he lives in Montana. Or if he's still alive."

"We don't know anything," I said. "Let's put out a bulletin on him."

"Will do," he said. "Want to tell the chief we're going to wait for Robin's forensics and Harold's report?"

"Let's see if he's got something else he wants us to do."

We walked over to the chief's office, where he was talking with his assistant, Margaret. He looked up at us and raised his eyebrows.

"Quick question, Chief."

He nodded for me to proceed.

"We ID'ed the vic from this morning. LaKadrian Williams. Used to play football at the university. Long record of using, some selling. When he was a student, he got in a fight with another student who's now a serious dealer."

"No forensics yet?"

"Robin's got the vic's drug kit. There might be something there. And Harold's gonna start the autopsy this afternoon."

"We've got a detail at the scene, right?"

"Yeah, we do."

The chief nodded. "Okay, let's wait until Harold calls it. If it's a homicide, it's yours. If it's an accidental OD, you're up for the next case."

"Chief, do you mind if we do a couple of interviews this afternoon?"

"Where?"

"On campus."

"Who do you want to talk to?"

"Both the victim and the guy he got in the fight with started at the university the same time. They both dropped out. Both got into drugs. Mary Dawson—the dean of students?—she might be able to help us see if there was any connection between the two guys. If the dealer sold bad product to the vic, we might be able to charge him with manslaughter, give him a long stretch." I paused. "It's on campus. Just a couple hours this afternoon. You phone us, we're here in ten minutes. Once Harold calls it, we'll know what we've got, and you'll decide how much manpower to put on it."

The chief turned to Ryan. "You okay with that?"

"Absolutely."

"Let's give Harold the rest of the day. If he doesn't call it by the end of the shift, talk to me tomorrow morning, start of shift."

"Thanks, Chief."

Two guys started at the same college the same time. They both got into drugs, got into it downtown, dropped out of college. Did Cory sell Lake the drugs he used to kill himself? That was a long shot. Even in a small city like Rawlings, there must be a hundred folks pay their way selling dope. But if Cory was still alive, still living in Rawlings, still dealing, there was a very good chance he remembered Lake Williams, knew what he's been up to lately, maybe knew who his source was.

And there was a very good chance Mary Dawson could help us find Cory McDermott.

# *Chapter 4*

"Good morning!" Mary Dawson welcomed us into her suite in the Administration Building. She had been dean of students at Central Montana State University for about ten years. Although her job description blah-blah'ed about how she was there to create a supportive learning environment for students to develop into skilled professionals and active, engaged citizens, she spent a lot of time mopping up when students got arrested, beat up, and, sometimes, killed.

On a light day, she responded when a student got caught cheating on a test or bullying a gay kid in a dorm, or when a student wanted a professor fired—immediately!—for making a snide comment about Jesus. When I called her twenty minutes ago to ask if we could meet for a few minutes, I made it clear it was about a student who had left the university a while ago. She was relieved and therefore happy to see us. Happy was her default.

"Detective Seagate," she said. "Detective Miner." Her colorful plastic bracelets jangled cheerfully as she shook our hands. She invited us into her office and gestured for us to sit. "You mentioned you wanted to ask about a student from a while back?"

"Yes, that's right."

"I'll sit at my desk, then, so I can pull up their record on the system."

"That would be great."

"What's the student's name?" She removed her glasses, which were attached to a gold chain around her neck, and put on a different pair.

"LaKadrian Williams."

She asked me to spell the first name. I did. As the system churned, she ran a hand through her professionally colored auburn hair. "It's a beautiful day, isn't it? I just love autumn."

"Me, too," I said. I saw no reason to tell her I didn't have an emotional attachment to any of the seasons. Except winter, of course. Winter is horrible. Luckily, it only lasts about eight months.

She turned back to her computer, read a bit, and sighed. "Oh, yes, I remember his case now." She read some more. "I'm afraid to ask. I assume he's in trouble?"

I shook my head. "He died."

She exhaled a long breath. "I'm so sorry to hear that." I had worked with her enough to know she was telling the truth. She didn't have to know a student to be upset when he died.

"The autopsy hasn't been performed yet, but we suspect he died of a drug overdose."

Mary Dawson shook her head. "You wouldn't believe how much I'm hearing about drugs these days … the last year or two, in particular. And it's not just the kids who used to get into trouble. It's kids who seem to be doing really well. Good grades, lots of friends. Then, all of a sudden, they're taking heroin or something, their families are ripped apart. I don't understand what's going on." She paused. "I'm sorry. You would know far more about this than I do. Excuse me for going on like that. I assume you want to talk about LaKadrian."

"Yes, Dean Dawson—"

"Please, call me Mary."

I smiled at her. Every time we bring her bad news, which is basically all we bring her, she tells us to use her first name. But I always start with the last name, just in case she's having a really shitty day and doesn't want to be pals. "Yes, Mary, Detective Miner and I were hoping you could help us understand a little about LaKadrian—he called himself Lake—and about another student, a Cory McDermott."

She jotted down Cory's name on a slip of paper. "Of course. I'll be happy to provide whatever information I can. Let's start with Lake since I have his records up. Do you have specific questions?"

"Would you verify what we already have on him? He was a transfer from a community college in California. He was on the football team. Left school during his third year, didn't get a degree. Is that correct?"

"Yes, that's correct."

"Okay, now, can you tell us what isn't on his transcript?"

She leaned back in her chair, took off her computer glasses, and put on her other ones. "Mr. Williams was on a full football scholarship, but he had trouble maintaining an acceptable GPA. He got into some trouble here …"

Ryan said, "You're referring to the shoplifting arrest?"

Mary Dawson nodded. "He took some team regalia from the bookstore. He said he thought it was okay to take team regalia because he was on the team." She started to roll her eyes, then caught herself. She must have remembered we were talking about a guy who had just died. "We got a call from the athletics department. They asked us if we would make an exception in his case—he came from a rough environment, he was having problems adjusting, *et cetera*. The charges were dropped. Then there were a couple of other things: some petty vandalism, drinking in the dorm, that sort of thing."

"But he kept playing?" Ryan said.

"Yes, the team disciplined him in various ways, including suspensions for two games, if I remember correctly, but he appeared to be most successful when he was playing, and he was a very good athlete. The coach told us they thought the best way for him to gain some self-confidence was through athletics, and they asked us to give him an opportunity to succeed."

"Mary," I said, "you seem to remember Lake's situation pretty clearly. Is all of that information on the records you just read off your computer?"

She shook her head. "No, unfortunately, I remember his case now because I was part of the investigation."

"He got thrown out?"

"No, eventually he lost his football scholarship, and he couldn't afford to stay without that support."

"Tell us about the investigation."

"Another student brought a complaint against him. A female. She accused him of rape."

"Can you tell us her name?"

"No, that information is protected. I can outline the situation in very general terms, but I can't provide any details."

I paused. "Mary, let me explain where we are. Lake died under mysterious circumstances. We haven't called his death yet. It could be an accident if it was an unintentional overdose, or suicide if it was intentional. Or it could be a homicide. If that's what the medical examiner rules, it would help us get a head start in assembling a list of suspects if we knew who the girl is." I didn't hold out much hope she would buy that reasoning, but it was worth a shot.

"I understand, Detective Seagate, but the university policies are crystal clear on this, especially when we're talking about sexual assault. If students thought their identities might be revealed if they came to us, they'd simply stop coming." She paused. "Here's what I suggest: If you determine that Mr. Williams's death was a homicide, talk to Timothy Giraldi, the university counsel. He'll know what to do. Of course we all want to help you catch a murderer, but Timothy will know whether you need some sort of court order." She put up her palms and nodded. "He's very good. He'll know what to do."

"That's great advice, Mary. Thank you. We'll contact him, if it comes to that. But let me get back to the complaint. Can you tell us—without any names or identifying information—a little more about the student's complaint against Mr. Williams?"

"She said he was becoming hostile and aggressive, subject to terrible fits of anger. And one time, she said, he forced himself on her sexually."

"Did the university find that he raped her?"

She shook her head. "The university didn't reach any finding. We convened the disciplinary committee, as we always do in such cases, and we scheduled the witnesses, including the two principals. But then the committee terminated the hearing …"

"Why was that?" I said.

"The student's father attended the hearing. I don't think I'll ever forget it. He went berserk, started to attack Mr. Williams. It took three of the men in the room to restrain him until the officers arrived."

"Did the father say anything during the hearing?"

She waved her hand dismissively. "He obviously wasn't thinking clearly. But right before he tried to attack Mr. Williams he said some nasty things about him—and about the university, and the process we were following."

"What kinds of nasty things?"

Mary Dawson adjusted the strand of fake pearls around her neck and shook her head. "How it was the university's fault for letting an animal like that on campus. How it was incredible that anyone would believe someone like that over his daughter. He was very upset."

"Did he make any specific threats against Mr. Williams?"

She paused. "I wouldn't characterize them as specific threats.

He did say this wasn't over, that he would get Mr. Williams."

"You said you shut down the hearing. That was because the father flipped out?"

"Campus Security removed him and brought him to their offices. His daughter was very upset about that. She was crying, out of control. She left the room."

"What did you do then?"

"We suspended the hearing. I said I'd follow up with the student and her father and report back to the committee and see what they wanted us to do next. Later that day I learned that the father had told us to go to hell—not his exact words, but that was the idea—and that he was taking his daughter out of school. I reported that to the committee, which decided to table the case until we received more information on what the student wanted to do."

"Did you ever re-convene the committee on this case?"

"No, we didn't. We never received any additional information from the student or her father."

"Did you try to reach out to her?"

"A number of times." She tapped her chest. "She never replied."

"Did she ever come back to the university?"

"I can't answer that. It's protected."

Ryan said, "Do you know if the athletics department was aware of what happened?"

"Yes, they were. We keep them up-to-date on any disciplinary actions involving student-athletes. That's part of the protocol."

"And that was when Lake lost his scholarship?" Ryan said.

"Some months later, I believe." Mary Dawson nodded.

"Even though he wasn't technically found guilty of anything?"

"The athletics department was very patient with Mr. Williams. Maybe this was the final straw. Maybe his level of play had become unsatisfactory. I'm not really sure. All athletic scholarships are year-to-year, and the athletics department has no obligation to report to us on whether they renew a student's scholarship for the next year."

Ryan said, "Do you have contact information on his parents? We need to inform them."

"Let me check his initial application." She hit some keys. "I've got an address at Riverside Community College, which won't do you any good." She read some more. "The last home address listed here is an Esther Capaldi in Los Angeles." She read us a phone number, which Ryan wrote in his notebook.

"All right, Mary," I said, "thanks for that. Could you look up Cory McDermott?"

She hit some keys, then read for a few moments. "Cory McDermott entered the university the same year as Lake, but he was a year or so younger—he wasn't a transfer. Football scholarship, like Lake, but he went on academic probation and never managed to pull his grades up. He stayed two years, then left." She looked up at me and Ryan. "It's such a shame when that happens. We have all kinds of programs in place, especially for the athletes. I know the athletics department does everything it can to monitor their progress. They have tutors on call, and when they learn that a student's in trouble ... well, it's just a shame." She paused a second. "Is Cory in some kind of trouble?"

Since Mary felt free to tell me why she couldn't identify the girl who accused Lake of rape, I felt free to tell her about my job. "Cory is a drug dealer. Has been for years. He's a bad guy. We think he might have sold Lake the drugs that killed him." Mary ran a hand through her hair and exhaled. "We don't have an address on him. We'd like to get him off the streets under any circumstances. That's why we'd like to contact the girl. If she knew Lake, she might know Cory. We're not gonna publicize her name or do anything to embarrass her. But it would save us a lot of time. We've got a bulletin out on him now. If we could get to him soon—before he has a chance to throw his stuff in the back of a pickup and hit the interstate—we'd have a better chance of putting him in prison."

Mary Dawson knit her brows. I could see she really wanted to help us but couldn't. "You understand I'll do anything I can to help you."

As Ryan and I stood, I said to her, "I do know that, Mary, and I'm sorry to put you in a bind like this." I pulled a card out of my big leather shoulder bag and wrote my personal cell number on it. I handed it to her. "Any time, day or night."

Ryan and I left the dean of students' office and made our way out to the parking lot in front of the Administration Building. We got in the Charger.

"Well, that's good to know." I turned to Ryan. "Cory was on the football team with Lake."

"Yes, that certainly is."

"What else did you get?"

"The girl was probably his girlfriend," Ryan said, "or at least a social friend. He didn't jump out of the bushes and attack her."

"Because she said he was getting angry and aggressive?"

"That's right. And the girl was white."

"Huh?"

"Remember what the girl's father said when he attacked Lake?"

"Something about how it was crazy that anyone would believe him over his daughter."

"How Lake was an animal," Ryan said. "Which is code for black—if you're white, that is."

"Okay, smart boy, how are we gonna find her?"

"I'll need twenty minutes ..." He raised an eyebrow, inviting me to ask him some more.

I just looked at him.

Finally, he spoke. "Of course, I'd be happy to tell you how: It'll be in the photos."

"What photos?"

"Game photos, publicity photos of the players going to the pediatric ward to meet with sick kids, photos of the team doing tourist things at away games."

"How are those photos gonna identify her? And before you answer, I just want to go on record: You're extremely annoying."

"You're a black kid from a bad background. You earn your keep playing football at a white-bread school—in Montana, of all places. What kind of white girl are you going to go after?"

I'm not nearly as smart as Ryan, and the gap between us is getting bigger because I'm getting older twice as fast as he is, but most days I can still think at a rudimentary level. "The kind who shakes pom-poms."

"Very good."

"Isn't that kind of a cliché?"

"Your point is that a black football player wouldn't want to hook up with a pretty white girl because the other players would make fun of him because it's a cliché?"

"Okay, let's go back to headquarters. I'll give you twenty minutes."

I drove us back and carded us in the rear entrance. We settled into our chairs. A little while later, Ryan leaned back in his chair and put his hands behind his back. He cleared his throat theatrically.

I looked at my watch. It hadn't taken Ryan twenty minutes; it had taken fourteen minutes. Like I said: extremely annoying.

# *Chapter 5*

Ryan said, "The student who said Lake raped her was named Alicia Weber."

"You found a newspaper story or something?"

"No, Karen. There are no newspaper stories." He spoke slowly and patiently, his tone just this side of obnoxious. "She never filed legal charges, and the university disciplinary committee never reached a finding."

"Let me see what you've got." I walked around behind him and leaned in to see his computer.

He hit a key, and the computer began to scroll through a series of photographs, one every five seconds. There were photos of the cheerleaders working the sidelines. Then there were photos of the cheerleaders and the players at banquets, at a middle-school football camp, at the zoo with a bunch of toddlers and moms, at a zip line near town. Each photo included the same tall, athletic woman with broad shoulders, high boobs, and a wide smile. Her fine light-brown hair was shoulder-length. She had wide-set grey eyes, pale skin with faint freckles on her cheeks, and a slender nose. In every picture, she was standing next to Lake. As the slideshow progressed, she and Lake got chummier. Then a photo showed Lake kissing her on the cheek; she was laughing and hugging him.

There was one more photo: a blowup of a portion of Alicia Weber's transcript, complete with a headshot in the upper left, showing her complete withdrawal from the university the fall semester, when the incident occurred, and her re-enrollment the next fall.

I stepped back and gave him a look.

"I rest my case." Ryan put up his palms and tilted his head.

I appreciate that Ryan saves me all kinds of time by doing stuff I don't know how to do, but sometimes his cheerful efficiency pisses me off. "Good work. But this was seven years ago, right? She might have a new name, a new address."

He leaned back in and hit some keys, which pulled up her wedding announcement from the newspaper. Alicia Weber had married Stephen Templeton four years ago.

"That's a new name, not a new address."

He raised his index finger and held it there. His expression said, Don't make me do it.

"You're hideous."

He gave me one of his big grins. "Say it, Karen: 'I am in awe of you, Ryan.'"

My phone rang. I walked back around to my desk. The phone screen read "Lab." I picked up and hit Speaker. "Hello, Robin."

"Bad news first?"

"Why not?"

"The fingerprints on the drug baggie are no good. By the way, it was heroin."

"And the good news?"

"She left her blood in the syringe."

"She?"

"You know: a female human."

"You saying there was no blood from the vic?"

"No, I'm saying it was a party: one male human and one female. The blood from the guy is probably the vic's, but I can't say for sure yet until you authorize me to type the DNA."

"Do it, both of them."

"You're welcome."

"Thank you." I hung up.

Ryan said, "Could be the woman out at the camp." He flipped a page in his notebook. "Kendra, they said her name was. Want to go out there?"

I thought for a moment. "No, let's see if Robin can identify her. If it's Kendra or someone in our system, yeah, we'll follow up. But if Robin can't tell us who it is, we'll have wasted a trip— the guys aren't gonna tell us anything."

"Talk to Alicia?"

"Yeah, let's try to figure out if Lake really raped her or she was just pissed at him—"

"For seeing other women?"

"Seeing them, screwing them, whatever."

"Then the father?"

"We'll give her a chance to level with us. If she bullshits us, we'll decide whether to talk to her father. That sound good to you?"

"Yes, it does."

"Okay," I said, "where do we find Alicia Templeton?"

"At Alicia Templeton Real Estate, of course."

"Of course. Bring the photos of her with Lake, in case the whole episode has slipped her mind."

Ryan copied the file to his tablet and we headed out to the parking lot and drove the twelve minutes to Alicia Templeton Real Estate, a narrow storefront in a sixties strip mall. A dozen property listings were taped to the inside of the window. We opened the glass door.

A woman of around thirty-five looked up from the reception desk. We introduced ourselves. She looked concerned. I told her there was nothing to be alarmed about, but that Alicia's name had come up in an investigation. She told us Alicia was out staging a property and gave us the address. It was a mile out of town, in a development called the Willows.

We drove over. There were no willows, but there was an Audi SUV and an unmarked panel truck at the curb. The front door was open an inch. I walked in and called out, "Hello?"

An Hispanic guy, late twenties, jeans and T-shirt, came out. "Can I help you?"

"We're looking for Alicia Templeton."

He shook his head, like he'd never heard of her.

"The real-estate agent? The woman who hired you?"

He nodded and smiled. "Sorry. In the dining room." He pointed, then walked off in the other direction.

The house looked about five years old, a standard three-bedroom, two-bath, two stories. No furniture. The off-white paint on all the walls looked and smelled new. We walked across the freshly cleaned beige carpets into the empty dining room, which had a hardwood floor. Beneath the glass chandelier, a tall, athletic woman was on her hands and knees, head cocked, her light brown hair grazing the floor. The hair was cut a little shorter than in her photos, but it was clearly the same woman. She seemed to be checking out whether the floor needed refinishing.

She looked up as she heard us approach. "Can I help you?" She offered us a business smile, half annoyed that we had stopped by unannounced and half hopeful that we were looking for a three-bedroom, two-bath. Her eyes darted from me to Ryan. She was trying to figure out what kind of weird couple we were. I was too young to be his mother but too old and too beat up to be his wife or girlfriend.

"Ms. Templeton, my name is Detective Karen Seagate. This is my partner, Detective Ryan Miner." She rose to her feet in a single motion, the way some fit young people can. Her expression was clouded. "There's no problem, Ms. Templeton, we just need to talk to you a few minutes."

Relieved, she exhaled, then smiled. "Thank goodness." I wanted to ask her which toothpaste she used. Her tangerine

blazer over a sheer white blouse said she was ready for business—
but still fun! Her figure was perfect, a little on the slender side.
She hadn't put on a pound since college.

"Is there someplace we can talk?" The guys were clomping
around as they carried furniture into the house.

"Let's go upstairs. They'll be down here a while."

Ryan and I followed her up the stairs and into the master
bedroom, which was empty. Light shone in through a big bay
window looking west.

"How can I help you?"

"We're working on a case, and your name came up," I said.
"LaKadrian Williams. He died."

I stopped right there. Telling a person that someone they
knew had just died won't necessarily tell you anything important,
but it's always a good idea to pay attention to how they react.
Alicia Templeton's eyes widened in disbelief before a look of
sadness came over her face. Either she didn't know he was dead
or she had put some thought into how she would react when we
stopped by. My instinct told me she didn't know.

"Oh, my God." She shook her head, her hair swaying. "What
happened?"

"We're not sure yet, but we think he died of a drug
overdose." Her gaze drifted off into the distance. "Have you seen
him lately?"

She came out of whatever reverie she was in. "Seen him? No,
not in years."

"Could you tell us about your relationship with him?"

She straightened her posture. "I don't have any relationship
with him."

"I mean, when you two were in college."

"He was a football player. I was a cheerleader." She put out
her palms, as if there was nothing more to it than that.

"Ms. Templeton, we can see you're pretty busy, getting this

house ready. So let's save everyone some time. Lake Williams died last night. He and a woman were shooting heroin in the homeless camp out in Ten Mile Park, which is where he lived the last few months of his life. We need to find that woman and talk to her about what happened."

Although Alicia Templeton didn't look even remotely like a junkie—her grey eyes were bright and focused, her skin clear, and she was full of energy—I saw no reason to suggest I had ruled her out as Lake's shooting buddy.

"You have to be kidding. You think I took drugs with Lake last night?" She smiled in disbelief.

I wasn't smiling. "Ms. Templeton, we don't think anything. We're just talking with you, seeing if you can help us understand what happened last night."

"I have no idea what happened to Lake. I haven't seen him in years. I didn't know he was homeless. Why are you asking me about this?" She seemed a little more upset by my attitude than she had been, a moment earlier, when she learned he was dead. That happens.

"Can you tell us why the two of you broke up?"

"Broke up? What are you talking about?"

"All right, Ms. Templeton. We'll stop here." I turned to Ryan. "We have Ms. Templeton's home address, right?"

Ryan nodded gravely. "We do."

"How about this, Ms. Templeton? We'll stop by this evening to talk more. You'll be home, correct?"

"What? Wh-what are you ...?"

Her arms were out in a gesture that said, This can't be happening. But in fact it was. Nothing works like a phony threat to stop by a married woman's house later to talk about a dead former boyfriend.

I pointed to the bay window, with a built-in bench topped by a custom-fitted cushion. "Would you take a seat, please, Ms.

Templeton?"

As she tucked a strand of hair behind her ear, I could see a slight tremor. She went over to the bench and sat down. Ryan closed the bedroom door, and I drifted over toward her. She sat with her knees together tight, her arms folded across her chest.

"Okay, Ms. Templeton. We don't need to stop by your house, interrupt your family time, if you'll work with us now. But you need to understand where we are. This is a police investigation. If you lie to us or withhold information that could help us understand what happened, that's obstruction of justice. At least a misdemeanor, could be a felony. You could be arrested and prosecuted." I paused. "Do you understand what I'm saying?"

She nodded but wouldn't make eye contact.

"Ms. Templeton, please look at me. Answer my question. Do you understand what I'm saying—about obstruction of justice?"

She raised her head. "Yes." Her eyes were glistening. I couldn't tell if she was thinking about Lake or the possibility of getting into some legal trouble.

"Thank you. Now, let me ask you again: Why did you and Lake break up?"

"He was fooling around with other girls."

"So you just broke up? That was all there was to it?"

"I don't know what you want me to say. We were college kids, we went out for a while, then we stopped. I haven't seen him in years."

"Ms. Templeton, I'm going to ask you the question one more time. Your next answer is important. If you lie again, we will take you in for questioning and have you make a formal statement. You'll have to send the furniture guys away and lock up the house. It could take some hours."

Ryan drifted over toward the window so that the two of us were standing over Alicia Templeton. Her body tensed up, and she looked frightened.

"So you just broke up?" I said. "That was all there was to it?"

She took a deep breath and exhaled. "Lake cheated on me. A lot. I knew that about him. All the players were like that. The girls on the squad knew that."

"The cheerleaders?"

"Yes, we all knew that. But, you know, it was exciting, going out with them."

"If you knew the guys cheated, why did you break up with him?"

She was silent a moment. "He became violent. He hit me a few times. He used to be the sweetest guy. He was so gentle. Then, all of a sudden, he would go crazy."

"What made him go crazy?"

"It could be anything. Something I did or said. Or wore. Or something that happened to him that day. A bad practice, a fight with another player or one of the staff. Or a bad grade on a quiz or something. Anything at all."

"Did he take drugs back then?"

"He used to smoke weed, I know that. All the guys did. And he had pills for the pain."

"Where did he get the pills?"

"I don't know. He didn't say. But all the players took pills. And I know they got injections, too. Painkillers."

The guys downstairs were laughing and speaking loudly in Spanish.

"Tell me about the disciplinary hearing at the university. You charged him with rape."

Sometimes people are so ashamed or embarrassed or traumatized about stuff that happened they won't bring it up, but if someone mentions it matter-of-factly so they don't have to say it themselves, they won't deny it.

"He hit me sometimes. But then he would be very loving. He'd want to make up with me. Sometimes it, you know, it turned into …" She couldn't say *sex*.

"All right, I understand. What happened at the hearing?"

I could see the gears turning. "How do you know about the hearing? That was supposed to be private."

I chose not to answer the question. I don't like people to think we're having a discussion. "At the hearing, did the university find Lake guilty of rape?"

"I withdrew the complaint."

"Why did you do that?"

"I realized I couldn't win. Everyone knew I was going out with him. I didn't have any evidence he was abusing me—I mean, I never filed any reports with anyone, never went to get medical treatment or anything. So I knew if I said he raped me, nobody would believe me. Besides, he was this famous football player. I was a cheerleader."

"What difference does that make?"

"The girls weren't stupid. Most of the players were just like Lake. I mean, fooling around whenever they wanted. Some of them were abusive, too. So if you dated a football player, you knew what you were getting."

"So you withdrew the complaint against him?"

She looked me straight in the eyes. "That's right."

When Ryan and I interview a liar, he likes to give them a couple of chances to tell us the truth. "It must have been very difficult in the room that day," he said. "You sitting across the table from Lake, all those administrators there. You with nobody there to support you."

She nodded. "It was a nightmare."

"Then seeing him on campus afterwards—that must have been uncomfortable," Ryan said.

She shrugged. "I moved on. What was I going to do?"

"Did you ever talk to your parents about it?" I said. "Your mom? Your dad?"

She shook her head. "They never knew about me dating a player. It was my problem, and I did my best to get through it."

"Okay, Ms. Templeton," I said. "Thanks for talking with us. We appreciate your candor. I don't think we'll need to bother you again." I handed her my card. "If you think of something that can help us, give me a call, please."

She sat there, the sun falling on the shoulders of her tangerine blazer. She nodded but didn't look up.

We left the house and got in the Charger. I turned to Ryan. "Well, we gave her every opportunity to be straight with us."

"We certainly did. We even told her we knew she was lying."

"You don't see her shooting up with Lake in his tent, do you?"

"Not any more than I see my wife there."

"But she's not leveling with us."

"No, she is not."

"She didn't deny that she charged him with rape. She just lied about withdrawing the charge. So it's about her father, right?"

Ryan nodded. "That's my guess."

"Could just be that Dad's got anger-management issues, right?"

"Or he's a racist, and she doesn't want us to talk to him."

"Or he's a murderer," I said, "and that's why she doesn't want us to talk to him."

"Want to head back to the station and see what we can learn about him?"

"I think we should."

# *Chapter 6*

"Were you able to get contact information on Lake's foster mother?"

Ryan shook his head. "I tried. Couldn't find her. Gave it to an admin to try. She couldn't, either."

"Talk about a motherless child." I shook my head. "How about Alicia's father? What's his name?"

"Ronald Weber."

"Is he in the system?"

Ryan studied his screen. "Two DUIs: one from eight years ago, one from four. And there was a road-rage incident five years ago."

"He hurt anyone?"

"No. It was a misdemeanor."

"Okay," I said. "Now we know he has an anger issue. Maybe alcoholism, too. Let's take a drive."

Weber Electric was a whitewashed concrete-block building on a short commercial road off of Veterans Parkway. There were three parking spots out front for customers, as well as six spots, alongside the building, for the electricians. Two company trucks were parked behind the building.

The modest reception area, with dark brown industrial carpet squares, fake wood paneling, and fluorescent-tube ceiling lights, looked like it hadn't been updated in fifty years. There was a receptionist's grey steel desk with a PC, three tall file cabinets, a couple of plastic stacking chairs, and a small table with a coffee pot and Styrofoam cups. No cream, no sugar, no napkins. No frills.

The receptionist, a thin young man with tight clothing, gelled hair, and thick black plastic-framed glasses, told us Mr. Weber was in his office in the back. He would go tell him we were here. Can he tell him what this was in reference to? No, he can't.

It took less than a minute for Ronald Weber to appear from the hallway that led back to his office. He was obviously Alicia Templeton's father. He had the same fine light-brown hair, but it was streaked with grey. Crow's feet framed his wide-set grey eyes. At forty-five, he looked like a former athlete, with a trim waist and broad shoulders. He shook our hands, repeating our names to be sure he got them correct. "Would you like to come back to my office?"

"Thank you." We followed him back.

He gestured for us to sit on the two old, nicked wooden chairs in front of his desk. He slid in behind his desk. He closed the open laptop. "How can I help you?"

"We spoke with Alicia a little while ago—"

"Is there anything wrong?"

"No, not at all. Sorry. Didn't mean to frighten you. It's about a case. LaKadrian Williams has died, and we wanted to talk to her to better understand what happened."

Ronald Weber closed his eyes, and his head slumped forward until his chin rested on his white shirt with a Weber Electric logo on the pocket. He didn't open his eyes. I started to count. I glanced over at Ryan, who was leaning in, trying to figure out what was happening with this guy. At five-Mississippi, Weber opened his eyes and took a deep breath.

"You okay, Mr. Weber?"

He looked deeply sad. "I'm very sorry to hear of his passing."

"Were you ... were you two close?"

"No." Ronald Weber shook his head. "Not at all. But I know

he was a troubled soul, and I'm sorry to learn of his passing."

I nodded. "We think he died of a drug overdose."

He was silent a moment. "Did he take his own life?"

"We're not sure. It's still very early in the investigation."

Weber nodded. "And you talked to Alicia because of her relationship with Lake in college?"

"That's right, sir. She suggested that she and Lake dated a little in college, but that she had no contact with him after that. Is that your understanding?"

He shook his head. "No, that's not what happened at all." He exhaled slowly, as if it was going to take him some effort to tell the story more accurately. We don't get that every day.

"What did happen, Mr. Weber?"

"It was more complicated than that. They were together for over a year. They broke up because he raped her."

"Oh, my God," I said. "That's terrible. I didn't know that."

He nodded his appreciation. "Lake started to have serious anger problems. He had become violent with her. And at some point he raped her. It was very traumatic for her, of course, as I'm sure you can understand."

I could. "Did she go to the police?"

"Her mother and I urged her to, but she refused."

"Why was that?"

"She couldn't explain why—at least, she couldn't explain it in any way her mother and I could understand."

"So she took no action—I mean, no action against Lake?"

"She agreed to bring it to the university. They began an investigation to determine if they should take any action against him, but the process never got going."

"What do you mean?"

He pointed to his chest with his thumb. "It was because of me. I lost my temper and started shouting. I wanted to kill him because of what he had done. I threatened him, got a hand on

him. Some of the men in the room restrained me until the campus
police came and dragged me off."

"Then what happened?"

"The police were very professional. They contacted Lake to
ask him if he wanted to press charges. He didn't, and I was
released."

"And with your daughter?"

"She didn't pursue the investigation at the university, and she
didn't want to have anything to do with me for a long time."

"Because you embarrassed her at the hearing?"

"I'm sure that was it—I mean, about me. Was that the only
reason she decided not to pursue the investigation? I really can't
say. I think what was going on in her mind was that there were
two guys in her life who had let her down. Both of the guys
violent, out of control. Neither of them acting in her interest. It
just kind of overwhelmed her, and she needed some time, and
some space."

"What did the university do then?"

"They let her withdraw from school that semester, and she
didn't attend the next semester, either. But the next fall she
returned and completed her degree."

"Was that the last of her relationship with Lake, as far as you
know?"

"Yes, as far as I know. When the baby came—"

"She had a baby? Lake's baby?" Sometimes I don't have to
fake surprise.

"Yes, she did. We're Catholic, but her mother and I counseled
her against bringing the baby to term. She insisted, and that's
what happened."

"Did Lake participate in the birth?"

Ronald Weber shook his head. "He had left the university by
then. Whether she told him about the pregnancy and her decision,
I don't know. But she never mentioned to me or her mother

anything about Lake participating."

"Does the child live with her and her husband?"

"No, she gave the baby up for adoption. She had it all planned out, and it happened soon after his birth. Almost immediately. She insisted we not see the baby, and I don't think she saw the baby more than a few times."

"Has she ever mentioned her son in front of her husband?"

"Not that I'm aware of."

"So you have no idea whether the husband even knows about the baby."

"I have no idea whether she has ever mentioned Lake or the baby to her husband. And unless she tells me, or he does, I will never know." He paused, his eyes shining with tears. "The last time she needed my help, I let her down. I am determined that will not happen again."

"Mr. Weber, I'm a little curious. You tell us you shouted at Lake and tried to attack him during that disciplinary hearing at the university. And we know you had a road-rage incident a while back. You had a couple of DUIs, too. Yet you seem very composed as you speak to us …" I let it hang there.

"I am a recovering alcoholic, and I work very hard to stay sober. I attend AA meetings seven days a week. And I have accepted Jesus Christ into my life. Jesus is my Lord and Savior. Without Him, I would not be alive today. I am certain of that. I would not be married, and I would not have my son and my beautiful daughter and her wonderful family—except for Jesus. I am aware that my failures made a terrible time for my daughter even more difficult, and it hurts me every day. Only Jesus's love and forgiveness enable me to get up and carry on every day."

I nodded. I hadn't seen Ronald Weber at any of my AA meetings, but I go to the same one every day, and there must be a couple dozen different sessions around the city.

"Mr. Weber, do you know anyone who would want to hurt

LaKadrian Williams?"

Ronald Weber tilted his head, as if he was thinking hard about my question. "The last time I saw Lake was that day at the university. I know he was dismissed from the team and left the university some months after that. But I don't know what he has been up to—what he had been up to—since then. It must be five or six years ago, now."

"It's seven years." I thought for a second. "You follow the team?"

He smiled, for the first time in the interview. "I love the Cougars."

"Even after what happened?"

He waved his hand. "I love the game. I used to play, in college. But more important than that, I believe strongly that college athletics gives a lot of kids the opportunity to attend college and get a degree, an opportunity they wouldn't have otherwise. A kid like Lake? He could have gotten an education here." His expression turned somber again. "There are a couple of kids every year who can't make it, but that isn't the system's fault. The system is good."

I spoke. "I'm sorry I interrupted you. I'd asked whether you knew of anyone who wanted to hurt him."

He shook his head. "No, Detective, I don't know anyone who would want to hurt him. If you'd asked me that question two years ago, I would have said I did—I wanted to hurt him. I wanted to kill him. But I have forgiven him, forgiven him completely, for what he did to Alicia. I don't pretend to understand what demons he was wrestling with during his life. But I do know he had demons, and I am thankful, at least, that he is now at peace."

I stood and offered Ronald Weber my card. "If you can think of anything that can help us understand what happened to Mr. Williams, would you please get in touch?"

He stood, took my card, and nodded.

Ryan and I headed back to our cruiser and got in. I just sat there, gazing at the cinder-block building.

Ryan turned to me. "Problem?"

"I can't quite get a read on him."

"That's not a problem." Ryan smiled. "That's a puzzle."

"What did you see?"

"I saw a guy whose story was a lot closer to what we know happened than his daughter's."

"Did you buy it?"

"I'm just browsing at the moment, thank you." He paused. "What about you? Is he a recovering alcoholic?"

"Yes, he definitely, absolutely might be a recovering alcoholic."

"Did he get something wrong?"

"No, everything he said was fine. He's thought about how his actions have hurt people in his life. He feels sorry he hurt them. He's trying to make amends. And the Jesus thing? That's part of the AA story. A lot of recovering alcoholics get into religion big time."

"It makes sense." Ryan rubbed his cheek. "If you're the kind of person who can go to the AA meetings, you're the kind of person who can see the value of an organized religion—the morality, the routine, the rituals."

"You didn't hear anything that raises a flag?"

"No, I didn't. He didn't say enough for me to tell whether he has a deep understanding of Christianity, but that's not the point. He could get that all screwed up and still be an honest, sincere guy."

"It doesn't bother you that he's wearing his cross on his sleeve?"

"Not at all. He doesn't sound like a Catholic, but if he's into one of the evangelical faiths, that's what you're supposed to do.

You know, spread the good news. Isn't that part of the AA Twelve Steps, too?"

"Yeah, I guess so. I'm not really into all the steps. To me, it doesn't make a lot of sense to say, 'I'm a total screw-up, so take my advice.'"

He gave me a sad smile. "Well, that raises all kinds of interesting philosophical questions that I'd love to discuss with you sometime."

"Yeah, that's gonna happen." I started up the Charger and drove us back to headquarters. Neither of us said anything on the short drive.

We got settled at our desks. "One thing Weber told us."

Ryan waited for me to form a thought. He has to do that a lot. "Yeah?"

"I get why Alicia didn't tell us about a baby."

"Well, we didn't think to ask that. We didn't know she had a baby with Lake."

"Obviously, I can see how for some people it increases the shame factor: She was screwing this guy, then he knocks her up. And if race is part of it in her circle, now she's got herself a mixed-race kid."

"From what her father said, I couldn't tell if Lake's race had any role in her decision to give up the baby."

I said, "Did you see Ronald Weber as a racist?"

Ryan shook his head. "No, I didn't. But maybe he's more evolved now. Or just smooth enough not to let anyone see it."

I started typing.

Ryan said, "What are you up to?"

I typed a little more. "I'm looking at the birth certificate for Jonathan Weber, who is now almost seven years old."

"Yeah?"

"The father is listed as LaKadrian Williams."

"We assume that is true, don't we? I mean, that he's the

father."

"Yes, we do," I said. "But I didn't assume she would list him."

"What does it tell you?"

"Not sure. It could be nothing."

"That's the great thing about this job," Ryan said cheerfully. "Everything could be nothing."

My ex-husband saw all my half-formed ideas as conclusive evidence that I was confused and stupid. Ryan saw them as my appreciation that human behavior is complex and subtle. Sometimes, I let myself think Ryan is right. Most of the time, I think he's just more polite.

# *Chapter 7*

"Harold called it yet?" the chief said.

"Not as of a minute ago," I said. It was just after eight, Tuesday morning. Ryan and I were checking in with Chief Murtaugh, like he asked us to. He had given us yesterday to try to figure out whether LaKadrian Williams's overdose was an accident, suicide, or homicide. Harold Breen, our medical examiner, hadn't posted the results of his autopsy.

"What'd you get yesterday?"

"We ID'ed the vic: LaKadrian Williams. He was a student at the university, football scholarship, started acting erratically, got kicked off the team, flunked out, became a junkie. His girlfriend, a cheerleader named Alicia Weber, accused him of rape. She went through channels at the university; she never brought it to us. But then she dropped the allegation after her father tried to attack Lake at the university hearing. When we interviewed her yesterday, she downplayed the whole relationship, said they were just going out for a while, then they broke up because of his behavior. Her story didn't square with the story from Mary Dawson at the university, so we tracked down the father, Ronald Weber. He's an electrician; owns his own company. He told us his daughter was lying. Lake raped her—as far as the father knows—then she dropped out of school, had Lake's baby, gave it up for adoption."

"You like Alicia?"

"Not as his needle buddy. She's no junkie. Real healthy,

athletic. Did she want to kill him? Can't be sure, but I don't think
so. She's moved on. She's a real-estate agent here in town.
Married. But what do I know?"

"How about the father? Why is he contradicting his
daughter?"

I turned to Ryan. "He's a recovering alcoholic," Ryan said,
"and he's found Jesus. He says she's spinning it because she's
ashamed of his actions when he tried to attack Lake. He's a new
man, now."

The chief looked at me. "And you buy that?"

"So far," I said.

"What do you want to do, then?"

My cell rang. I pulled it out of my pocket. "It's Robin." The
chief gestured for me to take it. I put it on Speaker.

"Seagate."

"Hey, Karen. Want to know who was hanging out in the tent
Sunday night?"

"If you don't mind."

"The guy was LaKadrian Williams. The woman was Kendra
Crimmons. They're both in our system."

"Is that Crimmons with a C?"

"Yeah."

"How'd you ID her?"

"From the DNA in the white blood cells. In the syringe."

"And you said the prints on the baggie were no good?"

"Right."

"Like she wiped them off?"

"The baggie closes with one of those plastic zippers, so I can't
tell."

"All right, Robin. Thanks." I ended the call and turned to
Ryan. "That's the woman lives out at the camp, isn't it?"

He nodded. "The guys called her Kendra."

The chief looked puzzled. "If she killed him," he said, "why wouldn't she just grab the drug kit when she left the tent? Throw it away someplace."

"Maybe she wanted it to look like a simple OD," Ryan said. "She wiped off her prints. She didn't know her DNA was in the syringe."

"Maybe it was really good heroin," I said. "She was too high to think straight. When she came back down, she realized Lake was dead. She wanted us to know he was a junkie, so she left Exhibit A there for us."

The three of us were silent for a minute. "Well, Chief," I said, "want us to keep working this?"

"Bring her in." He nodded. "Take a statement. Then talk to me again."

Ryan and I headed back to our desks and pulled up her record. She was forty-one years old, with a string of offenses going back twenty-five years. Her two main offenses were the familiar chicken and egg: hooking and using. Before she was sweet sixteen, she was arrested for prostitution and possession. She moved from her grandmother's house—her mother was already in prison, her father long gone—to the juvenile justice system. Group living didn't suit her tastes, and she escaped back onto the streets. She started selling drugs, as well as her body, and spent the next two decades in and out of prison and the emergency room. If Kendra Crimmons ever had half a chance, she blew it. But I doubt she ever had.

"Well." Ryan looked up from his computer screen. "That's a cheerful story, isn't it?"

"One or two more bad decisions in high school and that would've been me."

We got our coats and drove out toward the homeless camp in Ten Mile Park. The sky was overcast, the breeze picking up enough to rock the heavy cruiser a little bit. A half-hour later, we pulled into the empty parking area. The crime-scene tape and all the police vehicles were gone. We got on the main walking path, which we followed for a few dozen yards, then branched off to the left on a narrower path that we hoped would lead us to the homeless camp.

The clearing was a little less forlorn now that it wasn't raining, but the breeze ruffled the tents and snapped some of the laundry on the clotheslines strung between tree limbs. Plastic bags and other garbage swirled in the clearing as we approached the picnic table and the oil drum in the center. Three guys huddled around the drum, hands out toward the fire, as bits of paper rose into the wavy air.

I put my shield around my neck. One of the guys, who I recognized from yesterday, muttered something to the two other guys. I couldn't make out what he said, but it didn't sound like, Great news, they're back.

"Good morning," I said. They glanced at me briefly, then looked away. They didn't say anything, but they wanted us to know they didn't intend to help us more than necessary. Nothing personal against me and Ryan—just the result of having lost every fight they've ever had with the system. And here we were with gold badges around our necks that said System. "My name is Seagate. This is Miner. We need to talk to Kendra. Do you know if she's around?"

They all shrugged their shoulders. Ryan and I walked over to Kendra's tent, the grey one on shipping pallets. "Kendra Crimmons," I said, loud but polite and legal. "Rawlings Police Department. Can we talk to you?"

No reply. I tried again. Still no reply. The tent wall flapped in the wind.

Ryan walked around to the side and looked in through a mesh window. He shined a flashlight in, then turned to me and shook his head.

We walked back over to the guys at the oil drum. I pulled a

booking photo of Kendra out of my pocket and held it up so each
of the three guys could see it. "This is Kendra Crimmons. We
need to talk to her about Lake's death, couple nights ago."

One of the guys wore a go-fuck-yourself expression. Another
gazed off into the middle distance. A third one dragged a foot
back and forth, making arcs in the dirt.

"We're not here to arrest her," I said. "We're not charging her
with anything. We just need to talk to her. We're trying to figure
out what happened to Lake."

Ryan stepped forward until he was about a foot away from
one of the men. "You guys know this whole encampment is
illegal. You're doing illegal burning right here. You're camping
overnight. You don't have approved sanitary facilities. If we call
this in, the city has to act on it. They have to take it down." He
looked at them, but they didn't respond.

I reached into my leather bag and fished a twenty from my
wallet. I held it up. "Where can we find Kendra?" Now I had their
attention.

The guy who was scratching at the dirt looked at me. He
cleared his throat and pulled his hand out of his coat pocket. The
finger joints were swollen and red. He pointed to a green tent.
"Just to the right of that tent, there's a path leads to a dried-out
stream bed. That's where she hangs."

"She there now?"

He nodded, just a little.

I handed him the twenty.

Ryan and I turned and started across the clearing. He said,
"Now you're down twenty."

"Worth it to get the hell out of here quicker."

We passed between the green tent and a little shack made of
corrugated steel, plywood sheets, and plastic tarps. I spotted a
face looking up at us from the shadows inside the shack. We came
to the edge of the clearing. I couldn't see a path, but Ryan saw

one. "This way," he said.

I followed him as his black overcoat was swallowed up in the bushes and brambles. The wind was picking up, whistling and shaking the leaves on the bushes and the trees. Every so often I caught a whiff of sewage. We kept going, following the narrow path as it wound its way along. Soon it started to dip down, which I hoped meant we were close to the stream bed. The bushes started to thin out, then disappeared. Before us was the stream bed, about ten feet across, with a busted bicycle, two tires, and a rusted shopping cart scattered along the foot-wide strip of mud that ran down the center.

We looked around. No Kendra. "Shit," I said. "I want my twenty back."

Ryan picked his way through the busted crap and garbage, across the stream bed and up the far bank to get a different view. "There she is," he said. About fifty yards away, off to the east, was a pile of dirty rags near some ratty shrubs. It took me a few seconds to figure out what I was seeing. It was a person, lying on her side, her back to us, her knees bent and legs drawn in. Her baggy brown jacket and dark sweatpants blended seamlessly into the terrain.

I called out her name as we approached her, but she didn't move.

Ryan walked around her body to face her. "Let's hope she's alive."

"Yeah, let's hope that." But, to be honest, at the moment I didn't have strong feelings about the issue one way or the other.

"Ms. Crimmons." Ryan said her name, first softly, then with a little more energy.

I walked around to face her, too, but I didn't see any movement. I reached down and shook her arm. "Kendra, you in there?"

The way she responded told me she was officially alive, if only barely. Her dark brown hair, matted and oily, obscured most of her face. Slowly her dirty, crusty dark eyes opened halfway. She tried to focus on me but she couldn't quite make it before her eyelids closed slowly.

"Kendra, wake up." I could see she was slipping back to wherever she had been. I shook her arm again. "Kendra. Get up. We're cops. We need to talk to you."

This statement didn't work. "Help me get her up," I said. We lifted her into a sitting position, but her arms were slack and her chin sank to her chest. She was about a hundred and fifty pounds of filthy rag doll.

"Hold her in this position." I crouched down so my head was on her level. "Kendra, wake up." I slapped her face lightly a few times.

Her eyes opened a little, then she let out a yelp. "Crap." Her voice was low and craggy.

I recoiled from the sickly stench of cheap whisky and whatever other shit had been decomposing in her mouth in the couple weeks since she'd last brushed her teeth. I felt my stomach turn, tasting the sting of my own stomach acid at the back of my throat. I gagged a couple of times but somehow managed not to blow breakfast.

I used to drink, pass out, and puke, just like Kendra. Quite often, I would piss myself, too. One thing I remember about being so disgusting: You're oblivious to how disgusting you are.

After a moment, I turned back to face Kendra Crimmons. She looked more than ten years older than her forty-one years. Her skin was puffy and blotchy; her eyes, bloodshot. Her nose had been broken, at least once; her nostrils were half-blocked with crusted snot. Her teeth were a yellow-green, outlined with a dark brown line along the gum line.

"Kendra, can you hear me?"

"Yeah, you don't have to shout."

"All right, Kendra, my name is Detective Seagate. The guy behind you—holding you upright—is Detective Miner." She turned her head a quarter turn, just enough to confirm there was someone supporting her. "We need you to come with us. We're gonna go to police headquarters and talk to you about Lake."

"Gimme a second." Over the breeze I heard a rumbling sound coming from deep inside her. Her face contorted into a grimace as her torso convulsed. I managed to pull back just in time to miss much of the vomit and phlegm that sprayed from her mouth and ran down the front of her jacket and onto her sweatpants.

Ryan gathered a handful of dead leaves and grasses and wiped most of it off her jacket and pants. She used her sleeve to clean off her chin.

"Okay," she said, struggling to her feet. "That's better."

"Yeah, that's great." Ryan helped me lift her to her feet. After sinking to the ground a few times, Kendra managed to stay upright, as long as the two of us supported her. With only two breaks to snort some crud from her nose and hawk it back up, we covered the hundred yards back to the clearing. We walked her past the oil drum, her head bobbing up and down with her steps. She seemed not to notice the guys. They glanced up at her but showed no expression and said nothing.

We got her out to the parking area and over to the Charger. When I held the back door open so Ryan could shove her in, he said, "Want to pat her down?"

"I think she'd be fine with you doing it."

"Has to be a female officer." He smiled.

"You're gonna have to hold her up."

Ryan got behind her and supported her by the armpits as I took a deep breath and started the patdown. She had no weapons, no needles or other paraphernalia. Nothing illegal. She had part of a dinner roll, some half-eaten candy bars, an old handkerchief that for some reason smelled like diesel fuel, and, jammed in her underpants but sticking out of the front of her sweatpants, a small wad of bills. Rather than asking Ryan what he thought of the legality of checking it out, I decided to brush the wad with my elbow, knocking it free. It fell to the dirt.

Ryan picked up the money, unfolded it and started counting. "Eighteen dollars." He shook his head. "Hardly worth an illegal search and seizure."

"Yeah," I said, "that was wrong, what you just did. You should put it back in her pants."

# *Chapter 8*

As soon as we got Kendra Crimmons in the back seat of the Charger, she tilted and fell over like a sack of potatoes. She began to snore almost immediately, choking and waking herself up every few minutes. I lowered my window for the trip. Stopped at a traffic light, I turned back to see how she was doing. She was breathing. On the black vinyl seat cover, near her mouth, was a swirly red and yellow pool of something nasty.

At headquarters, we hauled her inside and got a female officer to clean her up and put her in one of the interview rooms. Ryan and I headed off to the bathrooms.

We met up again and opened the door marked Janitor that leads to the little hallway where we look through the one-way mirrors into each of our two interview rooms. Kendra was wearing a white jumpsuit. She was seated at the interview table, her head resting on her hands, which were folded on the table. Ryan turned on the speaker. She was snoring peacefully.

"Think she'd tell us anything useful?" Ryan said.

I shook my head. "More likely she'd just puke on us again."

We walked to the chief's office to find out what he wanted us to do. "Chief, we brought Kendra in—the woman shooting up with Lake the night he died?—but she's too drunk or stoned or something to give us a statement now. We're gonna let her sober up and have a go at her later, okay?"

"Fine."

"Meantime," Ryan said, "we should talk to the people who

run the football program. We've got one former player dead from an OD, another who's a dealer, and a cheerleader who said she was raped by one of them. Maybe someone there knew Lake."

The chief turned to me. "You okay with this, Karen?"

"Absolutely, as long as I can lead on all the interviews." I paused. "Is a football the round one or the pointy one?"

The chief knit his eyebrows. "I keep mixing them up. Maybe check the Internet?"

I nodded my thanks, then Ryan and I turned and headed back to the bullpen. Once we got settled, he said, "Mind if I take a couple of minutes to read up a little on the program?"

"Sure," I said. "I'll start writing up Lake Williams."

Forty minutes later, we headed out to the parking area for the ten-minute drive over to campus. "What'd you learn?"

"Andy Baxter, the head coach, came to the university a year before Lake enrolled, so he might be able to tell us something."

"I meant about the rape."

"That's if there *was* a rape." Ryan was laying down a marker: He wasn't convinced yet.

"Yeah," I said. "I got that."

"I meant, Coach Baxter would know about Lake as a player, a student, a guy."

"Anything in Baxter's record you want to ask him about?"

"Well, there is one thing: He used to coach at Arkansas Southern, which is FBS. CMSU is FCS." He paused to give me a moment to ponder that information.

I glanced at him. "Sorry, I drifted off when you switched to gibberish."

"His former school had a better program than his current school. Coaches like to move sideways or up, not down."

"Maybe he was a shitty coach?"

"No, he was a good coach."

"And you're gonna get him to tell you why he moved?"

"I'll get him to answer the question. Can't guarantee it'll be the truth."

"Open with this: 'Do all your players turn into junkies, drug dealers, and rapists, or just most of them?'"

"Give me a second. I want to write that one down."

Three minutes later, we pulled into a metered spot outside the football complex. I flipped down my visor to show the Official Police Business card.

The complex was a large, three-story brick, metal, and glass building connecting the football stadium and the indoor practice facility. Above the main entrance was a metal replica, about ten yards square, of the Central Montana State mascot, a cougar with a pissed-off expression. Beneath the cougar, shiny stainless-steel letters a foot tall identified the building as The Melissa and Carl Davis Football Complex.

I pointed to the letters. "Who are they?"

"Carl Davis is the president of the Cougar Athletic Association, the booster group."

"He must do a lot of boosting."

"Couple of years ago, on his fortieth anniversary with the group, he raised twelve million dollars to re-do the complex and build the practice facility."

We entered through the big glass doors and walked across the expansive entrance, over the face of the cranky cougar in the carpet. At the wide reception desk, I showed the perky young woman my badge and asked if she could direct us to the main office. She told us it was in room 301, up on the third floor. "You can take these stairs." She gave Ryan a broad smile as she pointed behind her to a wide stairway that arose out of the center of the lobby. Then she turned to me and pointed off to the side. "Or the elevator."

I thanked her and turned toward the elevator.

Ryan followed reluctantly. "We could've taken the stairs, you know."

"You see the way that girl looked at me? Like I was pushing a walker?"

We walked past a large glass display case full of trophies and footballs and championship rings. Widescreen TV sets on kiosks showed game films, a graduation ceremony with the seniors in caps and gowns under a goal post in the stadium, and videos of players doing charitable events at hospitals and football camps for handicapped kids.

"This whole building is about football?" I said. "If I'm captain of the field-hockey team, I don't see the inside of this building, right?"

"I'm sure they give public tours."

At the main office, the forty-something woman at the desk looked up at us. Her name tag read Helen. She took in the detectives' shields around our necks. "Good morning. Can I help you?"

Ryan said, "Is Coach Baxter available? We'd like to speak with him for a few minutes."

"I'm sorry." Her expression showed just the right amount of disappointment. "He's not available at the moment."

"Is he around?" I said. "I mean, here on campus? It'll only take a few minutes."

"No, actually, he's not." That was all Helen said. Apparently, it was none of our damn business where the boss was, and she wasn't going to tell us. She looked at her screen and hit a few keys. "He's expected back around one this afternoon. I think he could work you in then." She lifted her eyebrows so I would know she was making a significant concession.

"How about you tell me where he is right—"

Ryan touched my arm. "One o'clock would be great," he said to Helen. "We'd appreciate that."

She nodded and smiled at Ryan, then typed something. She

looked up at Ryan. "Could you tell me your names, please?"

Ryan told her. She typed. I couldn't see her screen. I imagine she entered "Detective Ryan Miner and Obnoxious Bitch." She smiled at him again.

Ryan pointed to the floor-to-ceiling glass wall that overlooked the practice facility. "This is incredible. Do you mind?"

Helen almost hopped out of her chair. "Not at all." She led him over to the glass. I drifted over, hanging back just enough to not get in Ryan's way. He had begun to work her.

Through the glass I could see a full-size football field inside a metal building that looked like an airplane hangar. Sunlight filtered through the frosted windows, which extended from just above the artificial turf all the way up to the ceiling, at least fifty feet in the center. Around the perimeter of the building, about twenty feet above the turf, was a catwalk. Six observation decks, each big enough to hold three or four people, jutted out from the catwalk.

Ryan spoke to Helen. "On the ceiling—are those cameras?"

"That's right," she said. "Ten of them. The video coordinator can sit in his suite down the hall and swivel them with joysticks. The goal is to capture the video and get it to the coaching staff before the players leave the field."

"This is an incredible setup." He shook his head in disbelief, his grin set at ten.

I started to worry he was laying it on too thick. But since he was always been very good at figuring out which button to push—and how hard to push it—I hung back.

Although the players wouldn't arrive for practice for a few hours, the field was full of activity. Six young guys were setting up equipment: sleds to push across the field, rope ladders to hop-scotch through, cones to slalom around, and chutes to duck beneath. Hurdles of all shapes and sizes to jump over, and mats for players to fall onto. Along the sidelines, guys were wheeling out nets for quarterbacks to throw balls into and nets for kickers to kick into. They were attaching battle ropes to brackets on the walls.

On the wall beyond the west end zone, past the goal posts suspended from the ceiling, a couple of workmen were installing a video screen as wide as my living room. An older guy in a sport jacket and slacks and carrying a cane was talking with one of the workers. I said to Helen, "What's going on down there?"

As she turned to answer me, I caught a flash of annoyance on her face, as if in talking to me she might slip out of the orbit of Planet Ryan. But she recovered quickly and offered an official smile. "We're installing a video setup like the ones in the stadium."

"Can you tell me who the guy is? In the sport jacket?"

"That's Mr. Davis."

"Thanks."

Ryan turned to the woman. "This is an unbelievable facility you've got here."

She brightened. "Did you play?"

Ryan said, "Not here. BYU. We had an indoor facility, but nothing like this."

"If you've got a minute, I'm sure Mr. Davis would love to chat with you."

Ryan broke out his kid smile. "You don't think he'd mind?"

She nodded confidently. "Trust me, Mr. Davis will talk football with anybody, anywhere."

Ryan turned to me. "That okay with you?"

"Sure." I put on an indulgent smile for Helen's sake, but I liked Ryan's decision to talk with the booster, as long as he was right here and we had time.

Ryan turned to Helen. "We'd love to talk to Mr. Davis—just for a minute."

She smiled and headed back to her desk. "I'll call the student at Reception. She'll let you in."

"This is terrific. Thanks so much," Ryan said. "And we'll come back at one to talk to the coach."

The woman gave him a warm smile and bowed her head slightly.

When we got back downstairs to Reception, the young woman greeted us and led us down the hall to a set of double doors that opened onto the indoor facility. I closed my jacket in the chill. The air had a vague smell of engine fluids, plastics, and sweat.

The guys setting up the equipment glanced up at Ryan and me as we walked past them, but they took no particular notice. They must see a lot of guests walking through the facility.

As we approached Mr. Davis and the electrical guy, Ryan said, "You mind if I lead?"

"You better. Only question I got is, 'You kill Lake Williams?'"

Carl Davis didn't see us approaching as he talked with the electrician. When the electrician stopped and turned to us, Davis turned, too. "Hello," he said, "I'm Carl Davis." He presented a warm, slightly crooked smile that crinkled up his eyes, which were cloudy and veiny with age. He had a half-dozen liver spots on his comfortably wrinkled face. His teeth, a little misaligned and discolored, were original equipment. I didn't see too many rich, successful eighty-year-old guys with the self-confidence to walk around looking like they're eighty. He tilted his head, a welcoming gesture that said, I bet we're going to be friends.

"Mr. Davis." I extended my hand. "I'm Detective Karen Seagate. Rawlings Police Department. This is my partner, Detective Ryan Miner."

Carl Davis made good eye contact, first with me, then with Ryan. He took a quick glance at Ryan's physique and outfit, then seemed to straighten up a little bit. It was like Carl Davis was looking at himself from fifty years ago. Ryan was wearing his usual shareholders-meeting outfit: tailored blue suit, crisp white shirt, maroon tie with a gold tack. Carl Davis looked ready for a photo at a dedication ceremony for the new building at a hospital or on campus he had endowed: a navy sport coat, pale blue shirt with a buttoned-down collar, a CMSU tie with the cougar logo on it, and grey wool slacks. He wore a black fedora, tilted a little, which matched the shiny black wooden cane with a silver handle. These two guys were cut from the same cloth.

"I'm very pleased to meet both of you," Carl Davis said.

"We're sorry to interrupt you." Ryan gestured to the electrician.

"Not at all," Carl Davis said. "They'll be glad to get away from an old man asking a lot of fool questions."

The electrician smiled indulgently and turned to go back to his job. "I'll catch up to you later, Mr. Davis." His name, Dave, was stitched on his navy blue work shirt, on the right chest. Over the pocket, on the left side, was the logo of Weber Electric.

# *Chapter 9*

I was planning to let Ryan work Carl Davis, the head of the Cougar Athletic Association, right here on the shiny green artificial turf inside the practice facility at Central Montana State University. But then I noticed that the company installing the expensive scoreboard in the practice facility was Weber Electric. That's the company owned by Ronald Weber, the father of Alicia Templeton, the former cheerleader. She's the one who might have been raped by Lake Williams but who definitely had his child, which she immediately gave up for adoption.

Because Rawlings is so small, most of the major tradesmen contract with the university, which has the biggest physical plant in the city. So the link between Weber Electric and the university was probably perfectly legit. But I did want to hear what Carl Davis had to say about the relationship. I decided to let Ryan talk football with Carl Davis for a minute or two before butting in.

Turns out—no big surprise—that Carl Davis was a college football player sixty years ago at the University of Montana. When Ryan started troweling on the compliments about the facility Carl Davis had built, Davis smiled his crooked smile and did some humble-bragging about how Central Montana wouldn't do too well on the field against BYU but that was no reason that his boys couldn't have facilities as good as the big boys had in Provo, Utah. The two men joked about the little Cougars and the big Cougars—apparently the two schools share a mascot.

It all reminded me of how my ex-husband used to spend

autumn weekends: making stupid, boring conversation with other guys about football as I pretended in my half-assed way to look interested. I won't blame football talk for me becoming a drunk, but it didn't help.

I could see, however, that Ryan and this old guy were building a bond, and I knew it might turn out to be useful. They seemed to go on forever about schedules, conferences, rules changes, and players to watch, but when I snuck a look at my watch, it was only four minutes. I stood there, shifting my weight from one foot to the other, resisting the urge to curl up on one of the mats and take a nap. In Carl Davis's defense, however, he never made any sexist comments, and he glanced at me occasionally so I wouldn't feel completely left out after he'd given up trying to involve me in the conversation.

Finally, I had to jump in. "Mr. Davis, I notice Weber Electric is doing the scoreboard."

He brightened and nodded his head, not because this was a fascinating insight but because he wanted to encourage me. "That's right, Detective. Weber does a lot of the work for the athletics department."

"Could you tell us a little about your relationship with the company?" Sometimes I like to use open-ended questions and watch how the person responds. If the university's relationship with the company was innocent, I expected Davis might ask me to clarify the question. But if the relationship was a little sketchy, he might get all defensive, unintentionally telling me what he didn't want me to know.

He pulled back a little. I couldn't tell if the question rattled him, or if it was the change in tone: how two guys chewing the fat about football somehow turned into a police interview. "Weber Electric?" His eyes drifted up to the criss-crossing tangle of steel beams holding the roof up. "Well, we've been using them—let me think—it must be close to thirty years, back when it was Ron's dad running the business. They've done a terrific job with all the electronics here and in the renovation of the complex. In the stadium, itself, too. It's quite complicated stuff—the lights, the electronics for the scoreboard. And all the gear for the locker rooms, the training rooms. Everything's electronic these days. I'll be happy to show you around if you'd like." He nodded and smiled, urging me to jump on his happy train.

"Did Weber do all the electrical work for the practice field? For the renovation of the complex? That must have been a tremendous project."

"I imagine they subbed out some of the work, but they've been our main contractor for a long time. Like this project here: the scoreboard. Weber did the scoreboard in the stadium, a really bang-up job. So when we decided to put one up in the practice facility, Weber was the obvious choice. We let them know what we wanted. Now, I'm not really up to speed on the details of the state contracting system; I'm more about fundraising and donating the money to the university. But I know they have to submit a bid just like everybody else."

Okay: Something about the bidding process was squirrelly. I don't know anything about how bidding works, but I figured the problem had to do with the university—or Carl Davis himself— steering the job to Weber Electric. It could be that Davis gave Weber special information that helped them write the proposal to beat out other electrical contractors.

Then it hit me: Davis's booster organization is about raising money, funneling it through the university to pay for athletics projects. If the organization was cheating somehow, it would be about pricing the bid. Maybe the Weber bids were too high, and Weber and Davis were skimming. But I realized that wasn't it: If another company found out that Weber got the job even though their bid was higher, they could complain, and the whole scheme would blow up. No, it was the opposite: The Weber bids were too low. That way, Weber got all the jobs and all the good publicity. That theory felt right.

"Does Weber undercut the other contractors?"

Carl Davis's expression turned cloudy for a moment. "You know, Detective, I really have no idea. My business expertise is personal financial planning; I don't know anything about this kind of contracting. But I do know that Ron Weber is a good friend of the program—he's a lifetime member of the Cougar Athletic Association. If he bids low on one of our projects—and takes a loss here and there—I'd see that as a contribution to the community."

Davis had just confirmed my guess. It was my turn to look puzzled. "How's that?"

"You have to understand the role of football and basketball in the community. If you want to see a live professional sporting event, you have to travel six hundred miles. Our two revenue sports—football, especially, but basketball, too—are the heartbeat of Rawlings for a lot of people. College athletics are a big part of what makes it so special to live here in God's country. The tailgating in the fall? That really brings us together, as a community. If Ron bids a little low, that's a donation to the university. It means we can build better facilities, which means we can attract better student-athletes. And that means more people in the stands. These two revenue sports subsidize all the other sports—and pay for a number of academic scholarships, too." He paused. "I see it as a win for everyone."

I caught a glimpse of Ryan out of the side of my eye. He looked a little concerned, as if he didn't want to piss Carl Davis off so soon. But I knew he understood what I was doing. And the fact that he didn't interrupt me to re-direct the conversation meant he was willing to let me keep going. "Do you know Ron Weber? I mean, socially?"

"I do. And I consider him a friend—not only a friend of

Cougar athletics, but a personal friend. And, I might add, he and his wife, Jill, were friends with my late wife, as well."

I moved a few inches toward him. "About seven or eight years ago, did Ron Weber tell you about his daughter getting raped by one of the football players?"

"My lord, no, he did not tell me any such thing." Carl Davis's right hand began to shake. He transferred his cane to his left hand and put his right hand in his pants pocket. "No, ma'am, he never told me anything about that." He swallowed hard. "That is very disturbing. Terrible."

"The player was named LaKadrian Williams. Do you have any memory of him?"

"You say seven or eight years ago?"

"That's right."

"He was a four-year scholarship player? Five years?"

Ryan said, "He was a junior-college transfer, but he lost his scholarship in the third year, left the university."

Carl Davis nodded his appreciation to Ryan for the information, then turned back to me. "I'm sorry, Detective. I'm eighty-four years old. I've met thousands of players over the decades, and my memory just isn't what it used to be." He paused. "Can I ask you why you're asking about this incident now?"

"LaKadrian Williams died yesterday. We think it was a drug overdose. He was living in a homeless camp out in Ten Mile Park. We just wanted to know if you could fill in any background on him."

Carl Davis's eyes began to glisten with tears. He wiped at them with his thumb and forefinger. The tremor in his right hand had become more pronounced. "When I hear about these boys getting themselves in trouble … I just don't know." He shook his head. "It seems like it's every year now. They get arrested, beat up their girlfriends. And drugs. So many drugs." He took a handkerchief out of his pocket and blew his nose. "I don't remember this boy. But raping Alicia? Ending up homeless? A drug addict? Don't get me wrong: I love what I do here—building these facilities. Like I said, I see it as a way to contribute to the community. But I work hard—and I know all the boosters do. Ron Weber does. I know that for a fact. Year after year. We work damn hard to give them every opportunity to make something of themselves. A lot of these boys, they don't have that much to begin with—except for their God-given talent. When I hear about a boy going wrong like that, throwing it all away ... it gives me a real hollow feeling inside."

I nodded. "Yeah, I get that. I absolutely do. I'm sorry to upset you like this."

Carl Davis waved it away. "Not your fault, of course. But hearing about the rape ... I know Coach Baxter, consider him a friend. And like I said, Ron Weber as well. To think that one of the boys did that to her. I've known Alicia since the Webers brought her home from the hospital." He shook his head. "It shakes you, it really does. But I have to tell you, I never heard word one about a rape. You know, a lot of things have changed over the time I've been associated with Cougar football. But I swear to you, on my wife's grave, all the athletics staff, from the equipment manager up to the A.D., and the university administration, right up to and including the president, I can tell you honestly, they have never tolerated sexual assault. Never. So when you tell me Alicia was raped by one of the players—I'm not saying it couldn't have happened. But the fact that Ron and Jill never mentioned it to me or my late wife ..." He tapped his chest with a fist. "It hurts me. It hurts me more than you know."

"Mr. Davis," I said, "we're really sorry we upset you with that information—and the death of Mr. Williams. But just to be absolutely clear: You can't help us with any information on his drug overdose?"

"To be perfectly honest with you, I didn't even hear about that death. Was it in the paper? On the news?"

"No, it hasn't been made public yet. We haven't completed the autopsy. We need to be able to say whether it was a suicide, accident, or foul play."

He leaned in toward me. "Do you think it might have been foul play?"

"We don't have enough information at this point. Like I said, the autopsy will tell us how he died. Anyway, Mr. Davis, we want to thank you for taking the time to talk with us. Sorry to tell you this bad news." I swept my arm out to take in the practice field. "You've got a beautiful facility here. Congratulations on that."

Carl Davis looked all of his eighty-four years now. His posture had slumped a little, and the tremor in his hand was fluttering the leg of his slacks. "I'm very sorry to learn of Mr. Williams's death. Very sorry, indeed."

Ryan said, "One more thing, Mr. Davis. Do you know if there are any players from Mr. Williams's time who are on staff here?"

Carl Davis took a deep breath and gazed at the ceiling again. "Seven or eight years ago," he said. Then he looked out at the practice field. His eyes lit up. "You see that man setting up the sled over there?" He pointed down the field. "That's Max Thomas. He's a defensive backs coach."

"You think he knew Mr. Williams?" Ryan said.

"I think he was Lake's roommate."

"Mr. Davis," I said, "thank you again. You've been very helpful."

Certainly more helpful than he realized—or intended.

# *Chapter 10*

Carl Davis collected himself and started walking slowly toward the guy from Weber Electric, the one he had been talking to when Ryan and I interrupted them.

My partner and I headed toward the wall of the practice facility. I picked up the grip on one of the battle ropes coiled on the floor, but my hand was too small to encircle it.

"Make it dance," Ryan said. "Go ahead."

I tried to pick it up, but I could barely lift it off the ground. "What the hell?"

Ryan raised an eyebrow. "Now picture one in each hand." He pantomimed the up-and-down motion of lifting two ropes high enough to get them to slap on the ground. "You rattled that nice eighty-four-year-old gentleman, you know."

"Thank you. He doesn't remember LaKadrian Williams but seems to remember he was called Lake."

"And that Max Thomas was his roommate? I'm having trouble remembering my roommate's name, and I lived with him for a year."

"Explain how he was telling the truth." I put down the heavy rope.

"It's possible he'd forgotten Lake. Like he said, he's met thousands of players."

"We never called him Lake. We called him LaKadrian."

Ryan shook his head. "That's not a giveaway. Everything about LaKadrian is stored deep in Carl Davis's long-term memory. It's locked away until someone opens it. Then, all the details come back, including his nickname."

"And the fact that he roomed with Max Thomas?"

"Again, possible. If something memorable happened involving those two players, yes, it's possible."

"'Memorable' as in Lake rapes Alicia Weber, so the football staff—with the full knowledge of Carl Davis—decides to cover it all up because he's a franchise player?"

Ryan stood there, looking down at the turf, his hands in his pants pockets. I heard a rumbling sound and felt the turf start to shake. Then I felt a breeze coming down from the ceiling. It was the big HVAC system turning on.

"Well?"

He took a deep breath, then exhaled. "Possible."

"If that's what happened, all that stuff Carl Davis just told us about how he didn't know anything about a rape—"

"And how seriously the staff takes rape—"

"Yeah, that's right. Bullshit. One-hundred percent."

Ryan looked at me. "We don't know that. We can't say the whole staff took rape casually. I'm willing to bet they follow rigorous protocols for all their athletes, all their sports. Even seven or eight years ago, every athletics program at every college and university was all over the Title IX provisions. And all the NCAA regs. When I was at BYU, we sat through endless orientation sessions. They gave us the notebooks, and we had to show we'd studied them."

"Which supports my point. Schools have to document how they've made good-faith efforts to prevent or punish any abuses. But if a school gets caught violating Title IX or committing a major NCAA reg—they come in major and minor, right?—"

Ryan nodded.

"If they get caught," I said, "the program could be in deep shit. So, even if they tried their hardest to punish the bad behavior, they still could face a lot of serious penalties, couldn't they?"

"Yes." Ryan held my gaze. "Fines. Lost scholarships. Forfeited victories. Ineligibility to play post-season."

"There's the motive to cover up the bad behavior. I'm not saying it happened. I'm just saying it's a possibility. Lake rapes his girlfriend—"

"*Maybe* he did."

"Lake rapes Alicia. At the hearing on campus, Alicia's father goes batshit, maybe says some racist things because he's not all that thrilled his little girl is screwing a black kid from LA or wherever. The football staff steps in, spreads some money around. All of a sudden, Ronald Weber falls into line, and Alicia withdraws her allegation. All for the good of the team. They tell Lake's roommate to keep his mouth shut and everything will work out for him."

Ryan frowned. "You saying they gave Max a job in exchange for his silence?"

"No idea," I said. "Max could've blown the whole thing up—but he didn't. So when he comes around, years later, looking for a staff job, they help him out. Listen, I never heard of the guy until two minutes ago. But if guys sometimes rape girls, despite the best intentions of the athletics program or the university—or their church or God, whatever—and if those rapes became public they could screw things up royally for those programs or the university, that's the motivation to get everybody behind the same story."

"Okay, I get that. So what do you want to do with Max Thomas?"

"I want to talk to him about his old roommate. See if he remembers him."

Ryan wasn't happy but he nodded. We started to walk over toward Max Thomas, who was leaning in, pushing a two-man sled across the turf toward the middle of the field.

"How heavy is that thing?" I said.

"Couple hundred pounds," Ryan said. "Five hundred when the offensive line coach climbs up onto it."

When Max Thomas saw us approach, he straightened up and glanced at the shields around our necks.

"Good morning," I said to him and introduced me and Ryan.

Max Thomas gave us a smile, told us his name, and we all shook hands. "How can I help you?" He was a good-looking man of about twenty-seven or twenty-eight, tall and beefy. His "Property of CMSU" grey gym shirt showed off a well-muscled torso. A thin sheen of perspiration covered his copper skin. His hair was cut short, his goatee carefully trimmed.

"Carl Davis gave us your name. We're investigating a case involving one of the football players," I said. "Mr. Davis said you might be able to answer a few questions."

"Hope it's nothing serious." He looked a little concerned. "I'll help you any way I can."

"We appreciate that. You're a coach here, is that correct?"

He nodded. "Defensive coach. I work mostly with the linebackers."

"Did Mr. Davis say you went to school here?"

Max Thomas smiled. "I did—and I do. I got my BA in history education here. Taught history and coached high school for six years, then was offered a position here. Actually, it's a graduate assistantship. I'm going for an MA in educational administration and doing the coaching."

A couple of guys setting up equipment started fooling around. I looked up and saw a football go sailing past one guy's head and knock over a cone. They started playfully yelling insults at each other.

"That's pretty good," I said. "And when you get that degree, what kind of education are you hoping to administer?"

He smiled broadly and tapped the sled. "This kind. My game plan is a career in college athletics. Step one: a full-time position on Coach Baxter's staff."

"And work your way up?"

"That's it. Defensive coach, defensive coordinator, head coach."

Like most people, he seemed happy to talk about himself, so I kept going. "Why do you think Coach Baxter hired you?"

"I keep asking myself that. I wasn't a great player. I was a *good* player. Not good enough to play on Sundays—not even close—but I studied the playbooks, kept my nose clean, tried to be a positive influence in the locker room. When the coach learned I was interested in coming back for my graduate degree, he thought I might be a good fit."

"He likes former players, I guess."

"All coaches look for former players—if they can contribute. And Coach Baxter really stresses the importance of education. He's up front with the guys about their football prospects. At a school like this, a player makes it to the NFL every ten, fifteen years—if that often. These kids are going to be working for a living, just like you and me. They've got to be prepared. That's a big reason you see Carl Davis around here all the time. He's kind of an example for Coach Baxter."

"How's that?"

"He got a degree—a real degree in a real field. Finance, I think it was. Started his own financial-services company, built it into a successful firm. Now, in his retirement, he does what he's always loved: helping the programs here at the university. He's active and alert. He's up every morning at dawn, does a half-hour on the stair-stepper, and plans how he can stay busy doing good for the university and for Rawlings. That's the message Coach Baxter wants the guys to hear; that's the life he wants us to build for ourselves."

"Sounds like the coach has thought it through." I paused a second. "Tell me about Lake Williams."

The smile slipped off Max Thomas's face. "Lake? My old roommate?"

"That's the one."

Max Thomas shook his head. "I really liked Lake. We all did, in fact. He was the one who was going to break out."

"How do you mean?"

"He had the raw talent. The speed, the moves, the instinct."

Ryan spoke. "What was his position?"

"Wide receiver. You see the pros doing this now—I mean, the one-handed grabs?—Lake used to do that all the time. In practice, out in the stadium." He swept out his arm to take in the practice facility where we stood. "This place didn't exist then. We did all our practices outside. It could be snowing, zero degrees. He's be out there, short sleeves, making showboat catches." Max paused and looked down at the artificial turf for a second. "Coach Baxter thought he had the ticket. We all thought that about him."

"But?"

"It didn't work out. First, he tore his ACL. Rushed the rehab, never got his speed back. Couldn't pivot on that leg. He wasn't the star he had been. And he wasn't real big on going to classes. He got put on probation a couple times. When the coach benched him, that seemed to ... I don't know, he lost his motivation or something. Pretty soon, he lost his scholarship, dropped out." Max Thomas shook his head and put out his palms in a gesture that said, What are you going to do?

"Did you two stay in touch?"

"For a while. My dad gave him a job in his tree-service business. You know, the guy who drags the branches over to the chipper? No skill, but my father gave him a buck more than minimum wage."

"How'd that work out?"

"It didn't. Lake was unreliable. Showed up late. Didn't show up at all. Got into fights with the other guys. My dad's tree guys, they're highly skilled. A kid comes along, gives them attitude, he's got to go. He lasted four or five months, which was a couple of months more than he would have lasted with anyone but my father."

"And that was the end of your relationship with Lake?"

"That's right. I tried reaching out to him, but his phone was disconnected, then I couldn't track him down. I think he was evicted. No idea where he is now." Max shook his head.

"Tell me about the rape."

Max's head pulled back. "What are you talking about?" His brows were tight. "What rape?"

"Lake was seeing a girl, a white girl. They were pretty serious. This is while he was still on the team. Do you remember her?"

Max closed his eyes, like he was trying to pull up a distant memory. "Wait a second. I think it was Alicia. I remember the name because my mom's name was Alice. Yeah, that's it: Alicia. She was a cheerleader, wasn't she?"

"That's right," I said.

He frowned. "And you're saying Lake raped her?"

"That's what she accused him of. Doesn't ring a bell?"

"Never heard about that."

"He's your roommate. And he never mentions a girl is accusing him of rape."

"I'm telling you, he never said anything about that to me." He was silent a moment. "You know, it wouldn't be the first time a girl accused a player of sexual assault. I'm not saying there aren't sexual assaults. Just that sometimes the allegations aren't true."

I nodded. "Any reason you think Alicia might've made it up?"

"Lake didn't talk to me much about his relationship with her. And, like I said, he never mentioned a rape charge. But Lake wasn't exactly what I'd call good boyfriend material."

"For example?"

"He liked girls. All the girls. There were maybe a dozen black girls on campus, if that many. Mostly student-athletes. You know, track and basketball. First semester here, he was out of control. He started going through them so fast the word got around. The ones who just wanted to party sought him out; the others avoided him. Pretty soon, he was making a name for himself on the field, getting more confident. He was in the school paper all the time, then in some national papers. You know, he'd never had any contact with white girls where he grew up. But they liked him here on campus, the cheerleaders especially. He met Alicia. But he wasn't into commitment. You know what I mean? I don't know what happened. Maybe she caught him fooling around behind her back. Maybe she got mad. A rape charge will get your attention."

"That could be it." I nodded. "That's probably it." I turned to Ryan. "You got that photo?"

Ryan pulled his phone out of his jacket pocket and swiped to the head shot of Lake Williams on the steel autopsy table. He passed his phone to Max Thomas.

When Max looked at it, his face contorted in pain. "What is this?"

"Is that Lake?" I said.

Max's face was frozen. He couldn't speak.

"Is it?"

Finally, he nodded, slowly and just a little. "It's Lake. He's changed, but it's him."

I held out my hand, and Max Thomas handed me the phone. I passed it to Ryan. "We'd like you to come into headquarters later today and make a formal ID of the body. Would you be willing to do that?"

Max stood there, staring off into the distance. "What happened to him?"

"Not sure yet. We think he OD'ed." I paused. "Did he take

drugs that you know of? I mean, when he was a student?"

"Pot, yeah. Most of the guys did. And the trainers had pain meds. When he had that ACL, I know he was on some pain meds for a while. Nothing else that I know of."

"We're gonna have an officer contact you about coming in to make a formal ID, okay?"

Max Thomas spoke in a low voice. "Of course. Whenever you need me." He wiped the back of his hand across his forehead, which was damp with perspiration. "I can't believe this happened."

I nodded. "It happened. We're sorry to have to tell you about it." I handed him my card.

Ryan and I thanked Max Thomas for talking with us. We started walking toward one of the big garage doors near the fifty-yard line that was open. We headed toward the Student Union to pick up some lunch.

I said, "Remember, right at the start of the interview, when I said it was about a player?"

"You mean, when he didn't ask which one? Or what he had done? Then, at the end, when he looked at the photo, he didn't ask when this happened, or where. He hasn't seen Lake in years, doesn't know where he lives," Ryan said. "Who doesn't ask those questions?"

"Someone who already knows the answers?"

# *Chapter 11*

The receptionist in the football complex—a different girl this time, but the same smile—phoned the main office to tell them we were here for our one o'clock appointment with Coach Baxter.

"Let's take the stairs," I said to Ryan.

"Because we took the elevator last time?"

"No, because I want to talk to you."

"Okay." We started up the stairs. "What did you want to talk about?"

"I want to make sure we're on the same page with this interview. We need to figure out why the coach took this job. You said you knew how to get him to talk, right?"

"I said I knew what questions to ask. But that I have no idea if he'll tell us the truth."

"You read up on him. Is he dirty?"

Ryan sighed. "Can't really say."

"Why not? You said he had some NCAA violations at his old school, right?"

"Every program has some violations. And most of them can occur without a coach's knowledge—certainly without his consent."

I stopped climbing. Ryan turned to face me. "But you did the research. You know what the NCAA did, don't you?"

"I do." He nodded. "I took notes."

"Well, what kind of shit was he into?"

"There are a lot of minor violations. Failure to report

recruiting expenses properly, contacting prospects at the wrong times. That sort of thing."

"Anything major?"

Ryan pulled his skinny notebook out of his inside jacket pocket and thumbed through it for a second. "The athletics department at Baxter's former university was accused of paying housing security deposits totaling over twenty-thousand dollars for student-athletes. That case took three years to resolve. The team received two years of probation, lost three football scholarships and twelve recruiting days the next year, and had to vacate the wins in those games in which those student-athletes competed. And the school was fined ten-thousand dollars."

"Anything else?"

"Fourteen players were found to be ineligible because they were not in good academic standing."

"Lousy grades?"

"Worse than that. A professor set up these special courses that only the football players could take. The NCAA said the courses were phony: no work, high grades."

"The coach admitted all that stuff?"

"He admitted it happened, not that he was responsible."

"He was the boss. How could he not be responsible?"

"It's called plausible deniability. The lower-level guys read the signals he's sending out—about what he'll tolerate and what he won't. Then they do what they think he's okay with. But they don't tell him what they're doing, so if they get caught, the coach can say—honestly—that he didn't know about it. I'm not saying that happened; I'm saying that's how it could have happened."

"In other words, he can cheat but still be honest, at least technically."

"That's right."

"The program got dinged bad for those violations?"

"Yes, they did," Ryan said. "But the biggest penalty, from the coach's point of view, at least, was that the president lost faith in athletics, decided to focus more on academics."

"Which was why Coach Baxter decided to leave?"

"We'll ask him."

"All right." We started back up the stairs. "If we get into technical stuff, I need you to take the lead. I have no idea how football works."

"I got it." He smiled. "I'll get him to talk."

We reached the third floor and entered the football office, where Helen, the secretary, looked up at us. "Let me see if the coach is in." She picked up her phone and started talking in a voice so soft I couldn't make out what she was saying. "The coach will be right out." She pointed to a couch and a couple of chairs.

It was less than a minute before Coach Andy Baxter greeted us in the reception area. "Pleased to meet you both." He gave us a boyish smile, but his dark, intense eyes were anything but carefree. His dark hair was thick and wavy, brushed straight back. He was a few inches over six feet, with a slim build. He wore a navy sport coat with an open-necked yellow knit shirt and tan chinos. When he shook my hand, I noticed his fingernails were bitten down severely, with dried blood in the corners. "Why don't we head back to my office?"

We followed him down the hall, and he invited us in. His office was a good twenty feet square. The far wall was a window overlooking the practice facility. One side of the office was dominated by a large oak desk with two wide computer screens. On the screens were game videos, paused. On the other side of the office sat a conference table, a small couch and some soft chairs, and bookcases full of game balls and a dozen trophies. Coach Baxter gestured for us to sit. We took the couch; he took one of the soft chairs. He lifted his right leg and rested the ankle on his left knee. The left foot started tapping.

"Thanks for making the time to see us, Coach Baxter," I said. "We won't take up much of your time. We've got some bad news about one of your former players: a man named Lake Williams."

Andy Baxter nodded. "Carl Davis called me, just a little while ago." He shook his head. "It's a terrible thing. Just terrible."

"You recruited him, is that correct?"

He nodded. "I had tremendous hopes for that boy. He had a rare talent. He didn't understand football when he got here—his films from junior college were a mess. But he had a sense of where the ball was going to be, which way to look back to pick it up, what the defender was going to do. You can't coach that. You can coach technique, but not that kind of instinct."

I said, "Max Thomas told us he rushed the ACL rehab."

"Yeah, he did." Coach Baxter's foot tapped quickly. "You have to remember, he was twenty-one, twenty-two. He was playing beautifully. He already had it all planned out: the Combine, then an early draft, a signing bonus. He wanted to put up some more numbers. I did everything I could—all of us did—to help him understand why he needed to go slow. But *slow* wasn't in his vocabulary."

"What can you tell us about the rape allegation against him?"

"Very little," he said. "I was informed, of course, that an allegation had been made. That's policy. Unfortunately, we'll get an allegation almost every year."

I think that last sentence was meant to suggest the allegations were bogus. I'm pretty sure it wasn't meant to say his players were rapists. "Did you know the student who made the allegation?"

Coach Baxter exhaled and shook his head. "I don't remember who it was."

"It was a cheerleader."

He nodded. "That's right. I remember that now."

"How did that case ever resolve?"

"I think she withdrew the allegation. Something like that."

"Did you kick Lake off the team because of the rape allegation?"

"Not at all. I believe he had academic issues. The scholarship was withdrawn for his academics, I think."

"Coach Baxter," Ryan said, "had you seen Lake Williams recently?"

"Not since he left the team." He picked repeatedly at the corner of his right thumbnail with his index finger. He glanced quickly at his thumb, then wiped away a drop of blood with another finger.

"Do you know anyone who would want to hurt him?" Ryan said.

"No, I ... Why are you asking that? Do you think someone might have killed him?"

"It's early in the investigation," I said. "We don't know yet."

"I can't imagine anyone associated with the team—players or staff—would want to hurt him. He was a good guy. Everyone would have wanted to help him."

His phone rang. "Do you want to get that?"

He brushed it aside. "It'll go to voicemail."

I glanced at Ryan to see if he wanted to ask some questions, like he said he would, but he shook me off. I stood, and Ryan did too. "Okay, Coach Baxter." I extended my hand to shake. "Thanks very much for talking with us." Then I handed him a card. "Please get in touch with me if you have any more information you think could help us."

"Of course, Detective."

Ryan turned on a medium-strength smile and pointed to the big window overlooking the practice field. "This is quite a setup you've got here."

"It's the best in the state." Coach Baxter returned the smile, glad to get onto a happier topic. "You should see the faces of the recruits when they get inside—when they see the whole complex, in fact. If we can just get the kids on campus, we're halfway home in signing them."

Ryan said, "Coach Baxter, if you can give us another minute. I've been reading up on the NCAA—the divisions, all the technical information. It's way beyond my understanding; I'm just a casual fan. Can you help us understand your decision to come to Central Montana?" Ryan took his notebook out, opened it up, and flipped some pages. "You used to coach at Arkansas Southern, which is FBS—have I got that right?"

Coach Baxter put on a friendly expression. I could see he would be good with non-football people. "Yes." He smiled indulgently. "I see you've done your homework."

"FBS is like the major leagues, if I understand it correctly. And you had a strong record there. You were really building up the program." Ryan put on a quizzical expression. "Now, CMSU is FCS." He glanced down at his notebook again. "FCS is less prestigious than FBS, correct? More like Triple-A in baseball. Can you help us understand why you wanted to come here?"

I didn't quite get what Ryan was doing. He knew college football inside and out, but for some reason he was pretending to be as clueless as I was.

Coach Baxter nodded. "Fair question. I got that a lot when Pat and I made our decision eight years ago." He ran his hand through his neatly trimmed hair. "You're right, we were making good progress at Arkansas Southern. But they had a new administration there, and the president wanted to go in a different direction."

"Which direction was that?" I said.

"Down in Arkansas, football is a religion, but the president decided not to make the changes that would have enabled them to become truly competitive—"

I said, "Such as?"

"They weren't willing to do what it took to be an FBS

powerhouse or to ever make it to a stronger conference. They wanted to put the money into academics, which I totally respect. So, we decided—my wife and I—that we weren't going to be able to pursue our own professional goals there."

"Did she work in the program, too?" I said. Halfway through the question I realized he might see it as obnoxious, which it was, so I put on a wide-eyed, ditzy expression.

Andy Baxter looked at me for a moment, not sure how to take my question. "No. Not officially, at least. Coaching a college football team is too big for one person. For me and most other coaches I've known, the spouses do a heck of a lot of work. There are so many PR responsibilities that go along with coaching—if I spoke to every group that invited me, I wouldn't have a minute to coach. So, from my point of view, without my wife's support and encouragement—and about thirty or forty unpaid hours a week of work for the team and the university—I couldn't do the job." He wore the self-satisfied smile that some guys wear when they praise their wives. He put his hands in his pockets and rocked on his heels. "We're partners in this, all the way."

Puke-inducing comments like that don't necessarily mean he's cheating on her. Not necessarily. It could just be the sort of thing that local bigshots say at donor dinners, and he thought he'd use it on me and Ryan.

I noticed that Ryan was wearing a bland, approving smile. I'd have to talk with him about why he had decided not to lay out chapter and verse on this guy's NCAA violations. In the meantime, however, I thought I'd give the coach one last chance to tell us about them.

"Coach Baxter, I do know football is real big down South. Why do you think the college decided to focus on academics rather than make a big push in football? Did you have any problems with the NCAA?"

Andy Baxter shifted his weight and waved the idea away with his hand. "Every program ... do you know much about the NCAA, Detective?"

"Almost nothing," I said. "My husband'll talk your ear off about it, but I don't follow the game."

"Well, it's quite a complicated relationship—between the college and the NCAA, I mean. The NCAA has a rule book—more than four-hundred pages—describing what a school can and cannot do, I mean, with recruiting, eligibility, financial aid, amateurism, benefits, practice-season limitations. The list goes on and on. The vast majority of the violations are just oversights, slip-ups. The school self-reports the violation, then the NCAA reads the report and imposes a penalty, usually a nominal fine. A few hundred bucks, most of the time."

I said, "So it's no big deal, you're saying."

"That's right. Most of the time, it's nothing. For instance, if a prospect comes to town and we pick him up at the airport and drive him to campus, we have to report the value of the ride in from the airport. If the prospect couch surfs at one of the student-athlete's apartments, we have to report the value of that overnight accommodation properly."

There are two ways to approach a guy who's bullshitting you. One way is to signal that you know he's doing it. You lose the element of surprise, but you might throw him off his rhythm so he implicates himself or gives you another angle to follow up. If Coach Baxter cheats on the NCAA rules—and you show him you know it—he might reach out to the staff members who help him cheat, and one of them might slip up and do something stupid.

The other way to deal with a bullshitter is to seem dumber than you are, then hope he'll underestimate you and make a careless mistake. For some reason I hadn't yet figured out, Ryan wanted to go dumb. So I was going to follow his lead. "Wow," I said, "that's kinda petty, isn't it?"

He smiled. "That's the NCAA."

"Coach Baxter." Ryan smiled. "Can you get us the game films for the years Lake played?"

The corner of Baxter's mouth tightened up, but he covered it up almost instantly with a smile. "Why would you want them?" He picked at his right thumbnail.

"I'd like to see Lake Williams play. I never saw him."

"How can that help you?"

"I'm not sure yet. Can you get them? They're all digital, is that correct?"

"Yeah, they are." Coach Baxter paused. "I'll have them copied to a drive for you."

"Thank you," Ryan said. "We'll arrange to pick them up. One other thing: your injury reports. Can we look at the reports for the years Lake played?"

Coach Baxter shook his head. "We're not required to submit them to the NCAA. We don't archive them. They're discarded after five years."

"Okay, thanks, anyway." Ryan nodded.

I turned to Ryan to see if he had any other questions. He shook his head.

"All right, Coach Baxter." I gave him a professional smile. "Thanks again for your time."

He nodded, and Ryan and I left his office and walked silently toward the staircase.

"What just happened?" I said to him.

"A lot of things, Karen." He wore an innocent smile. "You'll have to be more specific."

"Why were you such a little girl in there?"

"I find gender-based stereotyping highly offensive, Detective." Decent people like Ryan are especially good at faking righteous indignation. "I'd already figured out he's a liar."

"How's that?"

"That business about Lake and his ACL surgery. How Lake rushed the rehab? A head coach decides whether the player is ready to come back. He decides whether the player is ready to even practice. He decides everything. For an elite player like Lake, the coach is going to work closely with the medical staff to monitor the player's status."

"But if the player wants to get back in, he'll lie to the coach and the docs."

"That's right," Ryan said, "he will. But the fitness staff, the coaching staff, the doctors—they know the player is going to lie. So they don't rely on what he says. They can tell from looking at the leg's range of motion as he walks or jogs around the practice field. They know that if the player comes back too soon, he could risk catastrophic injury. It doesn't matter whether they like the kid. Even if they're even one percent unsure he's ready, they're not going to let him play."

"So the coach is a liar?"

"Way I'd put it, no matter what went wrong down in Arkansas, it wasn't the coach's fault. If someone paid for the players' rooms inappropriately, it was someone in Housing or on the football staff. If the players were taking phony courses, it was on the instructor. It wasn't the head coach. You noticed he said Lake flunked out?"

"Yeah."

"You remember what Mary Dawson said?"

"Uh ..."

"She said he lost his football scholarship. So the coach isn't even taking responsibility for throwing him off the team. Lake just flunked out—it's not the coach's fault. That's what I mean. So I just decided not to confront him."

"Okay," I said. "We didn't have any reason to confront him now, anyway."

"That's the way I figured it. We'll just hold onto that card.

When it comes time to play it, we will."

"So why do you want to see the game films and the injury reports?" I said.

"If Lake was playing hurt, I'll see it, and we'll know the coach wasn't looking out for his players."

"And the injury reports—is he telling the truth that he tossed them?"

"No. All of that would be archived. What the coach was saying is since the NCAA doesn't require that schools submit them, he can tell us they no longer exist. What are we going to do? We can't subpoena them; there's no probable cause."

"Which means you really want to see them," I said.

"I really do."

# *Chapter 12*

My phone screen read, Harold Breen, Rawlings Police
Department. I hit Talk. "Harold."

"Karen, we're ready to talk to you about Mr. Williams."

"Did a guy named Max Thomas come in and ID the body?"

"Little while ago."

"You posted the autopsy report?"

"Yes, I did. But I want to show you something in the lab. Can
you stop by?"

"Ten minutes?"

"See you," the medical examiner said.

Ryan and I made it back to headquarters and down to the
basement. We walked into Harold's cold, creepy lab. There was a
new corpse on a steel table, wheeled off to the side. Robin, the
evidence tech, was looking at some notes on a clipboard. A
woman I didn't recognize was seated in front of a microscope on
the desk that ran the length of the wall. Harold was standing next
to her, his hands on his hips, talking softly to her.

The three of them looked up, and the woman stood. She was
about forty, tall and thin. Blue jeans, simple blouse and sweater.
Her black hair was pulled back in a ponytail. She wore glasses, no
makeup. A visitor's badge hung around her neck.

Harold said, "Karen, this is Elizabeth Ouvrard. Liz, this is
Detective Karen Seagate. And Detective Ryan Miner." We all
shook hands.

I turned to Harold. "What's going on?" My version of

"Who's she, and what's she doing here?"

"Liz is a biology professor over at CMSU. I asked her to stop by to take a look at something and confirm I was interpreting it correctly."

I'd been on the force for eighteen years, but I couldn't recall Harold ever bringing someone in to confirm something. Usually, he went out to confirm things that other docs or medical examiners asked him about.

Harold turned to Liz. "Do you mind if we walk the detectives through this first?"

"Not at all." Liz Ouvrard answered briskly, her voice harsh and a little too loud in the tiled room full of metal. She seemed amped to be here with real cops consulting on a real case.

Harold said, "Robin, would you start?"

Robin nodded, tucking a strand of purple hair back behind her ear. "The heroin in the baggie was off the charts. Almost ninety-five percent pure. Only trace levels of adulterants."

"Ninety-five? Are you sure?" I said.

"Tried it three times, with different brands of test kits."

I turned to Ryan. "What do we usually see?"

"Fifty-percent pure is high in Rawlings. Twenty is typical."

"Where is a local junkie gonna get uncut heroin?"

Ryan shrugged his shoulders. "I don't know anyone in town big enough to place a special order. We'll need to ask around."

"Harold, is that what killed him?"

"Mr. Williams died of heart failure."

"From the heroin?"

"That's my guess. If he shot up a standard load of this heroin, his BP would have dropped through the floor almost instantly. His heart would have stopped. He would have died within two minutes."

"And the levels of morphine in his fluids?"

"The levels are consistent with a massive overdose. I checked the blood and the urine."

"You said on the phone there was something you wanted us to see?"

"I asked Liz to stop by. She's on an NIH panel that assesses grant applications for CTE research—"

I looked at him blankly. I knew the NIH was the National Institutes of Health. I didn't know what CTE was.

Liz Ouvrard saw my expression. "Chronic Traumatic Encephalopathy. CTE. Brain trauma from concussive and subconcussive hits to the head." She turned back to Harold.

The medical examiner said, "I took a slice of the victim's brain—standard part of the autopsy. When I saw the slide, I stained it and asked Liz to confirm what I was seeing."

"If you two would step over here, please ..." She led me and Ryan over to the microscope, then gestured for me to sit and look through it.

"What am I looking at?"

"You see those bodies shaped like pieces of popcorn? They're individual nerve cells in the brain."

About half of the popcorn pieces had brown areas in them. "Okay, what are the burned parts?"

"They're not burned. That's the stain Dr. Breen applied. The dark spots are tau deposits. Tau is a protein that helps the nerve cells communicate with each other. When the brain absorbs a lot of hits, the tau can start to clump up in the nerve cells. They're called tangles because they look kind of like tangles of yarn. Once they get tangled up like this, they start to impede the communication between cells."

I looked up at the professor. "Bottom line?"

"Bottom line: you're looking at Stage 2 CTE."

"Which means what?"

"Stage 1 is the onset of degenerative brain disease. Stage 4 is full-blown dementia. That's what we generally see in autopsies of football players and boxers who die in their forties and fifties. At Stage 2, the patient has noticeable problems: CTE presents with impaired judgment, impulse-control problems, aggression, and depression. Eventually—it can be years or decades after the repetitive injury—progressive dementia. The damage tends to start in the midbrain, then it moves out toward the subcortex and the amygdala—the areas of the brain that control anxiety and stress response. Eventually, it moves to the cerebral cortex, which controls learning, language, and memory. "

I turned to Ryan. "Lake Williams had violent episodes, right?"

Ryan's expression was grim. "Maybe as early as college. Definitely in recent years." He turned to Liz Ouvrard. "He could have had CTE symptoms in college?"

"We've seen it in high-school kids. We don't have a good, cheap way to test it on kids when they're alive, but we've seen it in a few autopsies of teenage football players. But college kids? For sure. In fact, we suspect that much of the damage occurs in high school. Kids that young don't think they can get hurt, so they take more hits than they should. And the vigilance by high-school coaches and staff isn't as good as it is in college or the pros."

Ryan spoke. "College coaches and the NCAA know about this, don't they?"

"Now they know quite a bit, and the NCAA has officially stopped denying the link, although they sometimes say stupid things. They've got pretty good concussion protocols in place. But when did Mr. Williams start college?"

Ryan said, "Counting junior college, about ten years ago. He played college ball about four years. Before that, we don't know. Probably three or four years in high school."

Liz Ouvrard shook her head. "Unfortunately, he could have been right on schedule to develop CTE. You have to remember, it's not just concussions that can cause this; we know that repetitive subconcussive hits can be just as damaging—maybe even more so because the player doesn't show any outward symptoms."

I said, "You mean, he doesn't get knocked unconscious, doesn't get dizzy and fall down or throw up or anything?"

"That's right." Liz Ouvrard nodded. "The skull is a wonderful bone, but when the head takes a big hit, the brain gets pushed up against the inside of the skull with a whole lot of force. If that happens repeatedly, you can progress to CTE." She paused a moment. "Do you know the position he played?"

"Wide receiver," Ryan said.

Liz Ouvrard nodded. "So he took some hits."

"I assume he blocked, too," Ryan said. "Since he had good hands, he might have returned punts and kickoffs."

She exhaled slowly. "He could have taken hundreds of subconcussive hits, maybe thousands."

I looked around. Nobody seemed to have anything else to say. I addressed Harold. "So how'd you call the death in the report?"

"Immediate cause: heart failure. Underlying cause: opiate overdose. Manner: undetermined."

Liz Ouvard said, "Why undetermined?"

Harold looked at me to answer. "If the victim didn't know how potent it was, it was accidental. If he knew and wanted to die, it was suicide. If someone gave it to him without telling him it was uncut, it was homicide."

Liz Ouvrard nodded.

Harold turned to me. "I'll update the report when you tell me what happened."

Ryan and I thanked Liz Ouvrard, as well as Harold and Robin, and headed back to our desks in the detectives' bullpen.

"Okay." We sat down. "Tell me how Lake Williams and Kendra get their hands on uncut heroin."

"I have no idea." He shrugged his shoulders. "Could have

been a mistake. His dealer handed him the wrong baggie."

"Or he asked for it. He wanted to die."

"Where'd he get the money?" Ryan said.

"He used to sell the stuff himself." I thought for a second. "Okay, let's try to figure this out. Leave aside suicide for a moment. Start with the simplest explanation: There's only the two of them. They wanted to get high and screw. They're dope buddies."

"So how come he's dead and she's not?" Ryan said.

"She didn't shoot up because she watched him take the first hit and flatline. She realized it was bad dope. She got scared, ran out of the tent."

"Then it's accidental death," Ryan said.

"He brings the dope. He's gonna give her some. In exchange, she's gonna screw him."

"I don't like it." Ryan shook his head. "She's too gross to want to screw. And Robin said they didn't screw."

"We're talking about the plan, not what happened. He was gonna screw her in exchange for some dope. He shoots up, dies. The plan changes. She makes sure we find the drug kit. She leaves. Simple as that."

"So the death was accidental," Ryan said. "Neither of them knew it was uncut."

"It's plausible. No crime committed at all."

"What about suicide?"

"Okay," I said. "His life has gone to shit: the CTE and everything else. He asks her to get him some heroin—"

"Or he gets it himself."

"That's right," I said. "Doesn't matter who gets it. He takes a big hit, dies."

"So why are his pants down?"

"He wanted to go out with a grunt, but he died before he could get it up?"

"Kendra pulled his pants down? To keep us scratching our heads?" Ryan said.

"Why does she want us to scratch our heads? She's not doing anything illegal. He wants to kill himself. He doesn't want to die alone. She's doing a nice thing, sitting there with him."

"She doesn't want us to put her at the scene," Ryan said. "She pulls down his pants so it looks like he's all alone and he's going to yank it."

"And the only reason that doesn't work is we find her blood in the syringe. Which she wouldn't have thought out."

"All right," Ryan said, "that brings us back to the main question: How come he's dead and she's sitting in Holding?"

"Shit." I slapped my knees. "We're gonna have to ask her."

Ryan called Holding and asked them to deliver her to Interview 1. Three minutes later, we entered the room.

Kendra was awake now. Really awake. She was twitching, scratching at her bare arms and her thighs. Ryan walked over to the controls on the wall and turned on the recording equipment.

"Kendra." I announced the time and the names of the people in the room. "We need to talk to you about what happened in the tent with Lake Williams."

"Wasn't me."

"Listen to me, Kendra. We have forensic evidence putting you in that tent with Lake. Don't waste our time here. You want us to go straight to charging you with murder?"

"What evidence you talking about?"

"Your blood and his blood were in the syringe."

"Maybe my blood was already in there."

"One more chance to start talking, Kendra, then we charge you with murder."

"What can you give me if I talk?"

"If you cooperate, we'll tell the prosecutor. That can make a big difference in the sentence."

"Not gonna be any sentence. I didn't do anything."

"If you don't start telling us the truth, there will be a sentence." I paused. "You can count on that."

"What can you give me now?" She scratched at her left arm repeatedly. Tiny drops of blood traced the long red marks.

"When you tell us the truth and we finish this interview, we'll see what kind of medical assistance we can get you for the withdrawal."

"I need to score. Give me my money and let me get the fuck out of here."

"Talk to us and we'll get you over to the hospital. Who brought the heroin: you or Lake?"

"Lake had it in his tent. I don't know how he got it. We were gonna shoot up. That's all it was."

"Why didn't you shoot up?"

"I did."

"The heroin was uncut. How come you're alive?"

"I just did a little."

"Why?"

"He didn't look too good."

"Did you try to revive him?"

"Didn't know what to do. I slapped his face a few times. Talked to him. I saw he was, like, unconscious or something. I got scared. Got the hell out of there. That's what it was."

"Why were his pants down?"

"We were gonna fuck."

"But you didn't?"

"He was passed out, whatever. He couldn't get it up."

"Did you have any reason to want to hurt Lake?"

"No, why would I want to hurt him? I just told you, we were gonna fuck."

"Did he ever hit you? Beat you up?"

"Everybody's got good days and bad days. He had a temper,

but there wasn't nothing wrong that day."

"Here's the problem we're having with what you just told us: If Lake got the drug, he would've known it was uncut and he would be alive now. The fact that you're alive now—and he's dead—makes us think you're the one knew it was uncut."

"It happened just like I said. Give me my money and let me get the fuck out of here. Did you take my money?"

"We got your money and your candy bar and your filthy clothes. When we release you, we'll give you all your stuff back. When we release you. We need to check out what you told us. But first we're gonna get you over to the hospital, see if they can give you something to take the edge off. You're gonna stay there, with an officer right outside your door, or here, in Holding."

"Just give me my shit and drive me back to my place."

"Can't do that. You don't understand what's happening, Kendra. We got you and Lake in a tent. He shoots up some uncut heroin. He's dead. We don't know what happened in that tent, but until we rule you out for killing him, we're not letting you go."

"Well, how the fuck are you gonna rule me out? I gotta stay here forever?"

"We get forty-eight hours to enjoy each other's company."

"Detective," I said to Ryan, "arrange to have Ms. Crimmons taken to the hospital."

I announced the end of the interview, and Ryan turned off the recording equipment and left Interview 1.

A minute later, two uniforms and Ryan returned. The two uniforms—Gonzalez and Murphy—escorted Kendra Crimmons out.

Ryan sat down. "Correct me if I'm wrong, but I don't think we know a single thing now that we didn't know ten minutes ago."

"Well, we know Kendra's got a pretty bad drug habit. But that she's thinking clearly enough not to implicate herself in any way.

She didn't supply the drugs. She didn't inject them into him. Hell, she didn't even screw him. All she copped to is she shot up a little herself."

"She knows we're not going to charge her with that."

"That's right."

Ryan said, "How are we going to verify her story about Lake getting the drugs?"

I shook my head. "I have no idea."

It wasn't until more than an hour later, when I was driving home, that I figured it out.

# *Chapter 13*

I pulled into a gas station, parked off to the side, and shut down the engine. I fished around in my big leather bag, found my phone, and called Dispatch.

"This is Seagate. I need to get in touch with Gonzalez and Murphy. They're transporting a suspect to the hospital. Can you connect me?"

In a moment I was talking to Maria Gonzalez. "Where are you now?" I said to her.

"We're processing Kendra Crimmons at the hospital."

"Have they given her any meds yet?"

"We're not that far along."

"Good," I said. "Put her in the patrol car and bring her back to the station. I'll be at Holding."

"You mean, after they treat her?"

"No, don't let them treat her. Change of plans. Thank the doctors or nurses or whoever and bring her back right now."

"She's pretty jumpy. What should I say if she asks what's going on?"

"I always go with 'no idea.'"

"Okay, Detective."

Then I called Ryan, who was still driving. "Ryan, I'm bringing Kendra back to the station. She hasn't gotten any treatment yet."

"What happened?"

"I figured out how to get her to tell us the truth. I'm telling you in case you want to come back for that. You're off shift. I don't mind doing it on my own."

"No," he said. "I'm a big fan of the truth. See you back at the station."

"Okay."

Ten minutes later, back at police headquarters, I asked the officer in Holding to process Kendra Crimmons and get her to Interview 1.

I was sitting in the interview room with Ryan when Gonzalez and Murphy brought her in. I thanked them and apologized for being a pain in the ass.

Kendra said, "What the fuck is going on? You said you were gonna get me over to the hospital." Both her arms now were red and raw from her scratching. Her eyelids were twitching pretty good, too. She wiped at her bloodshot eyes, which were tearing.

"Yeah, well, first we need to talk to you some more about Lake Williams."

"I told you everything I know."

"No, you didn't. You told us what you wanted us to believe. Problem is, it was all bullshit."

"What are you talking about?"

I turned to Ryan. "Detective, would you give us a few minutes? I'll look you up when it's time to begin the interview." I had a dummy folder with "Crimmons, Kendra" written on the tab. I opened it up and studied the scrap paper for a minute so Ryan could get set up to listen and watch through the one-way mirror.

"Okay, Kendra, here's where we're at. I was driving home, and something you said got me thinking. Couple times, you mentioned how you wanted us to just give you your money back and let you get the hell out of here. Remember that?"

"Yeah, why don't you fuckin' do that?"

"Now, what you wanted to do—I'm not judging or anything, but here's what I think your plan was: Buy some dope. Am I right?"

"You gonna arrest me for what you think I was gonna do?"

I smiled. "No, Kendra, but there's the thing. We entered all your belongings in the system. Except for your clothes and some food in your pockets, you had eighteen bucks on you. Eighteen bucks." I was looking at her hard.

She froze, for only a moment, and I knew I was right.

"So I thought, what kind of dope is she gonna be able to score with eighteen bucks? Then it hit me. You weren't talking about eighteen bucks. There's some other money out there, some other money you were afraid we'd gotten our hands on. But when we tracked you down at the camp you were so strung out you had no idea whether we'd found it." I paused. "Am I right?"

She shook her head. "No fuckin' way. Where the hell am I gonna get serious money?"

"That's a very reasonable question. Here's my answer. Somebody gave you some money to deliver the drugs to Lake. That person knew that Lake, being a drug addict, would shoot up right away—and then he would die." I looked at her. She was scratching at her arm, forming nasty new red marks. "You with me so far?"

"You're full of shit."

"Could be, but let's find out. You know why I asked my partner to leave the room?"

"Don't give a shit."

"It's because he's a Boy Scout. Actually, he's worse than that. He's a Mormon. I wanted to talk to you in private, just the two of us. Here's what's gonna happen: If I'm full of shit, and what you told us before was the truth, you just tell me. I'll get the two officers back here and they'll bring you over to the hospital. The docs will give you something to help you get through the night. And then we'll bring you back here to Holding. Tomorrow, at noon, I'll release you. And you can take your eighteen dollars and your candy bar and your filthy clothes and be on your way. We'll even drive you back to your tent."

"Why you gonna keep me till noon? Let me go right from the hospital. You don't have any right to hold me."

"You see, that's the problem. I don't think you were telling me the truth. So I have to do a little more investigating, and it'll take me until tomorrow, around noon."

"What kind of investigating?"

"You just told me what kind of investigating to do. You've got some money stashed out there. Otherwise, you wouldn't care if I released you tonight or tomorrow. How much is it, Kendra?"

"All right," Kendra said. "What if there is some money? How do you prove I didn't it get some other way? Some legal way?"

"Come on, Kendra, you're gonna go into the office and sell some stocks and bonds? Write some software? No offense, but I can't even see a john paying you five bucks for a suck. Whatever money you've got, you earned it selling drugs or—like I said— delivering the heroin to Lake. So these are your choices. You stick with your story, and I'll go find the dirty money, or you tell me the truth now.

"Here's the part you haven't figured out yet, the part I don't want my partner to hear. If you stick with your story, tomorrow morning, once the sun is up, I'm gonna get one of the drug-sniffing dogs, write it up as a sweep of the homeless camp, then walk on down to the riverbed where we picked you up. My guess is there'll be enough drug residue on any money you've touched it'll take the dog about thirty seconds to find it."

"Go ahead," Kendra said. "Find it, log it in. Give it to me when you release me at noon."

I shook my head. "Think for a minute, Kendra. Just sit there and think for a minute. Why did I ask my partner to leave the room? Why did I say I'd head out to the camp tomorrow, bright and early, just me and the dog?"

Her eyebrows were scrunched up for a few seconds, then she closed her eyes. "Fuck."

"Fuck, indeed." I paused. "I need you to make up your mind. My partner's gonna start to worry about what the two of us are talking about. What's your decision: stick with your story and let me go find the money, or tell us a better story?"

"If I tell you a better story, what happens to my money?"

"We log it in, with your eighteen bucks."

"No questions asked?"

"No questions asked. If we release you, you take the money with you." I looked at her. "The sooner you tell us a good story, the sooner you get to the hospital. You sit here for a while. I'll check back with you later."

Before I could close the file and stand up, she spoke. "Go get your stupid partner."

I turned to the mirror and waved him in.

Kendra frowned at me. "He heard all that? Everything you said was crap?"

"Most of it. He would've wanted half your money." Ryan came back into the room. "Turn the system on, Detective. Ms. Crimmons wants to amend her statement from earlier." When he did it, I announced the time and names.

I turned back to Kendra. "All right, Kendra, tell us the story. What happened that night?"

"That day, I was in town …"

"Where in town?"

"Lots of places."

"What were you there for?"

"Score some drugs."

"For yourself? For Lake?"

She shrugged. "Score some drugs. I didn't plan out who I was gonna share them with."

"Okay, go on."

"So I met with a guy I see sometimes. Bought some weed and some crystal off him."

"Where was this?"

"Down under the overpass. Near the skate park."

"So what happened?"

"He says, Want to make a quick fifty? I say, What do I gotta do? He says, Go over there, behind that concrete pillar. Wait ten minutes. A guy's gonna come up to you. He's got a business proposition for you. I say, I'm not gonna blow him outside in broad daylight, if that's what he wants. He said, Just listen to what he has to say. If you don't want to do what he wants, walk away. He holds fifty dollars in front of my face. I take it and walk over to that concrete pillar."

"Then what happened?"

"Ten minutes later, a guy comes up to me. He says, You know Lake Williams? I say, Why you asking? He says, You be in the parking area in Ten Mile Park tonight at ten. Someone's gonna drive up and give you something to give to Lake Williams. You bring it right to Lake. I say, Why should I do that? He says, The guy will give you five-hundred bucks. Cash. I say, Then what? He says, Then nothing. That's the deal. Deliver this thing to Lake tonight for five-hundred dollars."

"This guy you're talking to, who is he?"

"Never seen him before."

"Can you describe him?"

"White guy, maybe forty. Long hair, going grey. Needed a shave."

"What was he wearing?"

"Black jeans, dark jacket with a hood."

"Any distinguishing characteristics? Tattoos, scars, anything?"

"All I could see was his face and his hands. No tats there."

"How about his voice? Any kind of accent? Speech impediment?"

Kendra shook her head. "I think he smokes. You know, raspy voice. Smelled like cigarettes."

"And the first guy, the one you bought the dope from. What's his name?"

She smiled a little. "We don't do names. He calls himself Lucky."

"Tell me about him."

"Don't know anything about him. Tall, skinny. White guy. Maybe thirty. Gold loop earrings. That's all I know about him. It's strictly business. We don't hang out."

"Okay, that night, ten o'clock, what did you do?"

"Like he told me to. I'm standing by the parking area. A pickup pulls in, real slow."

"What kind of pickup?"

"Don't know. It was dark out."

"Could you identify the driver?"

"No, I walked up to the passenger side. Window slides down. An arm reaches out, hands me a baggie. Tells me to give it to Lake. Asks if I understand. I say yeah. Arm gives me five bills. Five hundreds."

"He didn't explain why he's giving you so much money?"

Kendra looked at me. "He didn't say. I didn't ask."

"What happened next?"

"The guy drives away."

"Did you get a look at his license plate? Any writing on the truck? Any damage you remember?"

"I don't see good enough to read license plates or writing on trucks. I used to have glasses, but not anymore. And why would I want to do that?"

"What did you do next?"

She scratched hard at one arm, then the other. "What he told me to do: Go to Lake's tent and give him the baggie."

"Did Lake ask where you got it?"

"You think homeless people spend all their time asking questions? 'That looks like a nice sandwich. Where'd you get it?'"

"Then what happened?"

"Like I said before: He shoots up, crashes pretty bad. I take just a little bit. When I come to, I see he's in trouble, I leave."

"You didn't think to call 911?"

"That wasn't my first thought, no."

"Here's what we're gonna do, Kendra. We're gonna send you over to the hospital, see if they can do anything for you. Then you're gonna spend the night in Holding. We'll feed you. Tomorrow morning, we'll talk again. You tell us where the cash is, we'll see that as a sign you want to cooperate."

"I didn't know the dope was so strong. I didn't break any laws."

"You mean, by shooting up as Lake crashed? Yeah, you got my vote for Citizen of the Month."

# *Chapter 14*

First thing Wednesday morning, Ryan and I walked over to
Holding, where we have four small cells. When the new police
headquarters was built eight years ago, we made sure to include
holding cells. In the old building, we had a single grey-bar cell,
where we could hold people for only four hours. If we needed to
hold them longer than that, or overnight, we had to ship them off
to County's jail, a couple miles away. We had to pay County a fee
for every person they held, and it cost us an hour of an officer's
time for the transport and the booking.

The officer in Booking opened the heavy steel door and we
walked into the cell, which was about ten by ten, with a stainless-
steel toilet and a concrete bed with a thin foam pad on it.

"Good morning, Kendra," I said. "You remember us?"

She was sitting up on the bed. She rubbed some junk out of
an eye, then studied her finger from a few different angles before
wiping it on her white jumpsuit. "Yeah, you're the two fuckers
who tricked me into telling you about my money, which I earned
legally."

"Okay, good. They give you something at the hospital to hold
you for a little bit?" She scowled, as if I was expecting her to
thank me for something that someone else had done. "How much
of what we talked about yesterday do you remember?"

"All of it." She spat out the words. "I'm a junkie, not an
idiot."

"Great. Let's start with you telling us about where you stashed the five-hundred bucks." Her expression said she really didn't want to tell us. "Remember the concept, Kendra. Someone killed Lake. Most obvious person is you. He used to beat you up. You buy the uncut heroin and go to his tent. He's so out of it he shoots it right up. It kills him. We go that route, you'll go before a grand jury, maybe face murder charges—at least manslaughter. One thing for sure: You'll be living in County for a while in a cell just like this one. One difference: County doesn't care about your habit. You see that drain in the floor?" I pointed. "Their idea of inmate welfare is to hose the cell down every once in a while."

Ryan said, "And your attorney? A public defender. He could be twenty-four, twenty-five years old, excited because he just passed the bar—on his third try. You could be his first case."

"Therefore," I said, "let's ratchet back the attitude. You don't like me? I get that. Just between us, I don't give a shit. I'm not crazy about you, either. But it's time for you to start acting a little smarter. You want us to believe you didn't kill Lake. You want to help us figure out who did. Where's the money, Kendra?"

She shook her head in disgust. "Down by where you grabbed me. There's a cottonwood. On the side away from the stream, there's a bunch of river rocks piled up. Dig down three or four inches. You'll find the envelope."

"And inside the envelope?"

"Five bills. Hundreds."

"All right. We'll get that envelope and log it in with your other stuff. Can you tell us any more about your dealer or the guy who told you to wait in the parking area?"

"Told you everything I know yesterday."

"If you're afraid one of them is gonna come after you, we can keep you in here until we pick them up."

She shook her head. "I can't ID them. I don't know them; they don't know me."

"You sure?"

"I'm more afraid of shooting some bad product. I don't know anything about the two guys. The one I scored from a few times is called Lucky. The other one, I don't know his name. Never seen him before."

I nodded. "We can hold you forty-eight hours. That's one more day. We're gonna use that time to try to figure out if anything you said is true. We'll start by looking for the envelope with the cash. If we find it where you said, that's a good sign. You think of anything else we can use to check out the rest of your story—you remember something about the pickup truck or any physical characteristics of the two guys—you bang on your door here and tell the officer you want to get in touch with Seagate. We'll talk. All right?" I turned to leave.

"What if I start to get the shakes again?"

"You'll shake. We can't keep bringing you back and forth to the hospital." I stopped and faced her. "You work with us, Kendra, a lot of good things can happen for you. We can help you get into a program. But if you keep wasting our time and mouthing off," I said, pointing to the floor, "aim for the drain."

Ryan and I left Holding and headed for the chief's office to brief him on where we were. Margaret, his gatekeeper, waved us in.

"Karen, Ryan." The chief looked up from his computer and gestured for us to sit. He raised his eyebrow to tell us to start.

"Harold finished the autopsy on Lake Williams yesterday afternoon," I said. "The vic's heart stopped when he shot up a load of uncut heroin. Harold wanted me and Ryan to see a slide of his brain. Turns out he had CTE."

The chief frowned. "He was less than thirty, right?"

"About twenty-seven," I said. "It was Stage 2, which is enough to explain some of the symptoms he was showing: confusion, violence, depression."

"Any evidence it was suicide?"

"We don't think so. We worked on Kendra Crimmons, his drug buddy. She told us one of her dealers put her onto some guy who gave her five-hundred bucks to deliver the drugs to Lake. If he had wanted to kill himself with drugs, he could've gotten them himself, without any help from her."

"And you believe her?"

I looked at Ryan, who shrugged his shoulders. "Her story is at least plausible," I said. "I don't see her as earning five-hundred, either dealing or hooking. She told us where she stashed the money, out at the camp. We're gonna run out there now. If the money's where she says, I think I'll believe her."

"She didn't identify who gave her the money or give you a motive?"

"Nothing."

"Is she holding back?"

"She's showing a lot of attitude, but I think this story might be true. She's learned not to be curious. Someone hands her some cash and tells her to give a baggie to Lake, I see her as doing it."

The chief sighed. "So you two are saying homicide?"

"If Kendra is telling us the truth—about a guy pulling up in a pickup and handing her money and the drugs—yeah, I think we are."

"What's your thinking on who and why?"

"We're not that far along," Ryan said. "Either someone wanted to kill him for something he already did, such as rape Alicia eight years ago—"

"Are you thinking Alicia herself?" the chief said.

"Or her father," Ryan said.

The chief turned to me. "But you don't like that?"

"No, we don't," I said. "Neither of them. Alicia seems to be living her life okay. I'm not saying it didn't screw her up, but we're not seeing what would cause her or her father to flip out now. More likely, someone wanted to prevent Lake from doing something he was gonna do. Or send a signal to someone else."

The chief said, "There's no test for CTE on live people?"

Ryan said, "There are some tests being developed, but there's no way a guy living in a tent in Montana is going to have access to that technology."

"So Lake wouldn't have known he had CTE."

I shook my head. "He would've known he was pissed off and violent, but he would've known that for the last ten years, my guess. Since the disease scrambles your thinking, he might not have been able to think it through. Besides, he was so young it probably never would have occurred to him to think CTE. Kendra told us he was violent sometimes but he was okay the day he died. Seems to me, you hang around with homeless people you're gonna see a lot of violence, depression, and confusion, anyway."

"Karen, you said the murder could have been to send a signal to someone. You got something in mind? Someone in the homeless camp?"

I shook my head. "They're real into the live-and-let-live philosophy. At least that's the impression I got. And I didn't see anyone there who's got five-hundred bucks to make this happen. Whoever wanted him dead is from outside. And has a pickup truck."

"Which brings us back to his college days," the chief said. "Someone he knew when he was in the world. So how are you going to work that?"

"Ryan says he can research the coach a little more. We think he's not being straight with us."

"What do you mean?" The chief looked at Ryan.

Ryan said, "I don't like his story about why he left his last job—how the school didn't want to let him build the program. He racked up some major NCAA violations and penalties at his last job, but he didn't mention them. We gave him a lot of opportunities, but he acted like all the violations were petty stuff."

"Being a coach carries a lot of PR responsibilities," the chief said. "You say he's in his forties?"

"That's right."

"Anyone that age in that job knows how to spin his story. That might be all it is."

"True," Ryan said. "The other way to crack this open is to find Kendra's dealer. He'll finger the guy who gave her the money. When we find that guy, we flip him."

"But you say she's not telling you anything else."

"Not at the moment," I said. "We might think of another way to come at her. We're gonna keep her in Holding until tomorrow morning."

The chief said, "Any ideas on how to get her to give up the guy in the pickup?"

"I already threatened to steal her money. That's why she told us about the dealer and the guy who made the deal with her out by the skate park. Right now, I don't think we have much leverage with her. There's no evidence she killed him—hell, there's no evidence for anything except she and Lake shot up some heroin that night. The only thing we can use to move her is to threaten to keep her locked up and make her go through withdrawal, which I don't want to do."

"I don't want to do that, either. See that she gets medical attention while we hold her. I'm fine with you keeping her a second night, but unless you can show probable cause that she killed Lake, we release her then."

"Absolutely," I said.

The chief smiled and stood. "All you need to do is figure out why the football coach wanted to kill a player who dropped out seven years ago and lived in a tent."

"I'm sure Ryan won't have any problem with that." I glanced at him. He gave me a no-problem nod. "Thanks, Chief."

Ryan and I went back to the detectives' bullpen, grabbed our coats, and headed out to the parking lot. It took us about thirty-five minutes to get out to Ten Mile Park. The extra five was the morning traffic.

We walked into the clearing, where a young guy was shoving paper and brush into the oil can to start it up for the day.

He looked up at us as we passed him on the way to the path down to the riverbed. "You looking for Kendra?" He put a lighter to the stuff in the can.

"No, we know where she is."

"I was gonna tell you, we haven't seen her in a while."

"We've got her."

"She kill Lake?"

"We don't know." We walked up to him. "Any reason you think she would?"

The guy shrugged. He was in his late twenties, thin and short. He had a patchy neck beard that covered up most of his old acne scars. He wore his green wool cap low on his forehead.

"What's that mean?" I said.

"Nothing."

He sounded like my son. When Tommy says Nothing, it usually means Something. "Did Lake ever get violent with Kendra?"

"Way we do it here, if she wants our help, she asks."

"Did she ask?"

"She didn't ask me."

I walked up closer to him. "What's your name?"

"Henry."

"Henry, I'm Detective Seagate. We're not sure what happened here that night. We know Lake died of a drug overdose, but we don't know if it was suicide or accidental. We haven't ruled out homicide. If you can help us, we'd appreciate it."

"I don't know anything." Henry scratched at his wool cap,

then looked in the can to see if the fire had started.

"If you and the other people here can help us, we can help you."

"How you gonna do that?"

"For one thing, if this was murder—and it was someone in the camp did it—I think you'd want him out of here, right? Now, once the public hears about a murder in an illegal camp in a city park, that's gonna make it harder for the city to let you all stay here. We can tell the city how you cooperated with us. Even if it was someone in the camp who did it, that's just one bad apple. But if we have to say you tried to protect one of your own—out of loyalty or something—how do you think the good citizens of Rawlings—the tax-paying citizens of Rawlings—are gonna react?" I looked at him. "So talk to me. Do you know if Lake beat her up?"

He nodded but didn't say anything.

"He ever get into it with anyone else? Any of the guys?"

Henry nodded again. "Lake wasn't the only one gets pissed off."

"Anyone talk about getting even with him?"

"Fights happen. Nobody I know ever said anything about getting even with him."

"Did you hear anything—a fight?—Sunday night? Anything unusual?"

Henry shook his head.

I handed him my card. "Let me know if you think of anything, okay?"

He nodded.

When we started walking across the clearing toward the path down to the riverbed, he called out to us. "Why you going down there?"

I stopped and turned. "You let me know if you think of anything."

When Ryan and I were about thirty yards down the path, I glanced back. The leaves on the brush rustled in the breeze. Henry was standing there, at the start of the path, scratching at his wool cap. I couldn't see his face closely enough to read it. Probably he was just wondering why we would check out Kendra's place down by the riverbed if we knew she wasn't there.

# *Chapter 15*

Ryan and I followed the path down to the dried-out riverbed at Ten Mile Park. "Where did Kendra say she stashed the money?"

"A cottonwood," he said. "Buried on the side away from the riverbed, under some river rocks."

I shaded my eyes from the sun and scanned the area near where we picked her up yesterday. There was scrubby brush on both sides of the riverbed, but I didn't see the cottonwood. "Let's head down to where we found her."

We walked the fifty yards to the spot where we picked her up, which I identified from the dried-vomit starburst in the sand. On the other side of the riverbed, I saw a cottonwood rising out of the undergrowth. We crossed the riverbed and headed toward it. Both of us circled it a couple of times.

"You see a pile of river rocks?"

Ryan started walking around the stunted tree in larger concentric circles. "I'm not seeing anything."

"Is it possible some animal has gotten here?"

Ryan shook his head. "Not unless Kendra buried some food along with the money."

"Kendra's sitting in Holding. Could she be stupid enough to send us on a wild goose chase?"

Ryan thought for a second. "Something's wrong here—"

"What is it?"

He pointed back across the riverbed. "Wrong tree."

We crossed the riverbed and found the cottonwood, half-obscured ten yards back in the brush. At its base, on the side away from the riverbed, was a small pile of river rocks, just like Kendra said. We dug down a few inches and retrieved the envelope. I snapped on a pair of gloves and opened it carefully to confirm it contained the five hundreds, then placed it in the open evidence bag that Ryan was holding.

This was our first break: Kendra was telling us the truth. Somebody gave her five-hundred dollars to deliver some deadly heroin to Lake Williams. Now all we had to figure out was who and why.

I steered the Charger out of the parking area in Ten Mile Park. "You figured out how to get Kendra to finger her dealer or the guy who paid her to deliver the drugs?"

Ryan was silent for a moment. "We agree that her story is plausible, right?"

"Yeah."

"Including the part that she doesn't have a name on the dealer, and she'd never seen the guy who gave her fifty dollars to wait in the parking area—or the guy in the pickup who handed her the drugs."

"Unless you explain why I shouldn't believe her."

"When you read Cory McDermott's record—the dealer who used to play football with Lake?—you said he didn't have an address or a phone. Presumably, he doesn't have a driver's license or a car registration."

"Not unless he's a true moron," I said. "Not valid ones, anyway."

"Let me check that right now." Ryan swiveled the laptop toward him, hit the keys for a moment, and waited. "License and registration have lapsed."

"Any leverage we can use to get Kendra to remember better?"

"I'm with the chief on this: I don't want to use her addiction to force her to talk. If we can help her get into some kind of city or county drug program, we should do it, no strings attached."

"Yeah." I thought for a second. We drove toward downtown under clear skies in light traffic. "Any reason not to let her walk?"

"Not that I can think of," he said.

"You want to have a go at Alicia again?"

"You don't like her for paying Kendra to deliver the drugs, do you?"

"No, not at all," I said. "I don't see her hanging around with junkies or dealers. But we do know she lied to us about her relationship with Lake. Said it was just casual, then it ended when she found out he screwed other girls. She didn't tell us her father freaked out at the rape hearing. Didn't tell us she had Lake's baby. Why not bring her up to speed on the investigation? If nothing else, it'll show her we plan on being a real pain in the ass. You know, if you want us to leave you alone, you need to start telling us the truth."

"What would we tell her?"

"I'd start with how we now think it was homicide," I said. "How Lake had CTE. If the fact that she didn't abort Lake's baby means there was something more to the relationship than she admitted, we might be able to read it in her face. Hell, she might even be willing to open up about his relationship with the coach."

"You mean, about whether the coach knew about his head traumas?"

"That's right," I said. "If Kendra was just an accessory, we need to start looking harder at the football program. Alicia could help us decide how hard to come at Coach Baxter."

"That reminds me: I want to root around a little more in the coach's background, too."

"Okay, you want to see if we can find Alicia first, then head back to headquarters?"

A half-hour later, we were at the little strip mall with the offices of Alicia Templeton Real Estate. We walked in and I asked if she was available. The receptionist told us she was in her office and picked up the phone to ask her to come out: The police detectives were here to see her.

Alicia Templeton greeted us with a white smile and a cheerful tone, but the tight eyes and forehead suggested the words were for the benefit of the receptionist. "Why don't we talk in the conference room?" She led us back to a good-sized storage closet with a round table surrounded by six plastic chairs.

"Sorry to barge in on you like this, Ms. Templeton, but we have some more information on the Lake Williams case we wanted to give you."

She sat there, her fingers interlaced on the Formica tabletop, her thumbs tapping together slowly. Her expression was impassive, but a deep sigh told us she didn't want to hear anything more about him, presumably because she had told us all she had to say yesterday and she wasn't really interested in him, anyway. "Go ahead."

"We have determined that Lake was murdered."

Her fingers stopped tapping, and her grey eyes widened a little. "You're kidding."

"He died of a drug overdose—from some especially potent heroin that someone gave him."

She frowned. "How do you know it was meant to kill him?"

"Someone paid a person to deliver the heroin to him. They knew he would shoot up and die."

"Do you know who did it?"

"No," I said.

"Do you know why?"

"We were hoping you could help us."

She shook her head. "Like I told you yesterday, I haven't seen him since college."

I nodded. "Yes, we do remember that." I paused. "Unfortunately, you weren't forthcoming with us yesterday."

She sat there silently: no protest, no denial, no explanation.

"For example," I said, "you told us you dated Lake for a while, then you split up because of his cheating and the abuse."

"That's true."

"You didn't tell us you had his child."

She flinched. "Where did you hear that?"

"Births and deaths are public records." I decided against saying her father told us. I wanted to save the father-daughter conflict in case we needed it later. "You're sticking with 'you dated for a while'?"

"First of all, that is none of your business whether I had a baby or not. Second, I happen to believe that abortion is wrong. That's all it is. And yes, I'm sticking with 'we dated for a while.' I can't believe you'd throw it in my face that I *didn't* have an abortion."

"Nobody is throwing anything in your face, Ms. Templeton. I'm just saying it's curious you neglected to tell us you had a baby with this guy you dated for a while—and put his name on the baby's birth certificate."

Alicia Templeton shifted in her chair, her hair swaying. "I don't see what any of this has to do with a murder. I have a new life now, with a husband and a little girl. Don't you think maybe you should move on, too, and worry more about why someone would want to kill Lake and less about my private life?" She was breathing heavily. A thin film of perspiration was forming on her upper lip.

I nodded. "One other thing we learned that we wanted to tell you about. You mentioned that Lake had a temper and was abusive at times. You should know that he had CTE."

She looked confused. "What's that?"

"The brain damage caused by head trauma. You know, concussions? We think it might have started as early as college."

"That might have caused his temper and the violence?" Her

eyes were shining.

I nodded but didn't say anything.

She started to weep, quietly. She wiped at her eyes with her fingers, then covered her face with her hands and began to sob.

I let her weep for a while. After about half a minute, she got it under control and straightened her posture. "I'm sorry ... I didn't realize ... That's very difficult to hear about a person. Any person."

I took that last part to be her way of saying her reaction didn't mean she really cared about Lake. He was merely one of God's children in distress.

"I understand." I glanced over at Ryan, who nodded to signal me to keep going. "Ms. Templeton, did you ever see Lake get hurt? I mean, his head?"

"All the time. He'd get hit helmet-to-helmet a lot. I'd see his head bouncing off the turf after a tackle. He would play on special teams, too: kickoffs, punt returns. I'd ask him not to do that, but he would say he needed to put up the numbers. Three or four times he returned a punt or a kickoff for a touchdown. He had a little notebook where he wrote everything down: the yards from passes, the special teams, the blocking for runners. When I asked him if he had to play all those different positions—I don't know what it's called—he would shrug and say it would pay off someday. It would break my heart, what he looked like on Sundays. Bruises all over his face."

Ryan said, "Did Lake ever talk to you about whether the coach wanted him to sit out some plays?"

"Lake told me the coach wanted him to put up the numbers just as much as he did. He would've been the first CMSU player to go pro in, like, twenty years. The first during Coach Baxter's time. The coach wanted to see Lake in the highlights reel on TV and on the web. The coach told Lake that it would be a win-win for both of them."

"When Lake tore his ACL," Ryan said, "do you think he rushed the rehab?"

"We weren't together then. But I do know—from the times he got hurt when we were—that he hated any kind of rehab. You know, physical therapy? He would always start working out on his own as soon as he could."

"So you don't know if Coach Baxter and the staff told him to take it easy on the knee after the ACL?"

"All I know is, the other times he was hurt, they left it up to him—when he could start practicing and playing again."

"Ms. Templeton." I wanted to change direction. "If I say the name Carl Davis, do you know who I mean?"

She tilted her head. "Of course, he's my godfather."

"We talked with him yesterday, over at the practice facility. He told us a very different story about the rape allegation than you did."

She frowned. "What do you mean?"

"You said you never even told your parents about Lake raping you. That's not true. Carl Davis knew all about it. He knew that your father tried to attack Lake in that room on campus. Now, help us understand this. Carl Davis wasn't at that meeting, am I correct?"

Out of the corner of my eye I caught Ryan glancing at me. His eyes showed a little concern. He knew Carl Davis wasn't at that hearing, and Carl Davis told us explicitly he didn't know anything about a rape. But I didn't believe Carl Davis. I knew Davis and Ronald Weber were business buddies. It just made sense that Weber would go to Davis about the rape.

"That's right," Alicia Templeton said. "He wasn't there … But how did he know about my father?"

"Your father must have told Mr. Davis."

She was shaking her head. "Why would he have done that?"

"Your father is close to him. Like you said, Carl Davis is your godfather. He's known you your whole life, known your father for decades. In fact, your father and Mr. Davis work together closely—on the Cougar Athletic Association. Your father's done a lot of the electrical work on the stadium, the practice facility, the renovations to the locker rooms and all. And Mr. Davis made it clear to us that he and his late wife were close with your parents. Maybe your father saw him as a father figure. Maybe your father thought Mr. Davis could help somehow."

"Help how?"

I shrugged. "I don't know. Your father was distraught about the rape—as any father would be. But since it was a football player who did it, and since your father was such a supporter of Cougar athletics and so close to Mr. Davis …" I let it trail off.

"What are you saying?"

"I'm saying that when your father is unhappy about something related to the football program, he goes to Carl Davis—and Mr. Davis tries to fix it."

"What does that even mean? How does Carl Davis try to fix a rape?"

"You can't fix a rape. But if a guy rapes his goddaughter—and that guy is a football player—maybe Mr. Davis can take some action to make sure that doesn't happen again."

"You're not saying Mr. Davis had Lake killed, are you? After all these years?"

"I am definitely not saying that. I'm just answering your question about why your father might have told Mr. Davis about what happened—he was really upset and thought Mr. Davis might be able to help. That's all I'm saying."

Personally, I preferred the theory that the football guys wanted to protect Lake because he was a great player. But that wasn't giving us a good motive to kill him seven years later, once he was living in a homeless camp. So it was worth a shot to plant the idea that we were looking at Lake's murder as revenge for the rape. I had no idea whether Alicia's father still wanted Lake dead. And, if he did, I had no idea whether he would go to Carl Davis for assistance, or at least for approval. I didn't know whether Alicia would take the theory to her father, and, if she did, whether he would deny he contacted Carl Davis and it would die there. If that happened, Alicia might conclude that I'm crazy or stupid or corrupt. I'd be okay with that. She wouldn't be the first.

But if there was any truth to the theory that Alicia's father worked with Carl Davis to kill Lake for the rape, it wouldn't take but a few minutes for the news to make its way to Carl Davis and then to Coach Baxter.

# *Chapter 16*

"Help me understand what just happened in there," Ryan said as we drove back to headquarters. "I thought we were working the theory that the football guys were protecting Lake because he was such a good player. Now you think maybe they had him killed?"

"No, I don't think that. But we believe Lake was murdered, right?"

"Yes."

"And we think Kendra delivered the drugs, but she didn't know the drugs would kill him, right?"

"Yes," Ryan said.

"We have no reason to think any of the other guys in the homeless camp put up the five-hundred bucks, right?"

"Right."

"Every other suspect is related to the football program, one way or the other: Carl Davis, Coach Baxter, Alicia, her father. We know Alicia lies to us, and we know her father vowed to get Lake. It's possible—just possible—that he waited until he got a chance."

"What would that chance look like?"

"No idea," I said. "Could be he found out Lake was living in the homeless camp. He stumbles on a way to use Kendra to deliver the heroin to Lake."

"How does he stumble on a way?"

I don't mind when Ryan asks me questions with sharp edges. It makes me think it through better. And if I can convince him what I'm saying is at least plausible, it helps both of us—and I feel less stupid. "He owns Weber Electric. He's gotta have at least one employee who buys pot from a dealer in town. Weber catches this employee with the pot and comes up with the plan for killing Lake. He okays the plan with Carl Davis and presents it to the employee. They work out the logistics."

Ryan nodded. "Since nobody would think Ron Weber has anything to do with the dealer crowd—"

"And since the rape occurred more than seven years ago," I said, "who's gonna suspect this hard-working business guy who does all the electrical work for the program?"

"All right."

"Let's go through the rest of them," I said. "We know Coach Baxter spins everything. Given what we already know about his NCAA violations, and what Alicia told us about how he let Lake get smacked on the head as often as he wanted, it's no stretch to say he's a total douchebag who exploited his players for his own gain. And if he's a total douchebag, maybe he'd be willing to help somebody solve a problem with a junkie dropout who nobody gives a shit about anymore."

"All right. Is Carl Davis a total douchebag, too?"

"I'm not sure. He might be the benevolent grandfather of the program, like he says. Or he might be the guy who rigs the bids on the program's facilities so that all the jobs go to his buddies."

"Which doesn't make him a murderer."

"True," I said. "But there's enough people involved that his fingerprints aren't gonna be on every decision. When he wants a problem solved, someone solves it—quietly." I paused a moment. "You know, when I floated the idea to Alicia, I hadn't quite thought it through, but talking to you now, I'm warming up to it. It's someone in the football program—or in with them. Doesn't matter if it was payback for something he did seven years ago or to keep him from doing something now that would hurt them.

It's someone in the football program."

We made it back to headquarters and carded our way in the rear entrance. As we set up at our desks, Ryan said, "I want to dig a little more into Coach Baxter. Can you give me an hour or two? We'll talk around noon?"

"That's fine. I'll bring the chief up to speed and spring Kendra."

Ryan settled in at his desk while I went to tell the chief we thought Kendra was being straight with us. He asked if we were willing to call it a homicide; I said we were. He told us to follow it where it led.

I headed to Holding, logged the five-hundred dollars with Kendra Crimmons's other property, and told them to release her. "Second thought," I said to the sergeant, "let me have five minutes with her first."

The sergeant unlocked the cell door. Kendra was rocking back and forth on her concrete bed, hugging her knees.

"Kendra, we're gonna release you in a few minutes."

"It's about fuckin' time. Did you find the money?"

"Yeah."

"Right where I said it would be?"

"Yeah."

"Are you gonna give it to me, or did you lose it along the way?"

As part of an effort to be less of a self-centered jerk, I try to see something good in everyone, especially the folks who have hit bottom, just like I once did. But Kendra wasn't making it easy. "I just logged it in. It'll be with your other stuff."

"Do I get some sort of payment for helping you out?"

I put out my hands. "For telling us the truth? The second or third time we asked?"

"I solved the case for you. Doesn't that get me something?"

"You didn't solve any case, Kendra. You convinced us you

didn't kill Lake Williams—at least for the moment. But you didn't tell us anything useful about the guys who hired you to deliver the heroin to him. Or anything useful about the guy in the pickup truck—"

"What the fuck was I supposed to tell you about the truck?"

"Some people, I don't know, they would've noticed the color of the truck or glanced at the door to see if there was anything written on it. Some people might have looked at the license plate as it drove off—"

"I told you, I don't see good enough, and I lost my glasses."

"But the real thing you screwed up, Kendra, is you were in the tent with Lake, watching him die, and you didn't call 911 or get one of the guys to help. What did you do while Lake was dying? You decided it must've been first-rate smack because of the way Lake responded, and you shot just a little, so it would get you off without killing you."

Kendra looked away. After a moment, she turned back to me and said, "Fuck you."

"Good point, Kendra. I'm gonna quote you when I write up that citizenship award."

She was gazing at the wall behind me.

"Listen, Kendra, I've contacted Human Services, with the city. They're gonna reach out to you and see if they can get you some help with the drugs. If you don't get on top of this, two weeks—a month, tops—we're gonna find you just like they found Lake. Will you let them help you?"

"You give me my five hundred, that's all the help I need."

I turned and left her cell, closing the heavy door behind me, glad to be done with her. Back in the bullpen, I was surprised that Ryan wasn't at his desk reading about Coach Baxter on the computer. I spent a little time talking with Harold Breen about changing the call to homicide. Then I did a little more paperwork on the case. I checked my watch: a quarter past noon. I called

Ryan.

"Karen."

"Ryan, what's going on?"

"I'm downstairs with Jorge. He's helping me make up a file."

"What?"

Jorge was our IT guy. He was always happy to help us with our cases. Apparently, that was more fun than teaching cops how to use a paperclip to open a stuck CD tray.

"I found out some things about Coach Baxter, then a kid from the university dropped off the drive with the game films on it. I'm making up a file to show the coach. I'm going to need about another forty-five minutes. Do you mind contacting the football program and setting up another interview with him?"

"Yeah, if he's around," I said.

"Make sure he's around. We need to see him. This afternoon. It's a murder investigation."

"You telling me I can be obnoxious?"

"This afternoon, Karen." He ended the call.

I didn't know what he and Jorge were working on, but Ryan's tone told me he was very unhappy with the coach.

I phoned Helen, the office secretary, and made it clear that we would meet Coach Baxter in his office in one hour or we would bring him in to police headquarters to interview him. Helen got my point and said he would be pleased to make the time.

Forty minutes later, Ryan returned to the detectives' bullpen. His expression was somber and determined.

"Everything okay, Ryan?"

He didn't say anything, but nodded a little.

I looked at my watch. "We've got an interview set up with Coach Baxter in eleven minutes. You got that file you want to show him?"

Ryan tapped his jacket pocket.

"You want to talk about it?"

"No."

"All right, then."

I've been Ryan's partner about three years. One of his best traits is his cheerfulness. I count on it. But a couple times a year, something inside him snaps. This, apparently, was one of those times.

On the drive over to campus, Ryan looked out the side window, motionless and silent. I turned the radio on. We arrived at the football complex and headed toward the building with the big cougar above the door. Ryan hung his detectives' shield around his neck. I pulled mine out of my bag and put it on, too.

The girl at the reception desk recognized us from yesterday and gave us a smile and waved us on. We took the stairs to the third floor. I stuck my head in the office. Helen told us the coach was in room 314.

The sign on the door said Conference Room. I knocked. A big guy, maybe thirty-five years old, opened the door. There were about eight guys, all about the same age, some black, some white, all big, sitting around an oval-shaped conference table. They all looked up at us. Coach Baxter rose from his chair. "Would you excuse us, guys? I'll get back to you." The men gathered their identical tablets and filed out of the room, nodding to us as they passed.

The coach gestured for us to sit. We took our places across the wooden table. "How can I help you?" He looked at me, expressionless.

Ryan spoke. "Coach Baxter, we're here to talk to you about the Lake Williams case. We've determined it's a homicide."

The coach frowned. He was quiet for a few seconds. "That is unbelievable."

Ryan didn't reply.

"What happened? I mean, do you know how he died?"

"As we told you yesterday, he died from heart failure after

injecting some uncut heroin. We know that an associate of his was paid five-hundred dollars to deliver the heroin to Lake. He injected it and died almost instantly."

"But you don't know who paid the associate."

"That is correct. But this investigation is now officially a murder case."

"How can I help?"

"We want to talk with you a little bit more about Lake and about your tenure here at CMSU."

"Are you seriously thinking I had something to do with killing him?" He started picking at a thumbnail.

Ryan stared at Coach Baxter for the longest time. "We're pursuing a number of theories of who might have wanted to kill him. At this point, these are only theories, and we are certainly not accusing you of anything. But just to be perfectly clear, this is not a friendly chat or a courtesy call. It is an official police interview. You need to be honest and forthcoming with us. If at any time we determine that you are not being honest and forthcoming, we will take you into custody and charge you with obstruction of justice and any other crimes we believe you have committed. Do you understand what I am saying?"

Yesterday Andy Baxter was the smiling, diplomatic head football coach. Today he was stone-faced and wary. "Yes, I do."

"All right. Let's begin. The athletic director here at Central Montana State University is John Freedlander. When did you first meet Mr. Freedlander?"

Ryan's gaze was steady. I didn't know the answer to the question, and I had no idea why he asked it.

"I first met John Freedlander in 1993."

"What were the circumstances?"

"He was the head football coach at Southwest Missouri."

"And you were …?"

"I was a freshman at Southwest Missouri. I was a player."

"You played one year, transferred to USC and sat out a year, and then continued your college career there as a quarterback. Is that correct?"

"Yes."

"Do you know when Coach Freedlander left Southwest Missouri?"

"That same year."

"Do you know the circumstances of his leaving?"

"Not in any detail. He and the university wanted to go in different directions."

"Do you know if Southwest Missouri incurred any NCAA penalties for violations in the years leading up to John Freedlander's decision to leave?"

"I was a freshman. I wasn't involved in anything like that."

Ryan nodded. "In fact, the program was charged with a number of major violations and incurred some significant penalties. If you look on YouTube today, you will see the video of John Freedlander giving an interview to one of the local TV stations. Do you know what I'm referring to?"

Coach Baxter paused a few beats. "Coach Freedlander had been under intense pressure for some weeks. He lost his cool that day and said some things he probably shouldn't have said."

"Such as the comment about how he didn't mind at all being paid by two different universities at the same time?"

"That's right." Coach Baxter's hands were balled into fists on the tabletop.

"What was Coach Freedlander referring to?"

"He had just been released from Southwest Missouri, but he had two more years left on his contract."

"And he had just accepted a new position. Therefore, his statement referred to the fact that he would be paid by Southwest Missouri for two more years, as well as by his new employer."

"That happens all the time in college athletics." Coach

Baxter's tone was clipped; he was working hard to keep his temper under control. "In professional sports, too."

"I know that, Coach Baxter. I'm just wondering why, yesterday, when we asked you about why you moved from Arkansas here to Central Montana, you didn't mention that you played under the man who is now athletic director here."

"It was one year. I was eighteen years old. I didn't see the relevance."

"That's interesting. I would have expected you to say you played for Coach Freedlander for only one year but that you had good memories of that experience. That you looked forward to working with him here as athletic director because you learned a lot from him when you were just starting out as a college player. But instead you said, 'I was eighteen years old,' as if you were caught smoking dope."

"That's ridiculous, Detective. John Freedlander was an excellent coach then, and he's an excellent athletic director now. I have learned a lot from him. You're taking my words out of context."

"Okay." Ryan nodded. "Glad we've cleared that up." Ryan stared at Coach Baxter, who held his gaze. I couldn't tell if the coach knew he'd just given up some points.

"Let's go on," Ryan said. "I want to thank you for putting the game films on the memory stick for me." Ryan removed the stick from his jacket pocket and stood up. In the middle of the conference table was a USB port that looked like a golf ball half-buried in the tabletop. Ryan slid the drive into the port. "I made up a little file." He pointed to the glass tabletop where Coach Baxter was sitting. Beneath the glass was a computer keyboard. "I want to show you that file. Would you mind if I sit where you are?"

# *Chapter 17*

Coach Baxter's jaw was thrust out, but he said nothing as he stood and walked away from his position at the computer in the conference room.

Ryan settled into the chair and looked down at the keyboard under the glass to orient himself to the system. He glanced over at Coach Baxter, who was standing a few feet off to the side, his arms folded across his chest. "You might want to sit down, Coach Baxter. This will take a few minutes." The coach walked to the side of the table and took a chair as far as possible from both me and Ryan.

Ryan had just accused Coach Baxter of trying to hide information by not telling us he played for the current athletic director, John Freedlander, more than twenty years ago. And he had suggested that Baxter's decision to come to Central Montana might have been strongly influenced by the fact that Freedlander was a crooked coach and would be a crooked athletic director— or at least know when to turn his back and let the new football coach do whatever he wanted. But right now, it looked like the thing that pissed off the coach the most was Ryan asking to sit in his chair.

Boys.

Sensing that he had just won this preliminary testosterone-spraying contest, Ryan put on a professional smile. "First, I want to thank you again for going to the trouble of putting the films on the stick for me. And for delivering it to police headquarters. You didn't have to do that. I said we'd come get it."

Coach Baxter looked like he couldn't bring himself to respond. He nodded his head, almost imperceptibly. Then, he gathered himself. "No problem," he said. "I hope you got what you needed."

"Oh, I did. It was very helpful."

Ryan's right hand was on the mouse, under the glass tabletop. He turned to me. "Detective," he said, "you might want to swivel around to see the screen."

A burst of white light coming from behind me threw a silhouette of my body on the opposite wall. I hopped out of my chair and took a seat off to the side. The screen, a painfully bright white, must have been six feet by four.

"Coach Baxter," Ryan said, "I've seen Lake Williams twice: once, dead, in his tent in the homeless camp in Ten Mile Park, and once on the autopsy table. Getting a chance to see him when he was young and healthy was really helpful." A clip from a game film came up on the screen. Lake was running down the sidelines, a yard in front of the defender. At just the right time, he turned his body and leapt into the air. The pass traced an arc six inches beyond the defender's outstretched hands. Without breaking stride, Lake pulled the ball in and raced down the sideline toward the end zone. Another defender was coming across from the other side of the field at an angle. Lake did a little head fake, sending the defender lunging in the wrong direction.

Lake swept into the end zone and headed toward the umpire, who had just raised his arms to call the touchdown. Lake handed the ball to the umpire and turned to accept the chest bumps and helmet slaps of his teammates.

I looked at Coach Baxter. I couldn't be sure of his expression. It looked like a smile, but his dark eyes looked troubled.

"Do you remember this one, Coach Baxter?" It was a play from the opponent's five-yard line. Lake was alone, off near the left sideline. The quarterback dropped back and looked at a wide receiver on the right, then pivoted and threw to Lake, who was covered by two defenders. The pass was a bullet, but it was off the mark, pulling Lake over toward the sideline. Somehow he grabbed it with one hand, pulled it in, and turned to step over the goal line. One of the defenders lowered his head and lunged at Lake, trying to push him out of bounds before he could cross the goal line. Lake transferred the ball into his right hand and reached over the edge of the foam pylon just before he took a vicious hit. The umpire raised his arms to signal the touchdown as the ball went flying out of Lake's hand. Lake landed hard and lay on the turf, motionless.

With the bright, flickering lights from the video screen dominating the room, I couldn't quite make out what Coach Baxter was doing. But he appeared to wipe a tear from his right eye. "Lake had all the tools."

"He certainly did." Ryan's voice was steady. "But he paid a price."

The next clip showed Lake taking a kickoff at the ten-yard line and heading for the right sideline. He saw three defenders closing in on him and pivoted to the left, crossing back into his own end zone and running all the way across the field to the left sideline, avoiding three more tackles. By the time he turned the corner to head down the field, four defenders converged on him. Two hit him below the waist, two above. He rose into the air and flew for a few seconds before landing, out of bounds, his head hitting the turf. The umpire called unnecessary roughness. Lake lay on the turf as the trainer rushed over to him. After the longest while, when Lake rolled onto his back and moved his legs, the crowd applauded that he was uninjured.

The next clip, which lasted only a few seconds, showed Lake catching a pass and taking a ferocious hit that left him motionless on the turf. Then another clip, and another, each one showing

Lake Williams absorbing brutal hits to the head from an opponent's helmet. Then a set of clips showing Lake's head bouncing off the turf.

"This one is really interesting," Ryan said. "I want you to look carefully." The clip showed Lake getting laid out from a blind-side tackle and being helped off the field by two trainers. His legs were rubbery, his head lowered, bobbing as he walked. "Pay attention here," Ryan said. It was a wide-angle shot showing another player coming in off the sidelines to replace Lake in the huddle. "Lake is number eighty-eight." Lake was helped over to the bench, where he collapsed. Two guys were supporting him, while another man, presumably the team physician, knelt in front of him. Ryan stopped the clip. "Watch what happens next, Coach Baxter."

The image of Lake Williams was fairly small and hard to make out, but he appeared to lean forward and vomit. The doctor stood and waved to someone else on the sidelines. The injury cart came wheeling over, and the assistants helped Lake onto it and lowered his body so that he was lying prone. The doctor climbed in the cart next to the driver, who steered it off the field and into the tunnel.

Coach Baxter said, "That's protocol. The doctor was bringing him in to examine him, run the concussion tests on him."

Ryan nodded. "Watch this next clip. You see the game clock? It says 3:19 left in the third quarter. That's exactly two minutes and fourteen seconds after he was taken off the field on the cart."

Coach Baxter said, "Well, that's not two minutes and fourteen seconds later in real time—"

"That's right, Coach." Ryan looked at him. "I checked the real-time footage of this game. It was five minutes and eight seconds later. Watch what happens."

The clip showed Lake walking slowly out of the tunnel, the two assistants flanking him. They were trying to hold onto his arms, to support him, but he shook them off. They kept their eyes fixed on him, as if they were trying to make sure he wouldn't collapse. Lake pushed them away and walked slowly to the sidelines and up to the coach.

"There you are, Coach Baxter."

The clip showed Coach Baxter slapping Lake Williams on the ass, then Lake trotting onto the field and joining the huddle. The crowd applauded. The quarterback clapped his hands, breaking the huddle, and Lake lined up on the left. The quarterback dropped back into the pocket and threw to Lake, but it was overthrown. Lake got his fingertips on it but couldn't pull it in. The defender tackled him, cleanly, and he landed, his head bouncing on the turf. He lay there for a few seconds, then slowly lifted himself onto his hands and knees. A teammate came over and helped him up. Lake began to walk in the wrong direction; the teammate directed him back to the huddle, which had already formed.

"Why are you showing me this, Detective Miner?" He put his palms out in mock confusion. "You realize I was present during every one of those plays, don't you, and that I called every play?"

"I am aware of that, Coach Baxter. I want to make the point that Lake Williams absorbed a very large number of violent hits—and I've shown you only a small fraction of them."

"All due respect, Detective, I have devoted my life to college football. It's what I do every day. It's the first thing I think about when I wake up, and the last thing when I go to bed. Are you accusing me of doing something wrong? What exactly is your point?"

Ryan didn't say anything, didn't move. He stared at Coach Baxter.

Three seconds elapsed, five seconds, ten.

The coach ran his hand through his thick hair. "If you're trying to show me that football is a violent sport—I'm well aware of that."

Again, Ryan was silent.

"If you're trying to make the point that I was negligent or didn't follow NCAA protocol, you're way out of line. The most important responsibility for every head football coach—and I assure you I take that responsibility very seriously—is the safety and well-being of my players. Nothing is more important than that."

Ryan didn't move, didn't say anything. He was starting to creep the coach out. Me, too, a little bit.

"You saw the films." Coach Baxter was leaning in toward Ryan. "I followed the NCAA protocol to the letter. Me, my whole staff. From A.D. Freedlander down to the equipment guys. To the letter, we followed it. There's nothing in those clips that violates a single sentence in the NCAA protocols. What do you want me to say, Detective?"

"I don't want you to say anything, Coach Baxter. You've said enough. I want to say something to you. You didn't take care of Lake Williams. You didn't take care of him. You should have. And you should be ashamed."

Coach Baxter shook his head in disbelief. "I don't know what's happening here." He turned to me. "Can you tell me what you and Detective Miner are doing?"

Even though I had no idea exactly what Ryan was doing, I trusted him. So I sat there and stared at him without opening my mouth.

Coach Baxter let out a forced laugh, like both Ryan and I were crazy. "I put the game films on a stick like you asked for, and you come in here and show me clips and tell me I should be ashamed. What are you doing? I said it once. I'll say it again. Everything you've shown in these clips is clearly legitimate, according to the NCAA. How do I know? Because they haven't called us on it. Not once. Not once."

Ryan kept staring at him.

"Look," Coach Baxter said, "I don't know what you want me to do. You want to report me to the NCAA for something, you go ahead. But I doubt if they're going to pay any attention to a police detective who doesn't like how I run my program."

"You're right, Coach Baxter." Ryan spoke slowly, with an even tone. "I'm just a police detective. But you don't have to worry. I have no interest in reporting you to the NCAA. I just wanted you to know that I think you betrayed Lake Williams."

"Well, you've made that point." He nodded. "If you have any other opinions you'd like to share, take them to the university attorney, Tim Giraldi. If you have nothing else, I'll ask you to excuse me—"

"I do have one more thing to show you. It won't take but a few seconds."

Coach Baxter sighed in exasperation.

The slide from Lake Williams's brain scan appeared on the screen. Coach Baxter frowned, squinting. "What the hell is this?"

"This is a slice from Lake Williams's brain. He had CTE. Stage 2. The dark spots on the nerve cells are the abnormal clumps of tau, which he got from the concussions and the sub-concussive head traumas. The CTE caused the symptoms he was already showing during his playing days: the anger, the violence, the confusion, the poor judgment. CTE was killing him a little bit every day, until Sunday night, when someone delivered some uncut heroin to him. Someone knew that he was a helpless junkie, that he would shoot it up immediately, and that he would die.

"I did a little arithmetic, Coach. In the eight years you've been employed at CMSU, you have been paid over four million dollars by the state of Montana. That's not counting performance bonuses, the radio and TV shows, and the money you've gotten from various equipment pimps. That's probably another two million. In that same eight-year period, John Freedlander, the athletic director, has earned one-point-seven million dollars. Each of your assistant coaches earns more than a hundred-thousand dollars per year. Lake Williams had no income, no health insurance. He died on a filthy foam pad in a camping tent in a public park.

"I'm here to deliver a very simple message. I think Lake Williams represented a threat to your program. I don't know what the threat was. I don't know whether it was Lake himself who was going to say or do something, or whether it was someone else. But I think someone associated with the football program decided to solve the problem by killing him. And I want to be very clear on this: If I find out that Lake was killed to prevent him from threatening the program, I will come at the killer hard, and I'll keep coming. And I won't stop until he is arrested and prosecuted."

I heard my phone buzzing from inside my big leather bag. I pulled it out and read the text message. "Coach Baxter, we have to go." I stood up. "Thanks for talking to us."

# *Chapter 18*

Ryan and I left the football complex and got in the Charger. I didn't start the engine. "I sense you're a little upset."

Ryan looked at me. "When I learned that Coach Baxter played for John Freedlander, who was as dirty as they come, and they both ended up here, it fell into place. Baxter has spent his entire career working the system, one step at a time, each job bringing him more money and more power. And he's done it on the backs of kids like Lake, who get nothing."

"I understand that," I said. "But he said he was always in compliance with NCAA regs. Like that clip you showed of Lake puking, then coming back into the game. Baxter said it was legal, that his guys were following the concussion protocols. Was he lying?"

"It's impossible to know. We have no idea what his guys did in the locker room. But that's not my point. I didn't say he was in violation. I said he didn't take care of Lake, and that he should be ashamed. The head coach tells his people how to behave—or at least sets the example. If his team physician saw the hit Lake took, saw him throwing up—there's no way he should have let Lake come back out of that tunnel. Of course the physician should have run the protocol on him, but he should have done more than that: He should have looked out for him."

"All right," I said. "Things are gonna start to pop now—I mean, now that you reamed out the coach. He's gonna be on the phone to Carl Davis and the rest of his senior staff to tell them there's a crazy cop coming after them."

"Fine. The programs and the NCAA exploit kids like Lake, then throw them away when they're broken. Let's see how they respond when they have to deal with the police."

"Yeah, okay, but we don't know they took out Lake. I'm not saying you're wrong. I'm just saying it could be Alicia or her father—or someone who had nothing to do with football."

Ryan nodded. "And when we arrest Alicia or her father, I will personally apologize to Coach Baxter. But until then, I'm following the money. Someone paid five-hundred dollars to deliver the drugs that killed Lake. It's not Alicia or her father. I know it." He was silent for a moment. "That phone message you got when we were talking to Coach Baxter? Was that just you trying to get me out of there?"

"No, it was headquarters. Remember Cory McDermott, the dealer who was on the team with Lake?"

"Yeah, did we find him?"

"Sort of. He's in the hospital. Someone beat the crap out of him."

"Can he talk?" Ryan said.

"He can. No idea if he will."

"So why aren't you driving us there now?" He gave me a small smile, which I took to be a good sign. Our partnership works because of our opposite styles. Ryan is calm, rational, and thoughtful. I'm … not.

I started the engine and drove us to the Rawlings Regional Medical Center. We walked in to the big lobby and got his room number: 413.

"What exactly do we know about what happened to Cory McDermott?" Ryan said.

"Only that he's in stable condition. He's conscious. One of the responding officers is there to brief us."

We rode the elevator to four and wound our way around the

hallway to room 413. An officer was standing outside the room. His nametag said Stewart.

"What happened?"

"We got a call about two hours ago that a guy was beat up in the alley outside Johnny's Lounge."

"The caller leave a name?"

"No. Me and my partner went to the alley. He looked pretty bad, so we called for an ambulance."

"Did he say anything when you were with him?"

"Nothing useful. We asked him who did it. Said he didn't know. How did it happen? He got jumped."

"During a drug deal?"

"No, he says he's not a dealer."

"So why did he get jumped?"

"'Because shit happens.'"

"How'd you ID him? He have a wallet?"

"He had a wallet but no ID in it. He told us his name. My partner remembered the name from the bulletin that you were looking for a Cory McDermott."

"Okay, thanks, Stewart. Good work. Tell your partner thanks, too."

He nodded and left.

We entered the room, which had a center aisle separating two rows of five beds each, the beds separated by thin cloth curtains on tracks. I approached a nurse, tapped my shield, and asked her to point us to Cory McDermott. She led us down the aisle and opened a curtain.

"Can you tell us his condition?"

She picked up the chart hanging on the end of his bed. "Couple fractured ribs and facial lacerations. Bruising all over his trunk suggests he was kicked around a lot. We've scanned him for organ damage, but we want to watch his blood and his vitals for a while."

"Is he on pain meds?"

She looked down at the chart. "Acetaminophen and codeine phosphate. That's Tylenol with codeine. He said he didn't want anything major, but he's had a pretty rough morning. The doc prescribed a fairly low dose."

"Can we talk to him?"

"Just a few minutes. He might fade in and out."

I thanked her, and Ryan and I walked up to his bedside. "Cory, my name is Detective Seagate. This is my partner, Detective Miner. Can we talk to you a few minutes about what happened?"

Cory McDermott had a bunch of tubes coming out of his arms and an oxygen tube hooked to his nose. The swelling beneath his eyes had already half-shut them. A set of butterfly bandages closed a one-inch gash on his forehead; stitches held together a longer, nastier laceration on his left cheek.

I looked at his earlobes, first one, then the other. They were both pierced, but there were no rings in them now. I glanced at Ryan, who nodded to tell me he caught that. Kendra said her dealer had pierced ears. Then again, so do a lot of guys in Cory's line of work.

His eyes were cloudy, but he seemed to be able to focus. He looked at me, then at Ryan. "Don't know what happened."

"Do you know where you were when you got jumped?"

"Downtown."

"Remember where?"

He tried to shake his head, but even that small movement caused him to moan. "No."

"Was it a drug deal?"

"I don't deal."

"C'mon, Cory. You've got five convictions for distribution. You're inside as much as you're out."

He looked at me. "That's why I don't sell drugs anymore."

I nodded. "Did you see the guys who jumped you?"

"No." It was barely more than a whisper.

"You can't say how many guys?"

"No."

"You got a customer named Kendra Crimmons? A woman, about forty. White." I turned to Ryan. "You got her photo?" Ryan passed me a mug shot of Kendra, which I held up to Cory's face.

He closed his eyelids again, then opened them slowly. "No customers."

"I want to ask you a few questions about Lake Williams." I think he looked a little surprised, but his face was so beat up and his range of expressions so limited, I couldn't be sure. "Tell me about him."

"Good player. Blew out his knee."

"Good student?"

"He tried, for a while, then he stopped. There were phony courses for the elite players. He got good grades." Cory McDermott paused to catch his breath. "After his injury, they put him in regular courses. He couldn't handle them."

"You mean he didn't have the time?"

"I mean he could barely read. Like most of the JUCOs."

"Did he take drugs?"

"Weed, like everyone. And whatever the trainers gave him. That's all I knew of."

"Cory, did you know about the rape charges against him?"

"He didn't have to rape anyone. He got more pussy than he knew what to do with."

"Yeah, I know the girls liked him. Did one of them charge him with rape?"

Cory McDermott shrugged his shoulders, just a little, then winced in pain. "Light-brown hair, I think. A cheerleader. Don't remember her name. She thought he was into her, but, like I said, he was all about pussy."

Various beeping sounds from the medical equipment in the ward filled the room. I glanced down the aisle at the other beds. Green and amber lights shone through the curtains, which were as thin as the gowns they give you where your ass hangs out.

"Lake had a roommate, a guy named Max Thomas. You remember him?"

"Yeah. Big, slow. A linebacker, I think."

"You think he knew about the rape charge?"

"Wasn't a secret. Coach didn't name Lake, but we got all kinds of lectures about character. Shit like that. They even brought in the old man to tell us we represented the school. We had to act like gentlemen. Some woman from outside the program, too."

"Who was the old man?"

"Mr. Davis."

"Was Lake close to Max?"

"I don't think Lake was close to any of the guys."

"But you'd see them together sometimes?"

"Yeah. Lake was good with all the guys. On the field. I don't know if they hung out off the field."

"You ever see them mix it up?"

"Lake had a temper. He got into it with a lot of the guys. Later that day, they'd be laughing like it never happened."

"You got in a fight with Lake, both got arrested. What was that about?"

"I've been in a lot of fights. It was years ago. I don't remember."

"Was it about you and Lake competing for territory? You were both dealing in those days."

He started to laugh, then grimaced. "Lake knew how to do two things: play football and screw girls. That was it. He couldn't even sell weed."

"Cory, Lake Williams died couple days ago."

He was silent a moment. "People die."

"People die?"

"Half the people I know, they're dead."

"You curious about how he died?"

"Not really."

"Because you already know?"

"Don't know. Don't care."

"He OD'ed."

"I believe it."

"What do you mean?"

"Like I said, all he knew was football and pussy. I knew he was done with football, so I figured the pussy disappeared, too. But dope? There's always dope. Dope is patient."

A nurse passed by. I waited a moment.

"I'm gonna tell you what I think happened, Cory. I mean, with you getting this beatdown. This didn't just happen to you. It wasn't a robbery. Two or three guys jump you in the middle of the day—downtown?—for no reason? They were sending you a message. You know who did it, and you know why."

He raised his eyebrows, just a little, before a look of pain swept over his face.

"Interested?"

"Sure," he said.

"You know Kendra. You're her dealer. Somebody paid you serious money to get some uncut heroin. Told you to get her to deliver it to Lake, to kill him."

He waved a hand dismissively. "If you say so."

"Who was it, Cory? Who'd you order the heroin for?"

"No fuckin' idea what you're talking about. I told you, I don't deal anymore."

"Yeah, yeah, you told me. If you don't deal, what do you live on?"

"This and that. Not really your business."

"Where'd you get your hands on pure heroin?"

"I didn't. You don't have a clue. There's no pure shit in Rawlings. There never was. This ain't Chicago, LA."

"Who jumped you, Cory? What were they telling you?"

"You're out of your mind. I want to go to sleep. Arrest me or go away."

"Was it a warning, Cory? Were they warning you what was gonna happen if you talked to us? Was it because Kendra told us someone hired her to bring the heroin to Lake? Did you screw this up? Were you supposed to get rid of Kendra so she couldn't talk to us?"

"Bye, bye." He closed his eyes.

"Because if you screwed something up, and that's why you took this beatdown, what do you think's gonna happen when you get out of here? They might come at you again. I'm not sure you can go another round with these guys. What if they decide it's safer to just shut you up, since you're the one who can lead us back to them?"

Ryan tapped me on the arm. With his eyes, he gestured to the nurse, who was standing at the end of the bed.

"I'm going to have to ask you to leave now, Detectives."

We thanked her and started heading down the stairs to the lobby.

Ryan said, "Too bad we didn't have a few more minutes."

"Well, he did tell us everyone in the football program— including Carl Davis—knew about Alicia's rape allegation—"

"Which means Max lied to us, too."

"Max said he didn't know about it?" I don't remember things as well as Ryan does. Or as well as I used to.

"That's what he said," Ryan said.

"Could be they've all been told to deny things like that. You know, for PR purposes."

"I guess. But Cory might have told us what really happened in the alley today."

I shook my head. "No, I don't think he was gonna fold. Hell, he could've been telling the truth: that the whole story of him supplying the dope could be crap."

"I don't know," Ryan said. "I like it."

"All we really have is Kendra tells us her dealer is a thirty-year-old white guy with earrings, and he's a thirty-year-old white guy with earrings."

"No, I think we have more than that," Ryan said. "He was on the team. He knew all the guys. He got thrown off the team because he couldn't pass his classes. He wasn't a good enough player to get the special treatment—you know, the sham courses—"

"Yeah, is that true? Only the best players get the phony courses?"

"I don't know. There weren't any phony courses at BYU, I'm certain of that. But I could see why only the best players got to take the phony courses. They're the players the program needs to protect. You can't let the whole squad take the phony courses and get all A's. Too many red flags."

"So after Lake blows out his knee and isn't valuable anymore, they throw him into the regular courses—"

"And since he can barely read, he flunks out," Ryan said. "That frees up the scholarship for the next recruit."

"The scholarships are only year-by-year, you said?"

"Here. Not everywhere. But make no mistake about it: The players may be called student-athletes, but they're putting in fifty hours a week on football. If they can't cut it as athletes, they're not going to be paid to be students."

"Even if they got hurt on the field?"

"Especially if they got hurt on the field."

"All right, like I said, the only possible link to Kendra is that he's a dealer and he used to be on the football team. But there's gotta be a few dozen other guys who could be Kendra's connection," I said.

We stopped when we reached the main floor.

"True," Ryan said, "but look how tight the pieces fit together. Cory knows Lake. That's for sure. If he figures out Kendra lives out there in the camp with him—which he could learn if she mentions it when he's selling her drugs one day—and he knows she has the conscience of a sheet of plywood—she's the perfect courier to get the drugs to Lake."

"But why would the guys in the football program know Cory?"

"Because he was on the team."

"Yeah, but that was years ago, and he didn't exactly impress anyone as a student or an athlete."

"If the football guys are corrupt—and this whole thing doesn't make any sense if they aren't—if they're corrupt, they might find it convenient to stay in touch with Cory."

"Why?"

"Because corrupt football and basketball programs use drugs and prostitutes to recruit high-school kids."

"I thought they used shiny locker rooms and equipment, like the Carl Davis facility."

"And drugs and girls."

"Shit," I said. "If they didn't do this at BYU, how do you know about it?"

"You don't read sports magazines, do you?"

A couple of nurses entered the stairwell and started walking up the stairs. We gave them a moment to get out of earshot.

"Okay," I said. "But the link between Kendra and Cory and the program is pretty thin."

"You know why I think it might be true? Because Cory made it clear he'd rather risk another beatdown than tell us who did it to him. If two junkies jumped him and stole fifty bucks, he would tell us their names and let us pick them up. But he's scared. I don't think he's scared of Kendra. And we know he's not scared of Lake. It's someone in the football program. He's scared of whoever's running him."

# *Chapter 19*

The next morning, when I pulled in to work, Ryan was already at his desk. We said our good mornings. "I was thinking about your piss fight yesterday with Coach Baxter."

"Yeah, I know." He nodded. "I was out of line. Now he knows we think someone from his program was involved in the murder."

"No, you got it backwards. The problem is we didn't go far enough."

He tilted his head. "Go on."

"The other day, we gave the coach a theory of the case: that Lake was a threat to the program. We told him an associate delivered the heroin to Lake. But we never named Kendra."

"Why does that make a difference?"

"He doesn't know how much we've figured out. He might think we don't like him because he's not a good guy who watches out for his players."

"Which is true."

"Yeah, but I don't give a shit if he's not a good guy. All I care about is if he—or one of his people—killed Lake. Listen, all you told him is he didn't watch out for Lake—"

"I said he didn't take care of Lake."

"Yeah, so he's a shithead—"

"So he should be ashamed."

"Same difference. Now, for a nice religious boy like you, that might be a first-rate insult, but if Coach Baxter is half the douchebag you said he was, maybe he's not shitting bricks right now. He doesn't know we've got a thread we can pull."

"Kendra?"

"That's right. With money changing hands, we're talking felony. If he was involved in paying Kendra to kill Lake, that's conspiracy to commit murder. If he knows we know about Kendra and the payoff, he'll know she's talking to us. That'll get his attention."

"Okay, how do we tell him?"

"I don't want to go back to him so soon," I said. "He'd just tell us to go screw ourselves, then he'd call in the university attorney. The attorney would phone the chief, and the whole thing would turn into a fight about two crazy cops who don't like the football team."

"Carl Davis?"

"I'm not sure what to make of Carl Davis. I mean, whether the word would get back to the coach."

"Davis told the coach that Lake was dead less than an hour after we told him."

"True, but I'm not sure how well the gears are turning in Carl Davis's brain. He might space it all out or screw it up. Like you said, we can't be sure Davis was lying to us when he said he didn't remember the Alicia Weber rape charge."

"John Freedlander, the A.D.?"

"No: too high up. He reports to the university president, right?"

"Yeah, he does."

"So that's what he would do: go to the president or the university attorney."

Ryan nodded. "How about Max, Lake's former roommate? We know Max lied to us when he denied knowing about the rape allegation—at least, according to Cory McDermott he lied to us. That gives us an occasion to talk to him. Do you think we can count on Max telling the coach?"

"Yeah, we can. Max is fully housebroken. His loyalty is to the program—he's an employee now, as well as a student going for a degree. If he can figure out how to alert the boss to a threat, he'll do it."

"We could tell him we want to ask him about some of the things Cory McDermott said—"

"About how the coach and Carl Davis spoke to the team about the rape charges," I said.

"And then we can ask him about Cory getting beaten up but not telling us who did it. See how he reacts to the idea that the program keeps a drug dealer on retainer." Ryan smiled. "Yes, I think our conversation with Max will get back to the coach."

"Call the program, will you? See if Max is available."

Ryan opened his notebook and found the number. He called, talked for a minute, and wrote something down. Then he hung up. "He's not expected in until this afternoon, but Helen gave us his cell."

I signaled for Ryan to pass me the number and punched it in. Max Thomas picked up on the third ring. "Max, Detective Seagate. We need to talk to you again." I hit Speaker.

There was a pause. "Okay, what about?"

"We'd rather do it in person. The football office told us you're not coming in until this afternoon. You can come in to police headquarters, or we can come to wherever you are. Your choice."

"I just arrived at the dojo. I was going to work out."

"All right, we'll stop by. We'll just need a few minutes. What's the address?"

"It's the Montana Taekwondo Training Center. On Sixth."

I looked at Ryan, who nodded. "We'll be there in about ten minutes." We ended the call.

It took us twelve minutes to get downtown. I parked in a

metered space right outside the address and flipped down my
visor to show the Official Police Business card.

The dojo was on the second floor of a seventies stucco
building that housed a shoe store and a cigar and tobacco place
on the street level. In the picture window on the second floor, a
small neon sign identified the dojo. Heavy training bags hung by
chains from the ceiling. We walked up the scuffed, poorly lit
wooden stairs to the second floor. It smelled a little funky.

At the little booth inside the door, the blond guy with tats on
his arms and a silver nose ring seemed surprised to see me and
Ryan. He started to ask if he could help us. I tapped on my
detectives' shield. I scanned the studio, which was just a big open
space covered in industrial tile, with large mats strewn around.

Max was the only person in the studio. Wearing a white gi
with a black belt, he stood in front of a heavy bag. He crouched
down into a defensive position, his forearms up. He swiveled
counter-clockwise on his left leg and leaned his trunk to the left.
His right knee came up, the leg parallel with the floor, the ankle
pulled in tight against the thigh. He held that position a second.
Then, in a blur, the leg extended, the top of his foot slapping
against the heavy bag. The sound of his flesh on the leather bag
echoed off the glass and the bare walls. He returned to the
defensive position, then reeled off another one.

We watched him do ten quick side kicks. His back was to us.
"He any good?" I whispered to Ryan.

Ryan is an expert in Krav Maga, an Israeli self-defense system
they use in the police academy. "He's excellent."

Max Thomas was breathing heavily from the kicks. He must
have seen our reflection in the picture window. He turned and
nodded to us. "Good morning, Detectives."

"Good morning, Max," I said. "Sorry to interrupt your
workout."

"Not a problem. Sorry there's no place to sit down."

"That's okay," I said. "We won't be long."

He wiped the sweat off his face with his sleeve.

"We wanted to talk with you about one of your old teammates, Cory McDermott."

Max Thomas shook his head. "Long time since I thought about Cory. What's he up to these days? He straightened himself out?"

"I don't think so. He's in the hospital."

"Sorry to hear that. He sick?"

"He was assaulted sometime yesterday, by at least a couple guys. They worked him over pretty good."

"Did he identify the guys?"

"That's the thing: He wouldn't tell us anything. He claims not to know who jumped him."

"You don't believe him?"

"No, we don't. In his line of work—selling dope, I mean—I would think he'd know how to avoid situations where he could get jumped. But he really doesn't want us involved." I paused. "Any thoughts on why he might not want to talk with us?"

Max thought for a second. "Well, if he's a drug dealer like you say, I can see why he might not want to involve the police. He'd have a hard time pressing charges, right? I mean, you'd want to know what he was doing when the incident occurred. And if he identifies whoever beat him up, there's a good chance those guys are criminals, too. They might come after him. He might figure it's safer for him to settle the score himself or, even better, just move on." He paused. "I really have no idea. I'm just guessing."

I nodded. "Makes sense. So, knowing him like you did, you can't help us with any leads?"

"I haven't seen him or heard anything about him since he left the program. I'm not in his world, and he's not in mine." He gave me a sad smile. "Sorry."

"I get that. One thing he told us. We were asking him about

Lake—you know, trying to see if the assault was linked to our case. He knew about the rape allegation against Lake ...”

"You’re referring to Alicia Weber?”

I nodded. "That’s the thing we were wondering about. When we talked with you the other day over at the indoor facility, you said you didn’t remember it. And you were Lake’s roommate.” I paused. "Doesn’t that strike you as odd?”

Max Thomas put on a thoughtful expression. "I don’t know. It was a long time ago. I haven’t been thinking about Lake Williams or Cory McDermott. I’ve got a pretty busy life.”

"I’m sure you do,” I said. "A lot going on, what with the coaching job and your courses and all. Still, Cory said it was an open secret how Alicia had filed this charge against Lake. Cory told us Coach Baxter talked about it in a team meeting—how you have to show good character, that sort of thing. Carl Davis made a speech, too. And the university sent some administrator; Cory didn’t remember her name. Point is, nobody was trying to cover it up. Yet you didn’t seem to remember the episode at all.” I cocked my head and put on my confused expression.

Max Thomas shifted uncomfortably and tugged at the ends of his black belt. He patted his chest with the thick piping on his gi jacket to blot the perspiration. "You’re right, Detective. I wasn’t being completely honest with you. I did remember those speeches, although it’s true that nobody ever mentioned Lake’s name in connection with it. But, yes, Lake did mention it to me privately. So I did know.”

"Why didn’t you tell us that the other day?”

"Coach Baxter told all of us—the students, the staff, everyone—that since there was no formal complaint against a player—”

"You mean, because Alicia withdrew the complaint?”

"That’s right. There was no outstanding complaint. He didn’t want us talking about it to anyone outside the program. He was emphatic that any talk about a sexual assault could cause enormous problems for the whole program—the whole athletics department, all the sports." He paused and looked down at his bare feet for a moment before raising his gaze to me. "Your question caught me off guard, and I just responded without thinking. But you're right. I'm sorry. It won't happen again."

I nodded. "We appreciate that. I understand why the coach wouldn't want anyone in the program talking to outsiders about something like a rape. But when my partner and I talk to you—at the indoor facility, here in the dojo, wherever—you have to tell us the truth. If you don't, you're violating the law."

He wiped at the perspiration on his face with his sleeve. "I do know that. It won't happen again."

"Now that this is a murder investigation—"

He started. "Excuse me, didn't you say yesterday that Lake died of an OD but you didn't know whether it was murder?"

I nodded. "Yeah, that's what we said. And that was the truth." I couldn't resist saying it. "But we discovered new evidence. It was definitely murder."

"My God, that's terrible. Can you tell me what that evidence is? I mean, are you permitted to say?"

I shook my head, disappointed. "We can't say." I turned to Ryan. "What do you think, Ryan? Just the outline?"

Ryan nodded. "I don't see how the outline could hurt."

I turned back to Max. "We learned that an associate of Lake's was paid to deliver some lethal drugs to him. That's how he died."

"An associate?"

"We can't go into any details. Someone from the homeless camp where he lived."

"Maybe it was a beef with someone in the camp?"

"We checked that out pretty thoroughly, but we concluded that nobody out there had the kind of cash this associate was given. Anyway, that's not the way they do things out there. If one of them has a beef with another …" I held up my fists.

"Who do you think … I mean, who do you suspect might have wanted to kill him?"

"We really don't know. We're working with this associate of his, but we don't yet have a suspect or even a motive. All we know is that Lake used to play football—and so did Cory McDermott—so we're investigating whether there's some connection with the football program. Problem is, we can't see any relationship between Lake and the program since … well, since you two played together. So we think maybe it goes back all those years. We just haven't figured it out yet." I shook my head. "Anyway, it's our job to figure it out, not yours." I gave him an official smile. "Appreciate you talking to us, Max. We'll let you get back to your workout."

We left the dojo and started down the stairs. "Think he's gonna tell the coach?"

"Within two minutes," Ryan said. After we made it down the creaky wooden steps to the street, I saw Ryan glance up at the window. As I unlocked the Charger, I glanced up, too. Max Thomas was standing there, between two heavy bags, his hands folded in front of him.

"He's waiting for us to leave before he goes back to the locker room to get his phone."

# *Chapter 20*

MacIntosh Skate Park was built about seven years ago on some crappy unused land literally in the shadow of a highway overpass. It was within sight of a small, ugly warehouse cluster, a scuzzy club that booked black-leather bands that wore masks, and a wide alley that periodically had to be swept of homeless people. The city thought—correctly, it turned out—that the kids would appreciate the low-rent, nonconformist vibe. The only part of the plan that didn't work out was the prohibition on dealing. The park quickly became a small but lively drug and prostitute bazaar after the skaters left at dark.

The moral crusaders in town openly complained about the open sinning, but some of the more pragmatic big cheeses pointed out that the city could either let the sinning continue under the overpass or shut the place down and watch the sinning return to the downtown convention district, home to the upscale restaurants, hotels, and shops.

Ryan and I stood under the US 53 overpass in MacIntosh Skate Park, where Kendra Crimmons told us she shopped for drugs and was offered money to deliver a baggie to Lake Williams. The morning traffic above us had died down, but the intermittent rumbling and whooshing sounds of cars and trucks still made it difficult to talk.

The first officer on scene was Imelda Ruiz. I asked her what had happened.

"We got a call from dispatch this morning at eleven fifteen.

We arrived six minutes later. There were about fifteen skaters gathered around the body. We got them away, taped off the scene. First we thought the woman was sleeping. There were blankets and things around her, and she was kind of curled up on her side, like you see now. We determined she was dead, called it in."

"Did you get a chance to talk to the person called it in?"

She pointed to a baby-faced girl who looked about seventeen. She was wearing black jeans and a sweatshirt. Dyed black hair stuck out from around her yellow wool hat. "Name is Janice Cutler."

We thanked Ruiz. "I'll take the girl," I said to Ryan. "You start with some of the guys, okay?"

Ryan nodded and headed off to a small group of skateboarders who turned to him and eyed him apprehensively.

I walked over to Cutler, who was standing on her own. "Janice, my name is Detective Seagate. Can you tell us what happened this morning?"

"I got here a couple hours ago, like I do most days. I walked over toward the bodega over there to get a Red Bull, which I'm finally gonna have to admit I have a problem with. Out of the corner of my eye I caught this person. Actually, first I thought it was just a pile of rags and whatnot. Then the pile of rags kind of formed into the shape of a person. You know what I mean?"

"Yeah, I know what you mean." Oh, Lord. "What happened next, Janice?"

"Well, I assumed it was just a street person sleeping it off. Street people like this general neighborhood, you know?" Janice had quite a lisp. I looked closer at her and noticed a silver stud in her tongue. It took me some effort to keep from asking her why the hell she thought that was a good idea. "I didn't do anything about it. I mean, I let the pile of rags sleep or whatever. About an hour later, I'm heading over to the bodega again, and it dawned on me maybe the pile of rags was in some kind of trouble. I mean, it hadn't moved. Well, it wouldn't move if it was a pile of rags, except for the wind, of course. Anyway, I thought that was unusual, given all the traffic noise. So a bunch of us decided to go over to her or it or whatever, see if we could wake her up. Couple of the guys started poking her—by this time we could see that she was a person, a female person at that. Some of the guys were shouting at her to wake up, like that was going to do it. Personally, I thought that behavior was totally unnecessary—"

"Then what happened, Janice?"

"So I leaned in to touch her neck—the carotid artery, have I got that right? There wasn't any pulse, and that's when I saw the blood on her jacket. In the vicinity of the middle of her chest, right below the sternum. The blood was in a circle, at least six inches across. I know you like to know those details. That's when I called 911."

"You ever seen this woman before?"

"It's hard to say. I mean, I can't say for sure. There are always quite a few street people," she said, making air quotes on the phrase, "but no, I don't think so."

"You mean, buying drugs?"

Janice shrugged. "I try not to judge. You never know the path they were on that took them there. Besides, I got my own monkey." She held up her can of caffeine.

"Yeah, that's a good attitude." I paused a moment. "You were here yesterday, too?"

"I'm here most days." She closed her eyes and shook her head. "You don't want to hear about it."

That wasn't strictly true. In fact, I did feel some sympathy for this girl. But I was on the job, and I didn't have time for this lonely, screwy girl. I had to figure out who killed the lonely, screwy woman. "When did you leave yesterday?"

"Four, maybe five."

"You didn't see her here yesterday?"

"One of my goals is to be more aware of my environment. I've been doing some reading about mindfulness—you hear of it?"

"So that's a no, right? You don't remember seeing her here yesterday."

"Like I said, I can't give you a definitive answer. If I were to say yes, it would get your hopes up and you'd want to ask me more questions, but then I'd have to disappoint you because I wouldn't be able to tell you where the woman was or what she was doing or anything at all useful to you. You've got really nice eyes. A little sad. I don't want to disappoint you like that."

"Okay, thanks, Janice." I handed her my card. "You or one of your friends remember anything, give me a call, okay?"

"Of course, Detective. Can I say I talked to a detective today? You're not working undercover or anything, are you?"

"No, I'm not working undercover."

"Do you know the name of the woman who was stabbed? Was she a criminal herself? Did you expect to find her dead?"

Did I expect to find her dead? No, I didn't. Should I have expected it? I would have to work through that with Ryan. "No. I don't know who she was. All right, Janice, thanks for that information. Listen, I think you might want to cut back on those drinks, you know what I mean?"

Janice nodded. "I know I've got a problem. It was really good talking to you." She gave me what I took to be a genuine smile. I could see her at ten years old, full of chatter and cute as can be. She stepped on the end of her skateboard, grabbed the other end as it rose toward her palm, and headed back to her friends.

When I turned to walk back toward Kendra's body, I spotted Harold Breen with Ryan and Officer Ruiz. Harold was on his knees next to Kendra Crimmons. When I got over to the crime scene, Harold had pulled the zipper down on Kendra's jacket and lifted the cloth away from the bloodstain, which was about six inches across, just like Janice said.

"Hey, Karen," Harold said when he noticed me standing there looking over his shoulder.

"Good afternoon, Harold." I leaned in. "Can you see anything through all the cloth?"

Harold shook his head. "It was a fairly good-size knife." He leaned in a little closer and slipped on his reading glasses. "From the way the sweatshirt is frayed around the tear, it might be a fishing knife with a serrated edge. Robin will figure it out."

"Can you give me a time of death?"

"Once I get her on the table and take a core body temp, I'll be able to give you a window."

"What can you give me right now?"

He removed the glove from his right hand and touched her forehead, then her neck. "No guarantees, but I'd say sometime between midnight and five AM."

"Huh." That put her murder before we told Max Thomas there was a courier who delivered the drugs to Lake Williams. "I want to check one thing before you bag her." I pulled a pair of gloves out of my coat pocket and snapped them on. I lifted the bottom of Kendra's sweatshirt and T-shirt and felt around until I located the top of her sweatpants. I pulled on the stretched elastic and fished around for a few seconds.

"What are you looking for?" Ryan said.

"Five-hundred dollars."

"And?"

"It's not there. We'll be sure to tell Robin to keep an eye out." I turned to Harold. "Do you know if Robin's been notified?"

"She's on her way." Harold wiped the perspiration from the top of his head.

"All right, thanks. Ryan and I will be canvassing the kids. We'll catch up with you at headquarters."

"Enjoy."

"I plan to," I said.

Ryan and I spent the next hour or so interviewing the skating crowd that hung out at MacIntosh Skate Park, but we didn't turn up anything useful. They all seemed to agree that Kendra's body, or the pile of rags, was there when they arrived for the day.

"All right, Ryan," I said to him when we met up again, "what have we got? What have we not got?"

Ryan sighed and scratched at his cheek. "What we know: Cory McDermott didn't kill Kendra."

"Because he's in the hospital."

"And the plan for Max Thomas to get on the phone to the football guys to tell them the cops knew about the courier who delivered the drugs to kill Lake? That didn't work, either."

"Because she was killed last night," I said, "before we interviewed Max at the dojo."

"Yes."

"Which doesn't change anything, really," I said.

"How's that?"

"The plan was that Max would call the football guys, which would spook them, and all hell would break loose. Well, all hell broke loose," I said. "It just broke loose earlier than we thought."

"Okay, but why did it break loose?"

"The person who set up the plan—getting drugs to Kendra to kill Lake—knows that she delivered the drugs—"

"Because Lake's death went out to the media yesterday," Ryan said.

"But that was only half the plan, because Kendra was supposed to shoot up the same heroin."

Ryan smiled. "But Kendra was still alive. And she was the weak link, since she was outside the football program."

I nodded. "That's the way I'd see it. Since she didn't do the right thing—OD'ing right next to Lake—they had to kill her.

Apparently with a knife."

"Harold will tell us if it was the knife. It could've been drugs. She had five-hundred bucks and hadn't had a hit in more than twenty-four hours. She told us as much: She was going to get high. So maybe she came here and got in trouble."

"Possible," I said, "but I don't think so. Whoever killed her might have found her here buying drugs, taken her behind one of the concrete columns, stabbed her there, taken her cash to make it look like a simple robbery during a drug deal. More likely, they killed her somewhere convenient and out of the way, tossed her in the bed of a pickup at two o'clock this morning, and dumped her here."

"If it was the guy who set up the five-hundred bucks to deliver the baggie to Lake, she would already know him," Ryan said. "All he would have to do is flash a few bills and she'd get right in the truck with him."

"Let's head back, bring the chief up to speed."

Ryan was looking off into the distance. He didn't move.

"What is it?" I said.

"Did we just get Kendra killed?"

I shook my head. "Kendra just got Kendra killed. We told her we could keep her safe until we picked up her dealer. But she didn't want to name him. She didn't want to work with us. We even offered to set her up in a rehab program. All she wanted was to take her five-hundred bucks and walk. This was on her."

He nodded, not fully convinced. I was okay with that.

We drove back to headquarters and went to brief Chief Murtaugh. We caught up with him in the incident room, where he had just finished up a meeting with a group of uniforms.

I filled him on everything since we had last talked, including Cory the Dealer getting the crap kicked out of him, our interview with Max the Roommate, and now the murder of Kendra the Courier.

"So what's your latest read on the case? I assume this is all related, right?" the chief said.

I turned to Ryan to let him respond. He nodded for me to answer. "It could be a coincidence: Kendra made her way to the skate park, with the cash in her pants, ready to score, and she got jumped. But we think it's related to Lake's murder: She was the loose end that needed to be tied up."

"And the drug dealer getting beat up? How does that fit in?"

"Well, we're not sure it does. Cory isn't telling us, which makes us think he's afraid of fingering the killer."

"You think someone was warning him to stay in line?"

I looked at Ryan. He nodded. "That's what we think now."

"If Kendra was a loose end that needed to be tied up, why didn't they do the same to Cory?"

I shrugged my shoulders. "Maybe she was expendable because she's untrustworthy—she was too easy to enlist to carry the drugs. Since she's a junkie, they knew she'd do or say anything if someone offered her drugs or cash."

The chief said, "You're saying Cory is more trustworthy, which I get. But that would also imply they want to keep him alive because of what he has on them—or what he offers them."

"We need to keep working on that."

"If he's a dealer, that might be the obvious answer."

"Ryan says some programs have been known to use drugs and girls to entertain recruits on campus," I said.

"I haven't heard that about CMSU, but I know it happens at other schools," the chief said.

"Well, we canvassed the skate park. We'll wait for Harold and Robin to see if there's any new forensics."

"Other than that," the chief said, "we'll just hope someone makes a move."

We thanked the chief and headed back to the detectives' bullpen. My phone rang. The screen read "Rawlings Regional

Medical Center." I answered and hit Speaker.

"Detective Seagate. This is Lauren Wintrow. I'm the shift supervisor of the nurses. We screwed up."

"Yeah?"

"The patient you talked to yesterday: Cory McDermott? We've misplaced him."

"What does that mean?"

"He's not here."

"And you've looked?"

"For the last two hours. We follow a protocol for that."

"I assume you have a protocol for not losing patients in the first place, right?"

"That's why I said we screwed up, Detective."

"When was the last time you know he was there?"

"Eleven fifteen last night was the last time a nurse signed his chart."

"When would be the next time a nurse would check him?"

"Between four and five this morning."

"What the fuck happened?"

"We don't know what the fuck happened, Detective. Listen to me. I already said we screwed up. He walked out of here sometime between eleven fifteen last night and four or five this morning. That's all I know. There's another way to look at this, Detective: If it was all that important that he stay in the hospital, you might have told us and put an officer on his door."

I paused a second. "What did you say your name is?"

"Lauren Wintrow."

"Lauren, you're right. I'm sorry for biting your head off. I realize you didn't screw this up. You're just the one who has to tell me. Thanks for letting me know. You learn anything else, call me right away, okay?"

"Yes, Detective. I'm very sorry."

I ended the call and turned to Ryan. "Well, that kinda changes things, doesn't it?"

"It certainly does." He flashed a big smile. "This is exciting!"

"What the hell is wrong with you?"

# *Chapter 21*

"If Cory walked out of the hospital before midnight, he could've made it over to the skate park and run into Kendra, right?"

"Absolutely," Ryan said.

"And he could've said to her, 'Hey, Kendra, wanna make some more money?' She would've been happy to see him. He stabs her, grabs the five-hundred she was gonna give him for a baggie full of heroin."

"And then Cory never needs to worry that anyone is going to identify him," Ryan said. "If he's the dealer for the football and basketball teams, he lives happily ever after."

"We gotta bring him in."

"I'll put out the bulletin." Ryan picked up his desk phone and punched in the number for the sergeant's desk to set it up.

It wasn't two hours later when I got a call from Reception. "Seagate."

"Detective, there's a Cory McDermott here for you."

"Great. Have the officer who found him bring him up."

"We didn't find him, Detective. He just walked in."

"Really?" I needed a second to take that in. "Okay, have an officer escort him up to the bullpen, please. Thanks."

Two minutes later, an officer led Cory McDermott into the bullpen. He looked even worse than he did yesterday in the hospital. His face was still swollen, but now the bruises around his eyes and his mouth were starting to turn purple and black from all the busted blood vessels. But he had put the gold loops back in his ears. He recognized me and nodded before starting to walk in my direction. With every step, he held onto a desk or a cabinet for balance. The twenty yards took him the better part of a minute.

I stayed in my chair. Ryan stayed seated, too. "Hello, Cory." I gave him an official smile. I wasn't interested in acting sympathetic toward him. I let him stand there. "What can we do for you?"

"Can we talk?"

"Sure," I said. "Go ahead. Talk."

Ryan got up and walked toward the wall. He took out his phone, presumably to cancel the bulletin we had on Cory. It took him only a few seconds. He came back to his desk and sat down.

"I don't feel so good," Cory McDermott said. "Is there someplace we can talk where I can sit down?"

"Yeah, let's go to an interview room." I stood and led him and Ryan to Interview 2. We all sat down. "What's on your mind?"

"I want to make a deal," he said.

"What kind of deal?"

His scowl suggested he didn't appreciate my attitude. "I want immunity for any charges related to selling the heroin."

"That's interesting. Yesterday you told us you didn't sell drugs anymore."

"Are you gonna talk to me or not?" His eyes were bloodshot, his voice weary.

"Okay, Cory. You willing to make a statement?"

He shook his head. "After we reach a deal."

"Doesn't work like that. First you have to tell us your story. We'll get it to our prosecutor. He'll tell us whether we've got a deal."

"This is off the record?"

"Off the record." I pointed to the controls for the recording system on the wall. "We're not recording this."

"How do I know you're not secretly recording it some other way?"

"Cory, listen to me. You tell us your story. We see if the prosecutor is interested. If you don't believe me that's how it works, walk out of here. We know you know how to do that. Get an attorney. Ask him. Or bring him with you when you come back."

I could tell by his expression that he wanted to start talking now, even though he was scared and ready to fall down from exhaustion and pain.

"Your call, Cory."

He sat there, tapping his fingers on the battered steel table.

"I got an idea for you," I said. "Make the story hypothetical."

"What?"

"Tell us you know a guy. Let's say he lives in New Mexico. He sells this woman some dope. Take the story from there. You know, so you're not saying this has anything to do with you."

Some criminals are surprisingly ignorant about the law. He could tell us he killed Lake Williams, Kendra Cummings, and his own mother. Until he wrote it down and signed it or said it into a camera, we couldn't do a thing with it.

He nodded. "Okay. There's this guy lives in New Mexico—"

"What's this guy's name?"

Cory looked at me, confused.

"Sorry, Cory, just messin' with you. What did this guy do, Cory? This guy in New Mexico."

"He supplied some heroin, which someone else took to a third person, who shot up and died."

"All right. This New Mexico guy, did he intend to kill the third person?"

"No."

"Did he know this heroin would be used to kill the third person?"

Cory thought for a second. "He knew what would happen if someone shot up with it. I mean, if they didn't know it was pure."

"But did the guy know that someone was gonna shoot it up, or did he think someone was maybe gonna cut it to bring it down to normal potency?"

"This guy in New Mexico wasn't really thinking in those terms. He was offered some money to deliver a product. That was the extent of it."

"Okay, so what does this New Mexico guy want?"

"He's willing to do the time for distribution, but he wants immunity from any charges related to the death of the guy who shot up."

"What's he willing to give the New Mexico cops?"

"He's willing to tell them about the people he works for. The ones who ordered the heroin."

"The ones who wanted the guy dead? The guy who shot up?"

"Yeah."

"Does he know why they wanted the guy dead?"

"They never told him."

"Is he willing to make a statement and appear in court, if it comes to that?"

"Yeah."

"Let's say the cops are willing to bring this to the prosecutor. There's another problem."

"Which is?"

"What's the point of getting immunity on the drug death if this guy stabbed the woman who carried the heroin to the junkie?"

Cory's jaw fell slack. "What the fuck?"

"Not sure what you're saying there, Cory."

"You think it was me?"

"Yeah, the thought did cross my mind."

"Why would you think that?"

"Well, for one thing, how do you even know Kendra's dead?"

"I just came from the skate park. That's all they're talking about."

"You walked out of the hospital late last night. You had plenty of time to see her at the skate park, where we know you often do business. You figure if you kill her right there, you're home free."

"Then why am I here?"

"In case we can't find the forensics to charge you with her murder, you want to go on record as saying you didn't do it—and make sure you get immunity on anything we might charge you with related to Lake's murder. You killed Kendra so there's nobody to testify against you."

"I'm not a murderer."

I shrugged my shoulders. "That's more for a jury to decide."

"So you're saying you're gonna charge me with killing Kendra?"

I shook my head. "I'm not saying anything about who we're gonna charge—for Lake or for Kendra. They're both open investigations."

"I already told you about selling the drugs that killed Lake."

"Well, not really. You told us a little about that story."

"How do I prove I didn't kill Kendra?"

"That's a tough one, Cory. Proving you didn't do something, I mean. Why don't you start by telling us everything that happened since you walked out of the hospital?"

He nodded. "I talked to the nurse, the one who checked in on me around midnight. She told me my blood tests and the imaging shit they did on me turned out okay. My organs weren't fucked up. Just the bruising."

"So you walked?"

"That's right. I don't get sick days from the company, like you do. If I don't sell product, I don't eat. I went to the park to do

"Where you ran into Kendra."

"No." He said it with some force. "That didn't happen. She wasn't there. I did some other business, I don't deny that. But Kendra wasn't there."

"How do you explain that's where we found her body this morning?"

"I have no idea. Maybe she was there after I was. Or they killed her and dumped the body there in the middle of the night. That way, you'd find it and think she got hit during a deal. Or, better yet, you'd pin it on me, which is exactly what you're doing right now."

"Why should we believe you?"

"If I killed her, like you said, why would I come in here? I'd get in my pickup and hit the road."

"You have a pickup?"

"Yeah, I do. It's not registered in my name—for obvious reasons—but you're missing the point: If I killed Kendra, I'd be long gone. I sure as shit wouldn't drag my busted body in here so you could charge me with something I didn't do. I'm here about immunity on Lake. That's it."

"You'd be willing to give us DNA?" I knew we already had his DNA from his previous convictions, but I wanted to see his attitude.

"Any fuckin' thing you want: hair, cheek swab, urine, whatever. I didn't kill Kendra. You're not gonna find my DNA on her. If you do, just lock me the hell up."

I glanced over at Ryan, who was taking notes in his skinny notebook.

"Listen to me, Detective," Cory said. "I came here to get out from under any accessory charges related to Lake. I'm willing to give you the name of the guy who ordered the heroin. Isn't that the guy you ought to be looking at?"

"After you tell us who ordered the heroin," I said, "what's your next step? Let's say we cut this deal with you where we drop the heroin sale down to distribution—and we don't go after you for killing Kendra. Then what happens?"

"Depends on what the judge does. Or a jury." Cory winced in pain. "I'll probably go inside for six months, maybe more because of my record."

"Yeah, then what? Aren't you scared of the guy you're gonna flip on?"

"When I get out, I hit the road. Maybe he'll see that it's best to just let it go. Maybe he'll make it a point to come after me."

"You're taking quite a risk. I mean, talking to us."

"I don't have a lot of options. When I found out Kendra was dead, I knew it might get back to me. You were already looking at me for selling the heroin to Lake. I knew what you were gonna do with Kendra: You were gonna put it on me. Which is exactly what you're doing. I'm willing to take the distribution charge, but if I just leave town now, you'll charge me with Kendra and do a national search for me. I'd rather help you get whoever killed Kendra, even if that means I go inside and then I've got them on my ass."

He did have a point. "Okay, Cory. Here's what we're gonna do. You tell us your story. We'll bring it to our boss. If he likes it, it goes to the prosecutor. If he likes it, he'll talk to you about charges. At that point, you'll need a lawyer. If you don't have one, the public defender will act as your counsel. You understand that?"

"Yeah, I understand that."

"Tell us your story."

"I have a contact. I supply drugs to the athletics department."

"How long have you been doing this?"

"Since I was booted off the team seven years ago."

"How are you paid?"

"Cash. Always cash."

"Tell us about the heroin deal."

"My contact wanted some product. I got it, like I'd done dozens of times before."

"Did you know it was for Lake Williams?"

"No. He didn't say, and I didn't ask. I supplied the heroin. Listen, if I'd known they wanted to kill Lake—or kill anyone—I wouldn't have had anything to do with that. I can't sell drugs to dead people. And I knew Lake. I wouldn't have hurt him."

"So, how do you even know it was your heroin killed him?"

"I don't. For all I know, he OD'ed on some other shit he got on the street. I have no idea how it happened. The only reason I think it might be my junk is that I know Kendra lived out in that homeless camp with him—and I know I didn't have anything to do with killing her."

I nodded. "Okay, Cory, who's your contact with the athletics department?"

He shook his head. "Not until I get the deal. In writing."

"You're kidding."

"If I give you the name now, you go out and arrest this guy or whatever. And I'm left swinging in the breeze."

"Like I told you, Cory, we can't do anything with the information you give us until you sign a statement."

"I'm not gonna take that chance. This guy's name is the only card I've got to play. Why should I trust you to take care of me after I play it? The prosecutor will figure out some way to screw me. You'll arrest my contact—and I'll do ten or fifteen years for killing Lake."

"Cory, you gotta trust somebody. You either trust the prosecutor to follow the law or you trust a guy who's killed two people already. A guy who knows there's only one person still alive who can finger him. You sign a statement here today, we can put you in protective custody until we pick up the killer. If you don't, you're on your own."

Cory shook his head. "I'm not gonna walk into a prison cell. Not gonna take that chance."

I turned to Ryan. "Would you escort Mr. McDermott out?"

Ryan stood and walked over to Cory and started to half-lift him out of the chair.

He looked at me. "What the fuck are you doing?"

"I'm doing just what I said I would do. When you give me the information, we can protect you. I'll get the statement to my boss, and he'll decide whether to bring it to the prosecutor. But you haven't given me the information. We're done. It could be dangerous out there, Cory. First Lake, then Kendra. You watch your back, now." I stood and walked out of the interview room.

# *Chapter 22*

"Bob Billingham," he said. "Pleased to meet you."

Billingham was a man in his late sixties, maybe seventy. He was about six feet, a little heavy in the middle, with jowls on his long face. He had a fringe of silver hair and a thin silver mustache that I didn't even notice until I got in close to shake his hand. He looked out over his reading glasses.

"Good to meet you, President Billingham," I said. "Thanks for making the time."

The CMSU president introduced himself to Ryan, then turned to Chief Murtaugh. "Robert, good to see you again. I hope you're well." They did the two-handed shake, with the left hand grasping the forearm. Billingham was too old for the pull-in hug, and Murtaugh was too aloof. The chief asked about the president's wife, and they spent a few sentences on small talk.

President Billingham gestured to the coffee service set up in the corner of his large, well-appointed office. "We have coffee, tea, hot chocolate, and water. Won't you help yourself as we wait for the others?"

"Will there be others joining us?" Chief Murtaugh said.

I had no idea who was coming. The chief had arranged the meeting late Thursday afternoon after we briefed him on the interview with Cory McDermott, the drug dealer who told us someone associated with the athletics department was his contact, and that the contact had been supplying drugs to the department for over seven years.

The chief told us he wanted us all to sit down with President Billingham to let him know where we were with the investigation of Lake's murder and to brief him on the incomplete and perhaps untrustworthy information provided by the drug dealer.

The chief thought it was important to have as strong a relationship as possible with the university. One result of that relationship was that the chief had persuaded the university to let us have a sub-station on campus to replace the rent-a-cops the university used. In the several years since Chief Murtaugh had been in Rawlings, his close relationship with the university had fostered a new criminal-justice program at the school, as well as various outreach activities that helped us raise awareness of drug abuse and sexual-assault issues on campus.

The chief's philosophy was to keep the communication open with the university. "I don't want Bob Billingham to read about this in the paper," the chief said to me and Ryan more than once when we worked cases involving students or faculty.

President Billingham said, "I've taken the liberty of inviting three others to our meeting: Carl Davis, the president of the Cougar Athletic Association; John Freedlander, the A.D.; and Andy Baxter, the football coach. If you have information about inappropriate activities involving any of our teams, I want the relevant staff here. I believe in transparency in working with all members of the Central Montana State community. Since I would pass along any information you relayed to me, I thought it would be best to invite them to participate in our meeting this morning so that they could ask you questions. I hope that's acceptable, Robert?"

Robert Murtaugh put out his palms in a welcoming gesture. "Yes, of course, that's fine with us."

A minute later, the three men arrived together. We had met and interviewed Carl Davis, the eighty-four-year-old godfather of CMSU athletics, in the indoor football facility named for him and his wife. And we had interviewed and royally pissed off Coach Baxter. But we had never met John Freedlander, the A.D. who Coach Baxter didn't tell us was his coach him when he was a freshman at a tiny school in Missouri.

We spent a minute shaking hands and wearing tight smiles. Then we all took seats at a big, round conference table. President Billingham began. "I have known Chief Robert Murtaugh since he came to Rawlings almost three years ago, but in that short time I have come to admire his professionalism—and that of his entire force—and to rely on his judgment and his counsel. Therefore, when he phoned me yesterday and suggested that we get together to discuss a sensitive and serious issue, I told him that yes, of course, I wanted to sit down with him. When I asked the nature of the issue, he told me that it had to do with some allegations regarding inappropriate behavior in the athletics department. He made clear that these allegations were merely that—allegations— as yet unproven. But the two of us agreed that that they were sufficiently serious to warrant a frank discussion that might lead to a plan to investigate them. I have invited you—Carl, John, Andy—in the spirit of complete transparency. You three will be the ones I rely on for advice—and the ones who will be instrumental in addressing the situation. Would you like to begin, Chief Murtaugh?"

"Thank you, President Billingham, for those kind words." He turned his gaze to the three others, who were seated next to each other opposite him. "I am glad that President Billingham invited the three of you. I share his confidence that together we can get to the bottom of this. If any crimes have been committed, the police will of course have a role to play. And if our discussion leads to the discovery of any problems in the university's athletics department, I am sure that President Billingham and you will be able to identify them and make them right.

"The two detectives with me today are the leads on a murder

case. The victim, as you all know, was LaKadrian Williams, a twenty-seven-year-old who had been a student-athlete at CMSU. He died four days ago of a drug overdose that we have ruled a homicide. While Detectives Karen Seagate and Ryan Miner were investigating the Williams case, another homicide occurred. The victim in this case, which has not yet been made public, was Kendra Crimmons. Ms. Crimmons, a forty-one-year-old drug addict, lived near LaKadrian Williams in a homeless camp in Ten Mile Park.

"Ms. Crimmons had no ties to CMSU. However, in the course of their investigations, Detectives Seagate and Miner interviewed a third person, Cory McDermott, who conveyed the information that I thought President Billingham needed to hear. Mr. McDermott, aged twenty-six, is a drug dealer. For one year, he was a student-athlete, playing football alongside Mr. Williams. Mr. McDermott failed out of CMSU, one year before Mr. Williams did. I'd like to let Detective Seagate take the story from there."

President Billingham broke in. "I'm sorry to interrupt, but how do you know Mr. Williams's death was a homicide?"

The chief said, "We know that someone paid Ms. Crimmons to deliver the drugs to Mr. Williams, and we have concluded that the purpose of that transaction was to kill Mr. Williams."

President Billingham sighed deeply. "Thank you. Please go ahead, Detective Seagate."

I began. "We'd been trying to locate Cory McDermott for a few days because we thought that since he knew Lake Williams and since we believed he knew Kendra Crimmons—and since he was a convicted drug dealer—he might be able to help us with the Lake Williams case. Wednesday, we learned that McDermott was in the hospital. One or more persons jumped him and beat him pretty bad. He denied having anything to do with selling drugs and said he hadn't seen Lake in years. Yesterday we learned that he had walked out of the hospital early Thursday morning, sometime before Kendra Crimmons was discovered dead in MacIntosh Skate Park, which as you might know is a late-night drug bazaar.

"Then, yesterday, Cory McDermott showed up at police headquarters with the story we brought to the chief. Cory told us that a contact of his—someone associated with the athletics program—was the one who ordered the drugs that killed Lake Williams. He confirmed that Kendra Crimmons was the courier, who was paid to deliver the drugs that Lake shot up. Cory wanted to trade the information about this contact for a lighter sentence for selling the drugs that killed Lake."

John Freedlander, the athletic director, spoke. "Detective Seagate, if I can interrupt for just a moment …" A big man, a few inches over six feet and a good two-fifty, he ran his hand over his grey buzz-cut.

"Sure. Go ahead."

"You're saying Cory McDermott wanted a lighter sentence. Can you explain that?"

"If Cory was charged with selling the drugs that killed Lake, he could be charged as an accessory to murder. Maybe even manslaughter. He wanted those charges off the table. He said he was willing to tell us who this contact was if we would drop the accessory or manslaughter and charge him only with distribution: selling the drugs."

"Do you believe he killed Kendra Crimmons?" Freedlander said.

"We don't know. He denied it. And his decision to walk into police headquarters to make a deal about the Lake Williams murder doesn't fit with a guy who just killed someone. We'd expect a person who did that would hop in a car and leave town."

"You said he wanted to make a deal by giving you the name of his contact. But he didn't give you a name, is that correct?"

"That's correct. He insisted that we sign off on a deal taking the accessory charge off the table first. We told him that's not the way it works. He has to tell us his story, and we decide—Chief Murtaugh decides—whether to bring the story to the prosecutor, who negotiates the terms."

"So how did you leave it with him?"

"We said goodbye and he left."

"I can't speak for anyone else from CMSU." Freedlander shifted his bulk in his chair. "But my own feeling is that this drug dealer made up the whole story. He told you he had a contact who is associated with CMSU. But when you told him you wouldn't cut him a deal until he gave you the name, he knew there was no point in naming anyone. You'd investigate, but you wouldn't find anything—because there is no such person. You called his bluff. He folded." Freedlander raised his eyebrows and leaned in toward me, as if to say, I've just cleared this whole thing up, no?

"That could be it," I said. "Cory McDermott is a bad guy, a multiple offender who's still selling lethal drugs in town. Maybe it was a Hail Mary pass—you know, see if we'd be so excited to get the name of the contact who ordered the hit on Lake that we'd cut him a great deal. It didn't work, so he slunk away. But there's one other thing he said that made me and my partner think it might be worth pointing out to our chief. Cory said he's been supplying drugs to the athletics department ever since he was kicked out of CMSU."

All four of the CMSU people pulled back. President Billingham knit his eyebrows and frowned in disbelief. John Freedlander sat back in his chair, as if that was the most ridiculous thing he had ever heard. Coach Baxter's dark eyes narrowed. Carl Davis shook his head in sorrow. The room was quiet for a long moment.

I thought it was interesting that none of them said, "Now,

why would the football and basketball programs be buying drugs?" Apparently, I was the only one in the room who, a couple days ago, didn't know the answer to that question.

John Freedlander took a deep breath. "That is an extremely serious allegation that he made. Unless he can prove that allegation, I would think the university would want to consider taking legal action against him." He turned to President Billingham.

The president said, "He hasn't made any charges publicly, John. You're likely right that Mr. McDermott is just angling for a more lenient sentence. If at some point he were to make such charges publicly, then we would certainly talk to university counsel about appropriate responses. For the moment, however, I want to make sure we are doing everything we can to assist the police in their investigation. Their investigations, in fact."

Carl Davis cleared his throat and placed his fingers on the edge of the table. Everyone turned toward him. "Bob, I realize that you haven't asked any of us to comment on the charge that this young man has made. But I cannot remain silent. I have been associated with Central Montana State athletics for more than forty years now. I have earned the right to speak, and I want to go on the record before you and the police officers. This charge is categorically false. There is no truth to it. Drugs have no role in the athletic programs. They never have, and, as long as I am alive, they never will." He turned to me. "Detective, I am not criticizing you for bringing this charge to Chief Murtaugh. I understand you have an investigation to carry out, and you're obligated to pursue every lead, whether it seems promising or not. But I promise you, this young man—this drug dealer—is a liar." Carl Davis lifted his fingers and slapped his palms on the table. End of story.

Coach Andy Baxter spoke. "I need to say something, too. I recruited Cory McDermott when I began here at CMSU eight years ago. It turned out to be a mistake: Cory was unsuccessful as a student-athlete. He was a poor student and a mediocre player. Detective Seagate presented the most compelling evidence that he is a liar: he is now a drug dealer. We cannot make the mistake of listening to his absurd allegation. Doing so would jeopardize the futures of the hundreds of wonderful student-athletes who add immeasurably to the lives of the entire CMSU community, on-campus and off."

President Billingham turned to the A.D. "Do you have something you want to add, John?"

"No, Bob. Carl and Andy said it. This man Cory McDermott is a criminal and a liar. Obviously, he harbors an irrational hatred for the athletic programs and for CMSU. I know that Andy treats all of his student-athletes with the utmost professionalism. I wouldn't have hired him if I wasn't absolutely sure of that. Andy did right by this young man; this young man is not doing right by CMSU."

President Billingham glanced around the room to make sure everyone who wanted to speak had done so. "Chief Murtaugh, I want to thank you and your detectives for bringing this matter to our attention. Obviously, we reject this young man's allegation, but I assure you I will investigate it further with my staff. Please know that you can count on our full cooperation as you continue your investigations. Do any of you have anything you would like to add before we adjourn?"

"I'd like to say something," I said. "I want to thank all of you for meeting with us. I'm sure you're gonna follow up with this on your end. That's what we have to do, too, on our end. We need to stay in contact with Cory McDermott because he remains a suspect in two criminal investigations. Even if his allegation about supplying drugs to your athletic programs is a lie—which I'm sure it is—we need to determine whether he supplied the drugs that killed Lake Williams and whether he killed Kendra Crimmons. If he participated in either of these crimes, we need to understand why. We plan to charge him, at least for criminal distribution of dangerous drugs. But if we can charge him with more than that, that's what we want to do."

President Billingham nodded. "Thank you, Detective Seagate. Thank you all."

A minute ago, the three football guys seemed confident they had discredited Cory McDermott. He was a drug dealer, a drug dealer who didn't even have the balls to name the CMSU contact who ordered the hit on Lake Williams. His story was obviously bullshit. There was no contact; Cory made it all up to lower his sentence. They had everything under control.

But now they knew Cory told us this contact had been buying drugs for the athletics department for years. Now they realized that, if we could prove this charge, the entire athletics program— and their own careers—would be destroyed. And they must have concluded that Cory McDermott was a much more serious threat than they had imagined a minute ago.

# *Chapter 23*

The chief was driving me and Ryan back from the university to headquarters in his BMW. He had a pretty nice department Buick he could use, but he preferred his own car. I don't blame him. The seats were leather, the dash was full of shiny wood, and it had a big screen with all kinds of lights and controls for music and navigation. Plus, there were no soda cans on the floor or candy wrappers stuck in the heater vents. I'd like this car, too.

"What did you think, Karen?" the chief said once we left the university and got out onto the four-lane that would take us back downtown.

"I think it's possible that Carl Davis doesn't know what's going on, and that he believes the athletics programs are clean. On the other hand, he did lie to us—at least I think he lied to us—when he told me and Ryan he didn't know anything about the cheerleader saying Lake raped her. He got all worked up about how rape is so horrible, just like he did a few minutes ago about how drugs are so horrible. So maybe that's just the way he talks." I turned around to address Ryan in the back seat. "You remember that?"

"Very clearly," Ryan said.

"Remind me," the chief said, "what makes you think Carl Davis was lying about the rape allegation?"

"Because he couldn't quite remember who Lake was when we brought up the topic, but later he told us Max Thomas, one of the assistants, was Lake's roommate when they were players. Which I thought was a pretty specific thing to remember from that long ago. He even remembered that LaKadrian's nickname was Lake."

"But you don't believe that the A.D. and the coach are being straight with us?"

"That's right," I said, "I don't. When we asked the coach why he came to CMSU, he gave us some vague horseshit, then we find out John Freedlander used to be his football coach. And both of them have racked up a lot of NCAA violations—major and minor ones. I think they're both dirty. Did you notice that only Carl Davis was really indignant about the charges? It was a matter of pride to him that the athletics were clean. Like I said, maybe that's just the way he talks. But the A.D. and the coach? They didn't even seem pissed that someone would accuse them of being dirty. They said Cory was a liar because he's a criminal. They didn't address the allegation itself."

The chief cocked his head to address Ryan, who was sitting in the back. "What do you think?"

"I agree with Karen. I think the coach and the A.D. are dirty. I don't know if one of them is the contact Cory referred to. I don't know if it was someone else. I don't even know if there is a contact. Regardless, I want to get Cory off the street; he's a dealer."

"Are we putting Cory in danger?"

"If they killed Lake and then they killed Kendra," Ryan said, "Cory could be next. He already got worked over. He has a right to know that we told them what he said. Here's the way I'd look at it. If the football guys are telling the truth that the athletics department is clean—they had nothing to do with killing Lake or Kendra, and there's no contact who buys drugs for the program—they won't hurt Cory. If they're lying—they ordered the two murders and there is a contact—they might start planning what to do to make sure Cory doesn't name him. But Cory has a responsibility, too. If he wants us to protect him, he has to start working with us. We spelled it out to him very clearly. But he's not there yet."

"That sound right to you, Karen?" the chief said.

"Absolutely."

"Good," the chief said as he pulled the BMW into his reserved spot in the lot behind headquarters and shut off the engine.

"Thanks for the backup, chief," I said. "We'll meet with Harold and Robin and see if they got anything off of Kendra. We'll try to get the word to Cory that we met with the president and the football guys and told them he's got a contact at the university. We'll try to get him to come in and make a formal statement."

The chief said, "Okay, keep me up-to-date."

Ryan and I headed to the bullpen, hung up our coats, and headed downstairs to see what the medical examiner and the evidence tech had found.

We caught up with Robin in her office. She had her headphones on. I had to rap on her door a couple times to get her to hear me.

"Hey, cops." She gave us a bright smile.

"You get a chance to process Kendra Crimmons?"

"Done."

"And?"

"She had seven dollars on her: a five and two one's. No drugs on her person. No defensive wounds. I can't tell you cause of death, but I wouldn't be surprised if the three knife wounds to her abdomen had something to do with it."

"Interesting knife?"

"Not really. Blade about eight inches, one inch wide at the hilt, serrated on one side."

"You find anything on her clothes to say she was killed somewhere else and dumped at the skate park?"

MIKE MARKEL

"Her clothes had so much crap on them I couldn't give you anything that would hold up in court. But no, I didn't find any exotic organics or minerals or anything that would put her someplace else. Nothing that would suggest she was transported in the trunk of a car or the bed of a pickup. If you want to find the killer—"

"We kinda would."

"Then you're gonna have to find an eyewitness or some CCTV footage or something. Maybe she's full of the same heroin that took out Lake. Harold might have that for you."

"I doubt it," I said. "If she was dumb enough to shoot up stuff she didn't trust, the guy wouldn't have had to stab her three times. But thanks for the help. We're gonna check in with Harold now."

Ryan and I headed down to the lab. We opened the heavy door and walked in. Kendra was already on the table. Harold was bent over her torso. I called out to him, but he couldn't hear me because he was running some kind of saw. Ryan drifted over to watch the action. I stayed near the door.

Harold stopped the saw and looked up when Ryan walked up next to him. He wiped the perspiration off his scalp and slid his safety goggles up on his head.

Ryan said, "You have a cause of death?"

Harold turned around to see if I was there, too. "Hey, beautiful." Then he turned back to Ryan. "I haven't called it yet because I don't have the results on the blood work yet. She might have OD'ed like her friend. But there were three knife wounds. One hit the liver and she bled out internally. But whether that came first or any drugs killed her, I can't say yet."

I said, "Over at the skate park you said time of death was midnight or early morning."

"Yeah, I'm sticking with that. Probably midnight to two, give or take."

"All right, thanks, Harold."

"Sure thing. I'll let you know when I enter the report."

Back at our desks, Ryan and I talked about how to lure Cory in. "How do we get him a message? We don't have any contact information on him." I said.

"We could re-post the bulletin that goes to all the uniforms and detectives. Include a booking photo. Say we need him to get in touch. We want to make a deal. Something like that."

I thought for a second. "He might misinterpret that to mean what we already told him: We want to make a deal but he needs to name the contact first. I'd be more direct: We told the coach what you told us."

"Yeah, that's better. If he's too stupid to understand what that means, we're not going to be able to help him. He's on his own."

I nodded. "Would you get that downstairs?"

He popped out of his chair and headed off to set up the bulletin.

Then we waited. It happens a lot. When we wait, we start working on the forms. For every investigation, we need to record every person we interview, every piece of evidence we discover, every lead we follow. Over the course of the afternoon, I checked in a few too many times with the sergeant downstairs to see if any officers reported any sight of Cory McDermott. Nothing. That didn't surprise me: He was all beat up, and he worked at night. It made sense that he was sleeping somewhere.

Even though it didn't surprise me, it did worry me. If one of the football guys killed Lake and then Kendra, there was only one person left who could implicate them: Cory. And if Cory took the beatdown because he neglected to kill Kendra, his decision to talk to the cops might have sealed his fate. We wanted to force the football guys to do something that would move our investigation forward. But if they took out Cory—and did it cleanly—it would shut down the investigation. Shit.

Around four o'clock, I said to Ryan, "I'm getting antsy."

Ryan looked up from his screen. "I see that."

"I think we screwed this up."

"How's that?"

"We told the football guys Cory says he's got a contact on the team who supplies drugs. We want them to make a move. And we've tried to alert Cory that we've told them. We've set up a race: Who's gonna move first? If the football guys know where to find Cory, they can kill him before he even hears from us that we want him to come in."

"Therefore?"

"Therefore we've put his life in danger unnecessarily."

"What should we do now?"

"Tell the football guys that Cory's come in and told us everything. He's working with the prosecutor to knock down his sentence."

"What's the 'everything' he's told us?"

"I don't know, but they will."

"What if the football guys don't believe us?" Ryan said.

"Unless they've already got Cory tied to a chair in a basement somewhere, they can't be sure he *didn't* come in and make a statement. They can't take the chance we're bluffing. This is a capital-punishment state."

Ryan leaned back in his chair and knit his fingers behind his head. "Let me think this through. Possibility One: They're telling the truth. They're clean. They didn't kill anyone. They'll thank us for getting rid of the contact. Possibility Two: They're dirty, and they're murderers. If they think he's already made a statement, they're too late. There's no point in killing him."

"That's right," I said. "If he's already made a statement, the whole scheme falls apart, and it's every man for himself."

"So we tell President Billingham that Cory McDermott is talking, and the prosecutor is working out the details of the deal.

Billingham tells the football guys, and if they're dirty they'll sacrifice the most vulnerable one." We were both silent for a minute. "What are we not getting?"

We sat there another minute. "Let's run this by the chief," I said.

We headed down to his office and ran the idea by him. He quizzed us a little bit. Although he doesn't at all mind lying to suspects and criminals, he doesn't like lying to good guys, like President Billingham.

"Yeah, Chief," I said to him, "but it's risky to tell Billingham the truth. He might decide his relationship with Carl Davis, the A.D., and the coach is too valuable for them to find out he was playing them. Or he might want to think about it a while. In the meantime, the football guys could get their hands on Cory. They've got his phone number; we don't. We think they were the ones who already beat the shit out of him. That was a warning. What do you think they're gonna do to him now?"

The chief sat there, his fingers lightly tapping his desk, his head bowed. He hit a few keys on his keyboard. "Let me call President Billingham."

"Listen, Chief, why don't you let me call him? That way, if it blows up, you can say it was my idea."

"I appreciate that, but no. It's my responsibility. I'll do it."

The chief picked up his personal cell and phoned the president. He relayed the message. When the president asked who the contact was, the chief was smooth: We couldn't divulge that information until the prosecutor works out the details with Cory McDermott's attorney. The president said he hoped he wouldn't be blindsided by a public announcement about the contact. Chief Murtaugh assured him he'd give him a heads-up. They ended the call. Then the chief made another call, this one to Larry Klein, our county prosecutor. The chief sketched in what he had just told President Billingham. Larry Klein said thanks.

"Thanks, Chief," I said. "Hope your idea works."

He smiled. "You'll be the first to know."

That night, around nine, after I'd returned from my eight o'clock AA meeting, I checked my voicemail. Carl Davis had left me a message.

# *Chapter 24*

The voicemail from Carl Davis was brief. "Detective Seagate, this is Carl Davis. Tomorrow, sometime before noon, please expect to receive a phone call from an attorney, Christopher Reid, relative to your investigations. Have a good evening."

I went online to look up Christopher Reid, an attorney in Rawlings. I tried Reid and Reed. There was no such person. I tried a national search for an attorney named Christopher Reid. Bingo. There were twenty-seven of them. Rather than looking through all of them, I decided to do what a normal person would do: I ate dinner, watched a little TV, and went to bed.

Friday morning, around nine-thirty, the chief called us into his office. We sat down. "I just got a call from President Billingham. He wanted to make sure we had heard from an attorney."

I said, "Carl Davis called me last night, around eight. He said a lawyer named Christopher Reid would contact me this morning."

"Who's he?" the chief said.

"I looked him up. Can't find a lawyer with that name in town."

"Who's his client?"

I looked at Ryan, who shook his head. "Presumably the contact who Cory didn't give us yesterday." He looked like he was trying to suppress a smile. "With any luck, we'll recognize him when we meet him."

The chief looked at Ryan with a stony expression. "I'll call

President Billingham and tell him we expect to hear from the attorney. Dismissed."

Around ten-thirty, I got the call from Christopher Reid. "Detective Seagate, are you and your partner available this morning at eleven-thirty? My client would like to come in and make a statement."

I wanted to say, "Who the hell is your client?" But since our story was that Cory already told us, I said, "Yes, that would work, Mr. Reid. Do you need directions?"

"No, thank you. We'll see you in an hour."

"Looking forward to it." I ended the call and glanced over at Ryan, who was wearing a huge grin. "If you say, 'This is fun, huh?' I will have you removed from the case."

"This is amusing, huh?"

"How so?"

"Well, the chief calls the university president and tells him we know who the contact is. The president must've called the football guys yesterday sometime after four. Since then, they've had a heart-to-heart with the contact and even hired him an out-of-town attorney. This attorney has flown in—"

"How do you know he's flown in?"

"I don't, but it makes for a better story. This attorney has talked with the contact, perhaps for just a half-hour on the phone, but maybe for hours, here in Rawlings, going over the options. The attorney is going to walk up to Reception in about fifty-five minutes. He's going to say to the officer, 'Christopher Reid, with my client, John Doe, to see Detective Karen Seagate.'" Ryan started to laugh. "You'll get a call from Reception, telling you who's here to see us—"

"That's right, we'll have about thirty seconds to prepare to take his statement, Jackass."

"That's Detective Jackass to you." Ryan was still laughing. "I don't know what you're worried about. We don't have to prepare anything. They're the ones who are going to do the talking. All we need to do is ask questions."

I gave him a look and went back to reading my notes. At eleven-thirty, I got the call from Reception saying a Mr. Christopher Reid and his client were here to see me. "Have an officer escort them to Interview 2, please."

Ryan and I set up in Interview 2. A few moments later, the two men arrived at the door of the interview room.

Christopher Reid was a man of about fifty. His grey hair, shoulder length, was starting to thin on top. He had on a western style jacket, a tan gabardine with brown suede yokes extending down from the shoulders to the middle of his chest. He wore a white shirt, with snaps instead of buttons, and a bola tie around the open collar. The fact that the brown slacks matched the suede yokes, the tooled brown cowboy boots, and the brown cowboy hat he held in his left hand suggested that this was a coordinated outfit. Apparently, he wanted to look like a Hollywood rancher. I hoped this meant he was very stupid.

Behind him, wearing a conservative dark suit and a coordinated dark expression, was Ronald Weber, the owner of Weber Electric. Weber, the father of Alicia Weber, now Alicia Templeton, the guy who tried to attack Lake Williams at the hearing at the university after Alicia accused Lake of rape.

I breathed a sigh of relief that there was in fact a guy who was willing to cop to being Cory McDermott's contact—and that Ryan and I knew who he was. What else he was willing to cop to, I didn't know. The fact that he came with an attorney suggested maybe he was going to cop to the two murders.

We all took our seats. Ryan started up the recording equipment from the control on the wall, and I announced the names of the four of us.

I started by asking Weber to identify himself and where he worked. He answered in a low, steady voice. I didn't get the feeling he was going to freak out or fall apart.

"Mr. Weber," I said, "have you ever purchased illegal drugs to provide to current or prospective student-athletes at Central Montana State University?"

"Yes."

"How often have you done this?"

"I can't say precisely. Maybe fifty times?"

"When did you start buying these drugs?"

"About seven or eight years ago. I don't remember exactly."

"Did you buy these drugs from Cory McDermott, a former student-athlete?"

"Usually, but not always."

"Did you buy these drugs at the direction of Carl Davis, the president of the Cougar Athletic Association?"

"No."

"Was Mr. Davis aware that you were doing this?"

"No."

"Did you buy these drugs at the direction of John Freedlander, the athletic director at CMSU?"

"No."

"Was Mr. Freedlander aware that you were doing this?"

"No."

"Same two questions about Andy Baxter, the football coach at CMSU."

"No and no."

"Are you saying nobody knew you were doing this?"

"Correct."

"Why did you do it?"

"To help make the Cougars more competitive."

"Explain."

"If the student-athletes are happier, they'll be more motivated. If the prospective student-athletes enjoy their visit, they'll more likely accept a scholarship offer and attend."

He presented this information like he was instructing his sales
staff how to talk to customers. He didn't appear to be
embarrassed that the practices he was describing were felonies, as
well as violations of numerous NCAA regulations.

I couldn't help asking one more question on this topic. "Mr.
Weber, if any of three gentlemen I mentioned found out you've
been doing this for some years, how do you think they would
react?"

The attorney gripped Ronald Weber's arm with some force.
"My client would only be speculating. I think that question is
outside of the parameters of this statement." Weber cooperated,
sitting there silently, expressionless, gazing at the wall behind me.

"Mr. Weber, how did you get the drugs to the current and
prospective student-athletes?"

"There wasn't one way of doing it. Usually, they called me on
the phone and we arranged a place to meet."

"And that's how you got drugs to recruits, too?"

"I never met with recruits personally. Current student-athletes
would deliver the drugs to the recruits while they were visiting."

"Did you do other things for student-athletes?"

He sighed, like I was asking for a lot of information.
"Prostitutes. Cash—"

"What do you mean by 'cash'?"

"Couple hundred dollars here and there, for incidental
expenses. Jewelry. Tats. Liquor. I helped athletes sell game jerseys
and rings."

"Anything else?"

"Abortions for girlfriends."

"You're a busy man." I took a second. "Where does all this
money come from?"

"Mostly from me. Some from other fans of the programs."

"How do these other fans get you money?"

"In envelopes. At games, tailgate parties, diners."

"Everything in cash?"

"That's right. No banks. No records. No paperwork at all. Cash."

"So you're saying that for seven or eight years you have done these activities without the knowledge of Carl Davis, A.D. Freeedlander, or Coach Baxter? Is that correct?"

"That is correct."

"Let me turn to the Lake Williams murder. Did you buy the heroin from Cory McDermott—the highly concentrated heroin that killed Lake Williams?"

"No."

"Do you know who did?"

"No."

"Do you know why someone wanted to kill Lake Williams?"

"No."

"Did you deliver the heroin to Kendra Crimmons to give to Lake Williams?"

"No."

"Do you know who did?"

"No."

"Were you aware that someone had bought the heroin and given it to Kendra Crimmons to deliver to Lake Williams?"

"No."

"This is ridiculous, Mr. Weber. You had no role in the death of Lake Williams, you don't know who did it, and you don't know why they did it."

Christopher Reid said, "Is that a question, Detective Seagate?"

"Let me turn to the murder of Kendra Crimmons. Did you kill her?"

"No."

"Did you know her?"

"No."

"Do you know who killed her, or why she was killed?"

"No."

"All right, you had no role in the deaths of Lake Williams or Kendra Crimmons, and no knowledge of any actions related to those murders? Is that your statement?"

"That is my statement."

"Can you tell us where you were Sunday night?"

"Sunday nights, my wife and I go over paperwork related to the company. She does the billing for me. We reconcile any problems."

"This was in your office or at home?"

"We do this from home, Sunday nights."

"And Wednesday night?"

"Around what time?"

"Ten to midnight."

"My wife and I were home. I watched a little TV. We went to bed as we always do, around ten-thirty, quarter to eleven. I'm up at six. In my office by seven."

"I want to ask you about the your daughter's rape allegation aganst Lake Williams. Did you believe, at the time, that Lake Williams raped your daughter?"

"Excuse me, Detective," Christopher Reid said. "Mr. Weber agreed to come in, voluntarily, to make a statement about the two cases you are investigating now. Why are you asking about something that happened seven years ago?"

I nodded. "It relates to Mr. Weber's motives. He said, in a hearing attended by about a dozen people, that he would kill Mr. Williams."

Ronald Weber turned to his attorney. "I don't mind answering." Then he turned to me. "Yes, I believed he had raped Alicia—and I still believe it."

"Would you describe your emotions at the hearing on campus about your daughter's allegation?"

"I was furious. I wanted to kill Lake Williams. For what he had done to Alicia."

"That's certainly understandable. Now tell me this, Mr. Weber. Why did Alicia decide to withdraw the allegation against Lake Williams?"

"I think she concluded that her allegations would cause more harm than good."

"Please explain."

"It was well known, within the football community and on campus generally, that Lake was her boyfriend. She decided that since there was no proof she had been raped—no physical evidence, no eyewitnesses—and therefore most people, including the faculty and administrators overseeing the hearing, would think that she was simply trying to punish Lake for the way he treated her."

"What are you referring to? How did he treat her?"

"He was unfaithful to her. He didn't try to hide it. And he abused her physically. On more than one occasion."

"But your daughter never pressed charges—about the physical abuse, I mean?"

"That's right. I'm not sure what she was thinking." He shook his head. "Maybe she thought she could help him learn how to deal with his anger issues. I'm really not sure what her thinking was."

"Did anybody give you money to try to persuade your daughter to withdraw the rape allegation against Lake Williams?"

"No, nobody gave me any money."

"Mr. Weber, here's what I think happened. First, about your daughter. I think somebody paid you to get your daughter to back off. Second, about Lake Williams. I think he came to you or to someone in the football program—sometime in the last few weeks, maybe days—and threatened to tell his story. He was in real trouble. He couldn't think coherently, couldn't remember things, couldn't control his anger. Somebody gave you money to buy the heroin and get it to Lake Williams, knowing that since he was a drug addict, he would shoot up and die. Third, about Kendra Crimmons. I think you killed her because she was the only one who could identify you. You found out that she had talked to us about being paid to deliver the drugs to Lake Williams. Therefore, she needed to be silenced. And fourth, about Cory McDermott, your favorite drug dealer. Two days ago, I think you and others beat him severely to send him a message: If he did not keep his mouth shut, he too would be killed. That's what I think."

Christopher Reid spoke. "The wonderful thing about the Constitution, Detective, is that you have every right to say that. Well, not exactly every right. But here in this room, you have the right to say that. Unfortunately, you do not have proof. You do not even have any evidence to support those charges." He stood up. "Therefore, we are going to leave now. My client was gracious enough to come here today to make a statement, which he has now done. The next move—if you can think of a next move—is up to you. My bet is that, since there is no evidence to support any of your claims, you will not be able to think of a next move. You will decide that it is time to turn your attention to figuring out who really did kill Lake Williams and Kendra Crimmons." He bowed his head in Ryan's direction. "Detective Miner, good day."

"No, Mr. Reid." Ronald Weber put his hand on the attorney's arm. "I want to tell the detectives what happened."

Christopher Reid turned to me. "Would you give us a minute, Detective Seagate?"

"Of course." I announced a break. Ryan turned off the recording system, and the two of us left the interview room.

We got to the passageway next to the interview room and looked in through the mirror. Christopher Reid and Ronald Weber were arguing in whispers. The body language, complete

with shaking heads and fingers poking in chests, made clear that
the lawyer was telling his client not to say anything else to us.
They had us right where they wanted us. But Ronald Weber
wasn't going to do what his attorney advised.

# *Chapter 25*

The pantomime performed by Ronald Weber and his attorney, Christopher Reid, was wrapping up. Reid lifted his arms, palms out, in a gesture of surrender. Weber nodded to signal that he had won.

Weber walked back to his seat at the metal table and sat down. Reid looked at the mirror, through which we had watched the proceedings, and waved us in. Ryan and I re-entered the interview room. While he turned on the recording system, I sat down and announced that the interview would now resume.

I looked at Ronald Weber. "You said you wanted to tell us what happened? Do you want to start with Alicia and the rape allegation?"

"I've already told you about that," he said. "Alicia withdrew the allegation because she concluded that nobody would believe Lake raped her. In hindsight, she was probably wise. She took some time off from college, then returned and graduated. She has a wonderful husband and a baby daughter. She has moved on."

"But you're sticking with your statement that you were not paid by anyone at the university to persuade Alicia to withdraw the allegation in order to protect Lake Williams?"

He looked at me. "I'm sticking with that statement because it's the truth."

"All right," I said. "Tell us your version of the story about how Lake Williams died."

Christopher Reid, who had been sitting there silently, his arms crossed before him, suddenly spoke. "Really, Detective, I ask that you show my client some basic respect."

I nodded my head. "Tell us about how Lake Williams died."

Ronald Weber began. "I had learned that Lake Williams was experiencing significant problems—"

"Hold on a second, Mr. Weber," I said. "'I had learned'? How had you learned?"

Weber shook his head. "I'm not going to say."

"Come on, Mr. Weber. Why is it so difficult to tell us the truth? Who was it: Carl Davis, John Freedlander, Andy Baxter? They didn't do anything wrong in telling you Lake was in trouble. It's what humans do. Tell us who it was."

"I told you I'm not going to say. But—just to be clear—it was not one of those three men."

"Did Lake come to you and tell you? Did Kendra Crimmons come to you?"

Christopher Reid spoke. "Detective, this is not a deposition. My client is under no obligation to answer any of your questions. He has indicated that he does not want to tell you how he learned that Mr. Williams was having problems. Move on, or I will strongly advise him to terminate this meeting."

"You're not making it easy for me to believe anything Mr. Weber is saying, Mr. Reid."

"That is your challenge, Detective, not my client's."

"Go ahead, Mr. Weber," I said. "You had learned that Lake Williams was in trouble."

"That's correct. I decided I was going to assist him in getting help—"

"You were gonna help your daughter's rapist?"

Ronald Weber stared at me. "That is what I said. I decided I was going to assist him in getting help. When we met before, in my office, I made it clear I am not the man I was those years ago. I have accepted Jesus Christ as my Lord and Savior. I have forgiven Mr. Williams, and I saw it as my Christian duty to help him if I could."

"So what did you do?"

"I was in the process of making inquiries about resources to help him."

"What kind of resources?"

"Drug and alcohol dependency and mental health resources."

"You mean, like AA?"

"AA and various outpatient and inpatient programs."

"But Lake Williams didn't have any money, correct?"

"That is correct. But I did."

"You mean, your own money?"

"That's right."

"You're telling me—with a straight face—that you were gonna pay to get Lake Williams into some sort of program that would cost hundreds, maybe thousands of dollars a week?"

"Yes."

"Okay. Now tell me how we get from you looking around for programs to help Lake Williams to him shooting up some heroin that kills him?"

"I don't know."

"What?"

"I said, I don't know what happened. I learned of his death on the news Tuesday night, or whenever it was announced."

"Okay, Mr. Weber, just so I'm sure I've got this right. How he died, you don't know. But how you learned that he was in trouble, you do know, but you won't say. That's your statement?"

"That's my statement."

I sighed deeply. "Let's talk about the murder of Kendra Crimmons. You don't know, or you know but you won't say?"

Christopher Reid said, "Detective, remember what I said about tone?"

"Yeah, I remember, but since your client isn't giving us

anything useful, I don't really think the big problem here is my tone." I turned back to Ronald Weber. "You said you were gonna tell us what happened. So tell us. What do you know about the murder of Kendra Crimmons, Mr. Weber?"

"I know nothing about her murder. I had no reason to hurt her. I never met her. I never even heard of her. I could not pick her out of a lineup."

"Well, you're not gonna have to pick her out of a lineup. Okay, Mr. Weber, I think we're done here. This statement will go to the county prosecutor, who will determine whether to press charges. Personally, I hope that you do face charges for the distribution of dangerous drugs and for pimping, both of which you have admitted. And for conspiracy to murder Lake Williams, for first-degree murder of Kendra Crimmons, and for the assault on Cory McDermott. Obviously, I think you're lying to protect yourself and the football guys at the university. Or you're lying to protect yourself from the football guys. The police department remains committed to solving all these cases. If you stick with this story, we will do everything we can to get to the truth and prosecute you to the fullest extent of the law. However, if you decide to help us identify others who have committed crimes related to any of these cases, we will recommend to the prosecutor that he extend to you every consideration. As you think about what you said to us here today, remember that you can amend your statement—in part or in whole—at any time." I paused. "Do you have any questions?"

"No, I do not."

We ended the meeting, and Ryan escorted Ronald Weber and Christopher Reid down to Reception. A little while later, we caught up with the chief in his office and briefed him on what Ronald Weber had said in his statement.

"Bottom line," the chief said, "you don't believe him."

"That's right," I said. "He said he was going to tell us what happened, but then he had nothing to say. I think the football guys paid him—or him and his daughter—to get her to back off on the rape allegation, and that the same guys had him buy the heroin and get it to Lake. Then he or someone killed Kendra and beat up Cory McDermott—as a warning."

"Where do we stand with the football guys and President Billingham? Have any of them contacted you?"

"No. All I've heard from any of them is the call from Carl Davis telling me to expect to hear from Weber's attorney. How about President Billingham? He didn't contact you after you called him?"

"No, he didn't."

"What do you make of that?"

"Well, we can assume that President Billingham was the one who started the ball rolling after I phoned him to say the drug dealer had made a statement about his contact in the athletic department. But I have no idea what he actually did or said. Maybe he called them all together. Maybe he just told John Freedlander, who told the others."

"So, we don't know the president's involvement—or whether he's in with the football guys, do we?"

Chief Murtaugh rubbed his forehead. "If you're saying we don't know if he's covering for his guys, that's right. We don't. But I think I have a pretty good relationship with President Billingham. It would be a lot easier for me to believe he's unaware of what his guys are up to than to believe he's in with them."

"Should we contact him and get him up to speed?"

Ryan spoke. "There's nothing to get him up to speed about. We have a drug dealer who said he has a contact at the university, but he didn't give us a name or any evidence. Now we have a local businessman who says he delivered drugs and girls to student-athletes. And we have an athletics department that retained a lawyer for this businessman. But he didn't give us any names or any evidence, either. He didn't implicate one person who works for the university."

"If I were the president of the university," I said, "I'd sure as hell want to know about the kind of corruption Weber described."

"Me, too," the chief said, "but Ryan's point is that Weber's strategy was to insulate the university employees by saying he might be willing to take the fall for the drugs and hookers but not for the two murders or the assault. Weber left it up to us to develop those cases on our own. He was betting we wouldn't be able to implicate him or the university employees on any of the important crimes."

Ryan said, "From what he offered about the drugs and the hookers, I don't even think he's vulnerable to any criminal charges on those actions. He gave us no details, and we haven't developed any ourselves. What can we charge him with?"

"So he was just jerking us around?" I said.

The chief sighed. "I think so. The only thing I take from your account of the statement is that the football guys have gotten together and dangled Ronald Weber in front of us. But since we can't charge him with anything, we can't get him to flip on the football guys by dealing down the charges."

"You're saying you don't want to contact President Billingham, then?" I said.

"That's right. I agree with Ryan. We don't have any new information that relates to university employees. We can't give him a way to pressure anyone to cooperate with us."

"Is there a way you can talk to him and figure out whether he's oblivious to what's going on or he's in with them?"

The chief and Ryan were silent for a minute. Finally, the chief spoke. "I can't think of how to do that. I don't want to get aggressive with him or let him think I'm accusing him of protecting some bad actors at the university. There's too much riding on our relationship with him to jeopardize it unless there's a clear, compelling reason to do so. Right now, I don't see that reason."

"Okay, chief, I gotta tell you: I don't know what to do next. If the university guys and Ronald Weber are playing chess with us, I think they're kicking our asses."

"You know what I want to do? Bring in Larry. If we're missing something, he'll see it. That okay with you, Karen?"

"Absolutely," I said. "Like I said, I got nothing."

The chief picked up his phone and speed-dialed Larry Klein, our county prosecutor. He put it on Speaker.

"Klein." His voice was a little garbled.

"Larry, Robert Murtaugh. Did I interrupt your lunch?"

I looked at my watch. It was a few minutes after noon.

"It's a tuna salad sandwich, soaked right through the bread. Talk."

"We've got a case we want to run by you. It'll take five minutes. Can we set something up?"

"If it's really just five minutes, and you don't mind taking a short drive, let's do it now."

"Great, where are you?"

"I'm at the Plaza. There's a conference here. But I'd love to leave the building. How about out near the fountains in ten minutes?"

"See you then."

The three of us headed out to the parking lot behind the building and loaded into the Charger for the five-minute drive to the Plaza. That's the auditorium and meeting facility the city built about ten years ago. It's got an indoor arena for concerts and shows and our minor-league basketball and hockey teams.

I parked us in the underground lot and we headed back out to the grey skies. We walked to the little brick plaza where, in the warm weather, tiny nozzles shot water out of the ground in synchronized patterns. Little kids loved it.

Larry was sitting on a bench. It was warm enough for him to open his black wool overcoat, revealing his usual black suit, white shirt, and black tie. His heels didn't quite reach the ground, but his toes were tapping the bricks. "Robert, Karen, Ryan. Sorry to bring you out here."

"Not at all," the chief said. "Thanks for giving us a few minutes of your lunch hour."

Larry Klein looked at me. "You want to go somewhere we can all sit down?"

"No, this is fine," I said. "We'll only be a couple of minutes. Chief, why don't you take a seat?"

"No, you sit. I've been sitting too much today."

I sat down next to Larry.

"The main case," the chief said, "is the murder of Lake Williams a few days ago."

"The junkie?"

"That's right. Then, yesterday, another junkie, Kendra Crimmons, who lived out in the same homeless camp as Williams, was murdered, too. She was the one who someone paid to deliver the heroin that killed him."

"Okay, what's the question?"

"We've been working the dealer who we think sold the drugs that killed Williams. He told us he's been supplying the football and basketball programs for years through a contact at the university, but he wouldn't finger the contact without a deal with you. We told him he needed to name the contact before we could bring you in. He refused and walked. But we think there really is a contact, and that the football team—the coach, the A.D., and the head of the booster organization—they're all dirty. So I called Bob Billingham and told him we know who the contact is—"

"Which you don't."

"Correct. Today, the contact appears, with an attorney, at

headquarters. The contact is Ronald Weber. He's an electrician. Owns his own company."

Larry raised his eyebrows. "I know him. He's my electrician."

"We think the football guys got together and they're offering up Weber to us."

"Is he willing or unwilling?"

"We can't tell yet. He seems quite disciplined, wouldn't you say, Karen?"

"If that means he's not telling us anything, yeah, he's quite disciplined."

"Problem is," the chief said, "Weber admits he's the contact, but he hasn't given us anything to charge him with. And he's adamant that the football guys don't know anything about all the drugs and hookers he's supplied to the kids over the years."

"Your move."

"That's the problem, Larry. We don't have a move."

Larry Klein nodded. "Sounds like they've thought it through. You can't charge him; therefore I can't deal with him to get to the football guys. Presumably, there's no documentation about the drugs and hookers."

"That's right. There's nothing written down. It's cash in envelopes."

"And no probable cause to search phones or computers or banks or anything."

"No. There won't be any trail to follow."

"Even if you think his story is implausible, there's no legal way to use it to get him."

"Larry," I said, "you mean a guy can walk into police headquarters, tell us he's been supplying drugs and girls to players and recruits for years, and we can't charge him with anything?"

"But he didn't do those things," Larry said.

"What?" I said. "He just admitted he did. Why would you say he didn't?"

"The same reason you said he did." He smiled, his eyes crinkling at the corners, his black plastic glasses riding up his nose a little. "You get what I'm saying? The fact he says he's a bad guy doesn't mean he's a bad guy. The fact he says he's a good guy doesn't mean he's a good guy."

I think Larry used to be a teacher somewhere before he came to Rawlings. Sometimes he likes to play these games where he pretends to say one thing when he really means the opposite. Then, while you're trying to figure out why he said that, you realize you just walked into a trap. I don't think he means to be a pain in the ass. It's just the way his brain works.

"So what are we supposed to do?" I said.

"His statement wasn't really a statement. There's nothing you can do with it. It's more of a declaration. What he's saying is you need to develop the evidence to bring charges against him and the others. He's not going to deliver them to you—and he's not going to sacrifice himself."

"What you're saying is, we got nothing."

"The technical term is *bupkis*." Larry Klein opened his empty plastic baggie and blew out the crumbs. He sealed it and put it back in his paper sack. "Any other way I can be of no assistance?"

# *Chapter 26*

"What the hell is going on?" I said.

"No idea." Ryan's expression was grim.

We headed out to the parking lot behind headquarters, got in the Charger, and drove out along the Rawlings River, some three miles east of town. Eagle's Nest was going to be the city's largest new residential development. Sitting in a little valley between the river and the foothills, it would have some two-hundred single-family units, a few dozen three-story condos, and a block of apartments, all of them served by a small shopping center with a few casual restaurants.

We drove in on the main street, which was already paved, a black strip that wound through the dirt and brush. The feeder streets, where the houses were starting to appear, were still hard-packed dirt. On some streets, the houses were just concrete slabs; on others, the framing was complete; on still others, the houses were weather-tight.

Even late on a Friday afternoon, the area was buzzing with equipment and workers in hard hats. Roller trucks were pulverizing the rocky dirt that would become new streets. Water trucks followed, spraying curtains of water to keep the dust down. Earth movers scraped the land, uprooting scrub brush and boulders to make a spot for new concrete slabs. Backhoes were digging trenches for fat white PVC runoff pipes. Dump trucks were building mounds of dirt thirty feet tall. Cranes were lifting pre-built roof trusses onto framed houses.

A few hundred yards in, we approached the construction trailers and the materials-storage area. We drove up to the two squad cars and got out of the Charger. Two officers—Lane and Welsh—walked up to us.

"This way," Welsh said.

Ryan and I followed them toward the materials-storage area, which was a half-acre of dirt enclosed within storm fencing about ten feet tall with razor wire on top. The gate, wide enough to handle any of the construction vehicles, was open.

The area was filled with raw lumber, trusses, rebar, stone, brick, steel I-beams, and all diameters and lengths of PVC piping. All the materials rested on wood pallets but were open to the elements. The two officers led us into a labyrinth of lumber. We turned a corner and almost stumbled on the body of Cory McDermott, lying between two stacks of two-by-eight-inch pine.

He wore jeans, a T-shirt, and a light jacket. His crotch was wet, and he smelled like piss. He was lying on his back, his legs bent, the right knee touching the dirt, the left knee resting against a stack of lumber. His arms were outstretched above his head.

Usually, I'm not that good at figuring out cause of death, but this one was obvious even to me. The bruising around the eyes, now purple with a hint of neon green, was from the beatdown the other day. But the three ligature marks around his neck, just below the Adam's apple, were new. One of the three marks was sloping upward. That usually means the killer was behind the victim, and that the victim had slumped forward so the killer was above him while he tightened the ligature. There was bruising above and below the ligature marks. Little red hemorrhage dots ringed his eyes.

Ryan leaned in to study Cory's neck. "No fingernail marks. He didn't put up much resistance."

"He might have been unconscious when he was strangled." I started looking around to see if the killer had left the ligature behind. It wouldn't be a rope, which leaves abrasions in the skin and tends to be thicker. The marks on Cory's neck were less than a quarter inch thick, about the diameter of a standard electrical cord. I scanned the dirt around the body. It was littered with tin strapping used to bundle lumber, but nothing like an electrical cord.

"Look at this," Ryan said. He pressed a gloved finger against Cory's cheek, then withdrew it. The spot on his cheek turned pale. "That's livor mortis. It only lasts around two hours after death." Ryan bent over and lifted Cory's right arm a few inches off the ground. He let go, and it fell to the dirt. "No rigor."

"He's been dead only a couple hours." I turned to Welsh. "You called this in about fifteen minutes ago, right?

"That's right, Detective." He was a young guy, no more than twenty-four or twenty-five. He stood straight, eager to help, and eager to look like a professional.

"How'd you know who the vic was? Did you find ID on him?"

"No, but I remembered I'd seen the face before. I went back to the patrol car and got on the computer. You'd put out a couple of bulletins. That was the face I remembered."

"That's good. Really good." I nodded. "Do you know who called it in to headquarters?"

Welsh pulled a small notebook from a back pocket. "Man named Al Stoughton. He's the construction-site manager. He's in the big trailer over there." Welsh pointed.

"Do you know if the ME has been notified?"

"He has, Detective."

"All right, Welsh. Appreciate it. Set up the tape, will you?"

He pulled his frame up even straighter. For a second, I thought he was going to salute me or something. I turned to Ryan. "Let's talk to the site manager while we wait on Harold."

We walked out of the materials-storage area. Off to the right, about fifty yards away, sat a cluster of construction trailers. A big one was set on blocks, not wheels. The sign over the door read, "Manager." I walked up the three steps and knocked. I noticed a set of three CCTV cameras mounted along the roofline of the trailer.

A baby-faced man of thirty, wearing a reflective vest, opened up. We introduced ourselves. He invited us to come in and sit in the two plastic chairs in front of his Formica-covered desk. A secretary, seated at another desk at the far end of the trailer, nodded to us.

"Mr. Stoughton, can you tell me what happened?"

He looked at his watch. "It was about an hour ago. I got a knock on the door. One of the workers, a framer, came running up to the door. Said there was a dead body inside the materials-storage area. I grabbed my phone, ran out there with him." He put out his hands. "I saw the guy, called 911."

"Did the framer say if he knew the guy?"

"Said he didn't."

"Is the gate to the area locked? Can only some guys get in?"

"It's kept open during the day, when we're all here. When I leave, around six, I make sure it's locked up. There's a lot of valuable stuff in there."

"So the workers don't have to check in or do anything special when they enter the area, is that right?"

"No, never had any problems with theft by workers during the day."

"I see you've got some CCTV on your trailer. Is it on during the day?"

He shook his head. "I turn it on when I leave." He looked down at this desk for a moment and shook his head. "Might need to re-think that."

"There's no security for people going in and out of the whole construction site, right?"

"No."

"During the day, have you got lunch trucks, things like that, coming in?"

"Yeah, we do. But again, no problems. And owners. Folks who've already bought their homes. Technically, they're not supposed to be driving around in here, but they're good people. Some of the really young ones—you know, like me, first house?—they're excited. They like to take pictures. As long as they don't get in the way, we don't stop them."

"I'm gonna ask a more difficult question. The victim, we know him. Name is Cory McDermott. He was a drug dealer."

Al Stoughton's jaw dropped. "Holy shit."

"Yeah," I said.

"I'm sorry for that language, ma'am. Just caught me by surprise, is all."

"Here's my question: Do you know why he might be here? Are you aware of any dealing going on here?"

"I'm going to be completely honest with you. There've been a few episodes of guys breaking out some beers on Friday afternoons. I've seen it. You know, they're sitting in their pickups before heading out. But I swear to you, I've never seen a worker either using drugs or buying drugs on site here. We're really strict with all the contractors: We catch any of their workers carrying out any illegal activities here—that would include drugs, prostitutes, fighting, anything—that worker is gone, and the company is put on notice how if it happens again, the whole company is banned. We're serious."

"Okay, Mr. Stoughton. Thanks for all the information." I stood up and handed him my card. "If you learn anything that might be relevant, give me a call, please. And keep in mind, this is a murder investigation. If one of the workers phones you and wants to say something but he's afraid he could get in trouble—you know, for buying drugs from the victim or something like that—just give him my number and have him call me directly. A lot of times, the people who help us solve cases like this were doing illegal activities when they saw what happened. Our policy is to get these folks to come forward, cut them some slack on their own infractions if they can help us. You understand what I'm saying?"

"I do, Detective. I understand completely."

We left the manager's office. Over by the entrance to the materials-storage area, I could see the medical examiner's green minivan. "Harold's here." We started walking over to the entrance.

The crime-scene tape was up. Harold was on his knees, bent over Cory McDermott's body. He looked up at me and Ryan as he heard us approach. "You know I'm on salary, right? Not commission. I don't need a new body every day."

"Hey, we're not manufacturing them. If we were, we wouldn't do it on a Friday. Ten-to-one, we'll be working the weekend."

"Is this the same case?"

"Yeah, it is. This is the dealer we think sold the heroin that Kendra Crimmons delivered to Lake Williams."

"You're kidding me."

"No, I'm not."

"Anyone else in the supply chain I'm going to examine in the next few days?"

"Can't make any promises, but I don't think so."

"The officers told me you had a quick look at this man. What's his name?"

"Cory McDermott."

"You need me on this one?"

"Ryan and I think we got this one figured out. Ligature strangulation. That caused the broken capillaries. And the loss of bladder control. Can you identify the ligature marks? Looks to us like it might be something like an electrical cord. Skinny, smooth."

Harold Breen shrugged his shoulders. "Sounds right to me."

"Time of death?"

The medical examiner lifted one of Cory McDermott's hands off the dirt and moved it back and forth. Then he pressed on the victim's cheek, just like Ryan had. "Two or three hours. Four, at the outside."

"What are you looking for in the autopsy?"

"I try not to look for anything in autopsies. Just follow the protocol and see where it leads me. This one looks straightforward. It was ligature strangulation. Assuming he didn't really die of a drug overdose while he was being strangled, the only real question is the official cause of death. It was probably asphyxia from cutting off his air pipe, but it could've been cerebral anoxia. Either way, someone strangled him, probably from behind, with a skinny, smooth cord of some kind. You get to figure out the interesting stuff."

"Such as?"

"For instance, he's got the petechiae from the strangulation, but why are his bruises two or three days old?"

"Because he got beat up two or three days ago."

Harold looked at me. "Hmm. I looked at his fingernails. I don't see any tissue there. And I don't see any scratches or fingernail marks or scrapes on his neck. And look at his shirt and jeans. His shirt is still tucked in."

"All of which says he didn't put up much of a fight."

"That's right," Harold said. "Is that because he was still hurt from the beating?"

"That would make sense. He was hospitalized but he walked out that night."

"Why would he do that?"

"He said it was because he needed to get back to selling drugs to make money. But we really don't know. Maybe it was to kill

Kendra Crimmons. Maybe he was gonna go after the guy who later killed him. Or he was trying to get away from the guy. He didn't tell us what was going on, and he refused to let us protect him while we investigated the two other murders."

"Well, all right, we'll put a rush on this one."

"Do you think you can get to it tomorrow?"

Harold Breen looked at me and sighed. "I'll see what I can do. I'll start the blood work this afternoon. That will help me rule out a lot of things."

"I do love you, Harold."

"No, you don't. If you did, you wouldn't present me with bodies on Friday afternoons."

I squeezed his arm.

Ryan and I left the materials-storage area. As I glanced at the construction trailers clustered off to the right, something caught my eye. "Ryan, that trailer, the blue one, third from the left. What does it say, over the door?"

He squinted. "It says Weber Electric, Inc."

We walked over to it and knocked on the door. No answer. I tried the handle. It was locked. Ryan looked through the window. "No one home," he said.

We walked back to the manager's trailer. We knocked. Al Stoughton opened up. "Yes, Detectives."

"Mr. Stoughton, have you seen Ronald Weber today?"

"Yeah, I think I did."

"Remember when that was?"

"A couple minutes after one this afternoon."

"That's pretty specific. Mind if I ask how you know that was the time?"

"I eat lunch at one every day. I usually get a lot of people drop by between noon and one—you know, to talk about this problem or that. So I gave up trying to eat at that time."

"So, Ron Weber. Did he stop by a little after one today to talk to you?"

"No, I saw him drive by. Out this window." He pointed. "In his pickup. I was about to start eating my sandwich."

"Thanks a lot, Mr. Stoughton."

When Ryan and I turned to leave his office, Al Stoughton looked a little confused that we seemed to be in such a hurry.

## Chapter 27

Ryan said, "Want to pick up Ronald Weber now?"

We were standing outside the construction manager's office. He had just told us he saw Ronald Weber early this afternoon in his pickup truck, right near the materials-storage area at the construction site. If Weber had just finished strangling Cory McDermott, he might have decided to drive into the fenced-off area—the gate was open, and there were no cameras to record anything—and drop off Cory's body. Then, later, before the CCTV cameras came on, he could retrieve the body and stash it better. That would enable him to lay down a decent alibi to show how busy he had been all afternoon. It wasn't a great theory, but it was the best we had.

"Before we go, I want to ask Harold a question." We hurried over to the materials-storage area. Robin had already arrived, and Harold was walking slowly over to his green minivan to head back to headquarters.

"Harold, quick question about strangulation. One of the guys we're looking at is old, over eighty. Could he strangle someone?"

"There's three factors: force, duration, and the nature of the ligature. If you've got a lot of force, you can kill somebody in less than a minute. If you have less force, it'll take you longer. The ligature? If it's a fluffy towel, you need to apply more force or hold it longer—"

Ryan said, "But if it's hard and skinny, like an electrical cord, you do more damage faster."

Harold smiled. "There you go."

I said, "So, an eighty-four-year-old guy?"

Harold shrugged. "If he really didn't like the victim, and the victim took a bad beating the other day, and he had a minute to devote to the task, and he had an electrical cord ..."

"All right, Harold. Thanks. Have a good weekend."

"Well, now you're just being cruel." He opened the minivan door, took a deep breath, grabbed the steering wheel, and hoisted himself up into the seat.

I turned to Ryan. "Okay, we don't know exactly who did what, but you agree they're working together?"

"I do. The chief calls President Billingham about Cory having a contact in the athletics department, and next day Ronald Weber turns up on our doorstep and says, 'It's me.'"

"Then we've got Carl Davis, the booster; John Freedlander, the A.D.; Andy Baxter, the coach; and Ronald Weber, the contact."

"I don't like Carl Davis," Ryan said, "despite what Harold just told us."

"Too old and frail?"

"Too centered. I agree with Harold that an eighty-four-year-old guy could strangle someone, given the right circumstances. But I see Carl Davis living a multi-dimensional life, with a family and a job apart from football."

"His name on the front of the practice facility looked pretty big to me."

"Sure, he's got an ego," Ryan said, "and the university has done everything they can to feed it so he keeps the money coming in, but I think he has an identity apart from football. I don't see him killing people who threaten or embarrass the program. That's my sense, anyway."

"When you say 'that's my sense,' what you're really saying is, 'I don't have any facts to back that up,' right?"

"Harold was correct: You are cruel."

"I'm not ruling out Carl Davis," I said.

"I wouldn't rule him out, either. He's my fourth favorite suspect."

"You think it's Ronald Weber?"

"No, I think it's a conspiracy, but Weber's not the killer—because of how they fed him to us. They know we can't prove him guilty through forensics or eyewitnesses because he didn't do it. We'll be chasing him down, while the real killer—"

"Or killers?"

"That's right," Ryan said. "There could be multiple killers."

"You see any of them willing to take the needle for the football program?"

"Well, I myself wouldn't kill anyone for football, but now you're getting into deeper philosophical questions—"

"Oh, God."

"Short answer, if a person has no moral core, he'd kill for anything. Or even for nothing."

I nodded. "If Lake had proof of something that would cost them their jobs and everything they've worked for over the decades, and they were total douchebags, why wouldn't they?"

"That's right. There could be more than one. We already know that Freedlander and Baxter go back twenty years. If the reason Coach Baxter came to CMSU is that he knew John Freedlander was his kind of guy, they both might be in this all the way."

"It could be weirder than that," I said. "Freedlander came here to CMSU before Coach Baxter, right?"

"Yes."

"So maybe Coach Baxter came here because he had blackmail material on Freedlander. Baxter knew he could get Freedlander fired at any time. That would give him the freedom to do whatever he wanted on his team without having to worry about

Freedlander enforcing any rules."

"Okay, where are we?" Ryan said. "Carl Davis, a long shot. Even with Cory McDermott beat up and sore, it's a stretch to see Carl Davis throttling him. But John Freedlander? Absolutely. Andy Baxter? Of course. Ronald Weber? Certainly."

"But you don't like Weber."

"No, I don't. I think they decided to plant Cory's body at the construction site so we would see Weber's company trailer. Add the ligature marks that match an electrical cord—"

"Not a necktie or a rope," I said.

"So we spend our time chasing down Weber. It's an old football move: a misdirection play. Look in one direction, which pulls the defenders that way, then pass in the other direction."

"How do you defend against that?"

"The only way is to see it coming: You don't pull your defenders, or at least not all of them."

"So what do we do?"

"We pull our own fake. We have to question Weber again," Ryan said. "They expect us to interview the most obvious suspect. We want to look like we're falling for the misdirection. But we also work the forensics hard." He paused. "Have you got a better idea?"

"Shit. Let's run this by the chief."

We headed back to headquarters and tracked down the chief. He was getting ready to head out for the weekend. He put his coat down on the back of his desk chair.

"I don't see that we've got a lot of alternatives," the chief said. "We can't arrest Ronald Weber, right?"

"At this point," I said, "all we've got is circumstantial evidence—and it's flimsy. Unless we can find some forensics linking him to one of the three murders, the only thing we can do is interview him again to let them know we like him more than we did before. Then we hope they make a mistake."

"Do it," the chief said. "You two able to work it this weekend?"

I looked at Ryan. He nodded. "Yeah, Chief."

"Call me at home if you need me."

Ryan and I headed to our desks. The bullpen was slowing down in anticipation of the weekend. There were no phones ringing, no conversations, no admins running around.

Ryan spoke. "Do you want to try to track Weber down or just phone him?"

"I don't have the energy to chase him all over town. He could be driving from one job site to another. He could be at his office—or home. Let's just call him." Ryan nodded. "Punch his cell in for me, would you?"

I picked up my phone and waited for Weber to answer. "Mr. Weber, Detective Seagate. We need to talk to you again."

"Again?"

"Yeah, there's been a new development we need to talk to you about."

"I'm heading home right now. Can we do it on the phone?"

"No, unfortunately, we need to do it here at police headquarters."

"Can it wait till Monday?"

"We need to do it here, Mr. Weber. Now."

"I don't know if I can get my attorney now." He was exasperated.

"I'm not saying you need to have him here."

"What if he's already gone for the weekend?"

"Mr. Weber, you need to be at police headquarters in the next fifteen minutes. If you're not, we're putting out a bulletin for your arrest. If you can't get your lawyer here and don't want to talk to us without him, you'll sit in a cell in Holding. We get to hold you for forty-eight hours while we develop our evidence. You hear what I'm saying, Mr. Weber? You don't want to be here late

Friday afternoon? Guess what: My partner and I don't want to, either. Everybody's tired. But if you don't want three or four patrol cars in your driveway—with lights and sirens—you'll be at police headquarters in fifteen minutes. Do you understand me?"

He hung up, but I think he answered my question.

Twelve minutes later, we heard from Reception that a Mr. Weber had arrived and would wait downstairs for his attorney, who was expected in less than ten minutes. "Send them up to Interview 1 when the attorney arrives, please," I said.

Weber was unhappy with us. That was good.

Ten minutes later, a uniform escorted the two men up to the interview room, where Ryan and I were already set up. I gestured for them to sit, Ryan turned on the recording system, and I announced the names and time.

Christopher Reid spoke. "Did you think of another question that you forgot to ask this morning?"

I smiled at him. "Actually, we wanted to ask Mr. Weber about another case."

"We had two cases this morning. Now there's a third case?"

"Yes. The body of Cory McDermott, your client's favorite drug dealer, was discovered this afternoon. So, let's start. Mr. Weber, tell us where you've been this afternoon. Every place you've been since you left police headquarters a little before noon."

"First, I went to Betty's Diner for lunch around noon. I drove over to the construction site at Eagle's Nest around one to talk to a few of my guys. There's a small job—we're upgrading a two-bay garage to 220 service—over on Madison. That was around two. I was at the office after that. Then you called me."

"And you can provide addresses and names of people who saw you at all those places?"

"You want to start with my credit-card receipt from Betty's?" He reached into his shirt pocket.

"That won't be necessary," I said.

"What would be necessary, Detective?" Christopher Reid leaned toward me across the table. "What exactly do you want from my client? Why are you asking him to account for his time?"

"Cory McDermott's body was discovered less than two hours ago. He was strangled less than four hours ago."

"The drug dealer? Why do you suspect Mr. Weber?"

I leaned toward him. "Maybe because Cory McDermott named Mr. Weber as his contact at the university, and Mr. Weber admitted he'd worked with Cory for some seven years in supplying illegal drugs and prostitutes to CMSU athletes and prospects, and because I said to Mr. Weber about four hours ago that I thought he was up to his eyeballs in killing Lake Williams and Kendra Crimmons and that I was gonna come after him as hard as I could."

"What evidence do you have that Mr. Weber was involved in Cory McDermott's murder?"

"Mr. McDermott's body was discovered near the materials-storage area at Eagle's Nest construction site, where his company is the lead electrical contractor. Also where Mr. Weber just said he was around the time of the murder."

"There's got to be ten main contractors there, plus a lot of subs every day. At least fifty guys at any one time. Are you going to bring all of them in?"

"Every one of them who's told us he's been buying drugs from McDermott illegally for seven years."

He smiled. "You say Mr. McDermott's body was discovered a few hours ago. I take it there hasn't been an autopsy yet, correct?"

"Correct."

"For all you know, then, Mr. McDermott might have died of a heart attack or a drug overdose."

"That's possible, but the ligature marks around his neck suggest he was strangled."

"And your theory of the case is that my client strangled Mr. McDermott at this construction site and dumped his body there?"

"It's too early for a theory of the case, but I think your client wanted to eliminate the last person who could implicate him in the murders of Lake Williams and Kendra Crimmons. I think your client confronted him and strangled him."

"And why did he do it at the construction site?"

"I'm not sure that's where he killed him. If the murder occurred there, it was because Cory McDermott confronted him there. If the murder occurred someplace else, it was because your client needed to go about his daily routine, where he could be seen by others. Your client killed him, tossed him in the back of his pickup. Then he dumped the body at the construction site. Temporarily."

Reid nodded his head. "Temporarily?" The sarcasm dripped.

"That's right. Mr. Weber knew we were looking at him, so he had to kill McDermott today, before he provided any evidence that would prove Mr. Weber's involvement in the other murders. But your client also had to lay down an alibi. He disposed of the body at the construction site. He was going to come back later, retrieve the body, then dispose of it permanently. He just didn't count on one of the construction workers stumbling on the body this afternoon."

Christopher Reid smiled. "That's an excellent theory, Detective. Ingenious." He stood and picked his cowboy hat off the table. Ronald Weber stood, too. "When you develop some evidence to support it, will you get back to us?"

"Don't worry," I said. "We will."

"I need to say something." Ronald Weber put out his hands to tell everyone to stop. I could see perspiration shining on his forehead and above his upper lip.

Christopher Reid broke in. "Ron, let me handle this. I've got this under—"

"No, Mr. Reid. I appreciate what you're doing for me, but I have to speak now. You and the police here are talking about me like I'm a piece on a chessboard. They've got a theory of the case; you say the theory's no good because they don't any proof. But all of you are forgetting something: Three people have been killed. That's not a theory of the case. That's a fact. Three people, dead. Now, I came forward—voluntarily—to admit that I broke laws when I bought those drugs off of Cory McDermott." He turned to face me. "If you want to prosecute me for that, go ahead and do that. I am willing to pay the price for those crimes. But I am not a murderer. I did not kill Lake Williams or Kendra Crimmons or Cory McDermott. I don't care where Cory McDermott's body was found. I am innocent." He was breathing heavily now. "I am innocent."

"Who did kill them, Mr. Weber?"

He looked at me, his eyes intense. "I do not know. But it wasn't me."

I believed him. But I didn't let him see that.

# Chapter 28

Ryan and I sat in the interrogation room. An officer had escorted
Ronald Weber and his attorney, Christopher Reid, out.

"You believe him?" I said.

"Yes and no."

"Yes to what?"

"Yes that he didn't kill Cory," Ryan said.

"And no that he doesn't know who killed him?"

"That's right," Ryan said. "I believe the whole thing—from
Lake through Kendra to Cory—has been orchestrated by the
football guys so that nobody can be prosecuted." He paused.
"And you? You believe him?"

"Yes and no."

"Same as my yes and no?"

"Did you research Weber's attorney, this Christopher Reid?"

"A little. Why?"

"Where does he live?"

"Billings. Why?"

"When I was laying out the theory about Weber stashing
Cory's body temporarily at the construction site, you notice that
Reid seemed to know quite a bit about the site: how there were a
bunch of other contractors, must've been fifty guys working the
site? That strike you as odd?"

Ryan took a deep breath. "Well, it does now. You phoned
Weber less than an hour ago. He and the attorney wouldn't have
had a chance to speak for more than five or ten minutes before

they showed up here, right?"

"Yeah," I said.

"And if the attorney simply said to him, 'Tell me where you've been since this morning,' I can't see Weber going into all that detail about Eagle's Nest."

"So Weber coached him on the story," I said. "How Cory's body was in the materials-storage area, and how Weber drove past the manager's office."

"Wait a second." Ryan was rubbing his forehead. "I buy that Weber coached Reid on the story, but I don't know what Weber said to Reid first."

"What do you mean?"

"Did Weber say, 'I killed Cory and dropped his body at the site, and I want you to know what happened'? Or did Weber say, 'We're working on a misdirection play and I want you to understand it'? One of the other guys killed Cory and dropped him at the site, then Weber drove past the construction manager's trailer when he knew the manager was there eating lunch. That way, the police will like Weber but they'll never be able to arrest him because they can't collect any forensics because he didn't do it. Nobody will be charged, and the case will go cold."

"It's the misdirection," I said.

"How do you know?"

"Because a criminal attorney never wants his client to admit he's guilty. That's for a judge or jury to decide. The attorney simply wants to mount the best defense he can."

"But an attorney isn't permitted to argue facts he knows to be inaccurate," Ryan said.

"That's why this is a good misdirection. Weber says— truthfully—that he didn't kill Cory but admits he was driving past the manager's trailer on the way to talk to his employees. The lawyer says to him, 'You didn't kill Cory McDermott, and you didn't drop his body at the construction site, right?" Weber says,

'Right.' The lawyer doesn't say, 'Okay, then, who did kill him—'"

"Because that's for us to find out," Ryan said. "Christopher Reid is working for Ronald Weber, and if Weber said he didn't do it, that's good enough—legally and ethically—for the attorney."

"Exactly," I said. "Now, I wouldn't be surprised if Weber— alone or with some of his buddies—filled the attorney in on the plan, but as long as nobody literally says, 'I killed Cory,' the attorney is free to mount the defense—and charge them four-hundred bucks an hour."

"So what next?"

"If this is a misdirection, the only way we're gonna figure it out is with forensics."

Ryan nodded, and we left the interview room to see if Harold or Robin had anything for us. Robin's door was open.

"Tell us something good, Robin."

She looked up at me. "You're asking me to make something up?"

"Shit."

"Cory McDermott had nothing on or in his clothing that can help us. He didn't have an ID or a wallet. There was nothing on the outside of his jacket—no organics or particles—that you couldn't explain by looking at where he was lying. He had some wood fibers that matched the lumber right next to him, and some concrete dust that was all over the surface of the materials-storage area. But there were no defensive wounds on him, no tissue under his nails, no prints on his neck from the killer. The killer didn't seem to break a sweat in getting behind him and strangling him."

"You didn't find a ligature?"

"Like a three-foot length of electrical cord with the words Property of Weber Electric and the vic's DNA and the killer's prints?" She waited a second for me to respond. Then she said, "No, I didn't."

"Did you think to call the hospital and get a list of his injuries from the beatdown the other day?"

Robin winced. "That's a great idea. You mean, to see if there were any new injuries that might tell us something?"

"Yeah, that's what I mean. Did you think to do that?" My tone came out a little nastier than I intended. It was late Friday.

She smiled. "Actually, I did. There wasn't anything new, except for the ligature marks and the related blood vessels."

"All right, Robin. I appreciate you staying late."

"If an older person like yourself can stay late, I can, too."

I squeezed her shoulder. "You're the daughter I'm glad I never had."

Ryan and I headed down the hall to Harold's lab. It was cold, smelly, and noisy. Harold was leaning over Cory's body. I turned to Ryan. "Go over and talk to Harold, would you?"

The medical examiner looked up when Ryan walked up next to him.

"You didn't have to do this now," Ryan said.

"Well, you and Karen are producing bodies so fast, I thought I'd do this one now. You know, so I'm ready when you bring me the next one Monday morning."

"I think this one should be it," Ryan said.

"That would be nice." Harold wiped the perspiration off his scalp with his sleeve.

"Anything for us yet?"

"I took the blood, the stomach fluids, and the urine and put a rush on them. I don't see any signs that he was drinking. The tox results should be ready by Monday. I just thought I'd take a quick look at his throat."

"And?"

"You're how old?"

"Thirty."

"That's when the two halves of your hyoid bone fuse."

"What does that tell you?"

"If your hyoid bone is broken, that's the obvious sign of ligature strangulation. But since Mr. McDermott's hyoid bone wasn't yet fused, the strangulation didn't break it."

"Are you saying he wasn't strangled?"

"Oh, no, he absolutely was. I can't say if that killed him—he might have had a heart attack or a stroke five minutes before he was strangled—but someone definitely strangled him. There's a lot of trauma to his windpipe. And the bruising around the ligature marks shows he was alive when he was strangled."

"Okay," Ryan said, "then we've got at least attempted murder."

"Yes, we do. Once I rule out drugs or coronary issues or a stroke, I can call it officially. But for now, you and Karen should be looking for someone who wanted to kill him, twisted a ligature around his neck, and yanked it hard and held it tight for a while."

"You'll let us know if it's one of those other things, right?"

"I'll let you know either way."

"And that information about the hyoid bone fusing at age thirty?"

"That was just a gift for you. Because I knew you're approximately that age and you're curious about things like that." He turned his head to face me. "Unlike your squeamish partner."

"Thank you for not giving me any gifts, Harold." I waved from the other side of the room.

"I could tell you a lot of interesting things about your body. You're in your mid-forties, am I correct?"

"We're in kind of a hurry. I'll stop back when I'm in my mid-fifties, Harold."

Ryan and I headed upstairs to the detectives' bullpen and sat down at our desks. It was five-thirty.

"Think we should call the chief?" Ryan said.

I thought for a moment. "What have we got? Ron Weber says he's innocent but isn't telling us who's guilty, right?"

"And Cory was strangled."

I shook my head. "That's not enough. We don't have any decent forensics. We can't arrest anyone. There's not even enough to hold anyone. So what do we tell him?"

"Ronald Weber has told us—twice—that he delivered illegal drugs to players and recruits. Is that something we should tell President Billingham?"

"I'm not sure there's anything to tell yet," I said. "We don't have specifics, so we can't charge Weber. And even though it's hard to believe the A.D. and the coach didn't know this was going on, until we have evidence they *did* know, we can't move against any of them."

"In other words, all of this can wait until Monday?"

"I think so. What is the chief going to do this weekend to move the case along? What is President Billingham going to do this weekend about his A.D. and his coach?"

"Okay." Ryan smiled as he walked over to the coat rack. "This is working out better than I thought." He slipped into his coat. "See you Monday, Karen."

"Yeah, see you." I watched him leave. I was the only person left in the big room. The two second-shift detectives were around somewhere, but they weren't here. There were no admins, no uniforms. There were no phones ringing, no printers humming. I walked into the break room. There was no coffee left in the pot, which someone had turned off but not cleaned. There were no donuts or pastries left in the boxes.

Ryan was on his way home to his wife, Cali, their two infants and the newborn. The chief was … I didn't know where the chief was. When he first came to Rawlings, almost three years ago, he lived in a residential hotel down near the airport. But I didn't know if he ever got an apartment or bought a house. I realized that I had never asked him, not even in a casual, polite way. I had never offered to help, never shown any interest.

I drifted down to the incident room. Abrams and Wilkerson, the second-shift guys, were in there, looking at a big map of the city stuck to a corkboard. Abrams was pushing some pins in it as the two of them talked. They looked up when they saw me.

Wilkerson said, "I hear that Williams case—the junkie?—turned into a real sack of shit." He gave me a sympathetic frown.

"No big deal. Just three bodies this week."

"Three? I thought it was two."

"Third one this afternoon. The dealer who supplied the drugs that killed Williams."

"I'm sorry," Abrams said.

"Not your fault." I smiled. "Think of it as job security."

"Sounds like it." He nodded. "Is there something we can help you with?"

"No, sorry to interrupt. I'll let you guys get back to it."

I headed to the bullpen, grabbed my jacket, and headed home. It wasn't yet six o'clock. I cut open a bag of frozen chicken carbonara, tossed it in a casserole dish, and nuked it. I watched the timer count off the eight minutes, then slid the dish onto a plastic cutting board and carried it out to the TV tray set up in front of my chair. I turned on the TV and skipped through the channels. I stopped at one of my favorite cooking shows. It was an old French guy. He had some dish in the oven, and three other things on the burners of an enormous stove.

Around seven-thirty I headed out to my AA class. A bunch of people greeted me in their gentle, busted-up way. Most of them called me by name. I didn't remember any of their names, even though I'd been coming to this meeting, seven days a week, for more than a year, and seen the same people almost every night. As usual, I didn't say anything during the session, didn't talk to anyone during the little break, didn't stay for coffee at the end.

I was changing into sweats a little after nine when my cell rang. The screen said "Murtaugh, Robert."

"Hey, Chief." He never calls me at home—unless I'm supposed to be at work.

"Hi, Karen. This is Robert Murtaugh."

"Yeah, my phone tells me that. Is everything okay?"

"Yes, everything is fine. Hope I'm not disturbing you calling this late. I know sometimes you go to an eight-o'clock meeting."

"No, you're not disturbing me. I got back a few minutes ago."

"I just wanted to see how things went in the interview with Ronald Weber."

"Yeah, Ryan and I discussed whether we should call you but decided it could wait until Monday." I filled him in on what had happened. "So we didn't think we could charge Weber, and we didn't think we had enough to bring to President Billingham."

"You're probably right." He was silent a moment. I was about to say something when he spoke again. "Karen, I should have said something to you at headquarters. I should have." He was silent again.

This didn't sound like it was going to be good news. "What is it, Chief?"

"I just want you to know that I'm aware of how hard you're working ... I mean, with the AA. I feel bad that I threatened you—when you came back to the department—about how you had to do the AA or you were gone. You're an adult ... a responsible adult. You've proven that. I want you to know that, Karen. I'm proud of you. Of what you've done."

The tears rolled down my cheeks as I struggled to clear my throat quietly. "You did the right thing, Chief. I'd have been dead by now. I needed to do the AA. You knew that. And I needed to work again, too. That was you taking a chance on me. You saved my life, Chief."

The line was silent a moment. "I'll see you Monday, Karen."

"Thanks for calling, sir."

I knew right away that the chief hadn't really called to find out how things went in the interview with Ronald Weber. But it wasn't until a couple of days later that I realized he hadn't called to talk about AA, either.

# *Chapter 29*

It was a little after eight on Saturday morning when I got a call from Chief Murtaugh. "I'd like to see you and Ryan in my office, please. Thirty minutes?"

"Sure, okay. Want me to call Ryan?"

"No, I've got it."

"See you soon."

A half-hour later, Ryan and I were in the chief's office.

"Sit, please," the chief said. No small talk. No "Sorry to drag you in on Saturday."

"What's up?" I said.

"Just got a call from President Billingham. Early this morning, Ronald Weber was in a car accident. He's badly injured, but he'll live. It was a DUI. BAC of one point six."

That's twice the legal limit. "Sorry to hear that," I said.

"Chief," Ryan said, "why is the university president calling you about a car accident?"

"Because his A.D., his football coach, and the president of the booster organization said Weber told them that we're harassing him. Weber is talking. He said we're accusing him of three murders, and that's why he got drunk and got in an accident."

"Come on," I said. "That's bullshit. Weber came in on his own—with an attorney from Billings, by the way—and admitted he's been supplying drugs and girls to players and recruits for seven years. Did he mention that?"

The chief held his gaze but did not respond.

"Sure, we ran a theory by them," I said. "Weber and his lawyer wanted to know why we were looking at them, so I told them why we think Lake Williams and Kendra Crimmons and Cory McDermott are all the same case, and we think the football guys are in on it. But that's what happens in an interview room. You know that. Especially when the suspect walks in with a criminal attorney. But I'm not taking responsibility for Weber deciding to get drunk and crash his car. That's him, not me."

"Nobody's accusing you of anything, Karen—"

"Sounds like President Billingham is."

"*I'm* not accusing you of anything. But President Billingham asked if we could brief him on the case. He's got himself a serious personnel problem, with his two biggest athletic staff members and the booster demanding to know what's going on. What I'd like to do is sit down with him and present our side of the story."

"I don't think we should back off a murder investigation because he's got a personnel problem."

"I'll repeat what I said, Karen: We're going to present our side of the story. We are not going to back off the investigation. President Billingham will be right here ..." He looked at his watch. "In fifteen minutes. If you two want to be present, you're invited. If you don't want to be here—whatever reason—I can handle it myself. Your choice."

I looked at Ryan. He nodded. "We'll be here."

"You understand the ground rules. He asked to be briefed. We're going to brief him. He's going to be a professional. We're going to be professionals." The chief looked at me, then at Ryan.

"Yes, sir," I said. "Fifteen minutes."

The chief looked at his watch. "Good. Dismissed."

Ryan and I headed back to the bullpen.

"What the fuck?" I said.

Ryan sighed. "That question's a little too open-ended. Can

you narrow it a little?"

"I get it, Ryan. You went to college."

"You went to college, too. Karen. We've been working this case for a week now, and despite the fact that we've got three vics—"

"I didn't pour the booze down Weber's throat and hand him the car keys."

"Yeah, I think everyone realizes that. What I was saying is, we've done good work on this case. We don't want to jeopardize it by losing our composure in front of the university president—and in front of the chief. So if you want to be pissed off, could you do it in the next fourteen minutes?"

"Can I call you an asshole?"

"Why should this morning be any different?"

"You know, you can be an asshole." I smiled. "Okay, I get your point. I'll behave."

"The way I look at it, this meeting with Billingham just confirms our theory of the case. They're working together. The fact that they went to Billingham as a group tells me they're connected with Weber—"

"And they've been doing some bad shit."

"Exactly," Ryan said. "If Weber were the only bad actor, they'd have cut him loose. But they're going to bat for him—a guy they know has just admitted he commits felonies *for them?* What does that say to you?"

"Two things," I said. "They know what he's been doing, and they know that if they don't protect him, he'll flip on them."

"That's the way I see it, too. I don't know which one of them killed the three—and we don't have the evidence to charge any of them with murder—"

"Yet," I said.

"I'd be more comfortable if we leave off the 'yet'—especially when we talk to President Billingham. But it's fairly obvious they're worried about their careers. And that's a point that might interest him."

Ryan and I spent the next few minutes at our desks, looking over our notebooks but not saying anything. Then we walked to the chief's office and sat in the waiting area where Margaret usually sits. The chief's door was closed.

A minute later, the door opened and the chief invited us in. President Billingham wasn't there yet, and the three of us sat down to wait. Soon he arrived and we shook hands. We sat in the soft chairs arranged around a coffee table.

"I appreciate your taking the time to meet with me, especially on a weekend," President Billingham said, making eye contact with all three of us. His eyes looked bloodshot and weary.

"Not at all," the chief said. "We're happy to help you understand where we are in the case. Would you like us to review the three crimes?"

"I'm familiar with only two crimes. You've briefed me on LaKadrian Williams, the student-athlete, and the homeless woman, Kendra Crimmons. There's a third crime?"

The chief nodded for me to respond. I said, "Yesterday afternoon we recovered the body of Cory McDermott, the drug dealer. He's the one who told us there was a contact who was supplying drugs to the athletics department."

"How does Mr. Weber relate to these crimes?"

"Ronald Weber told us he is that contact. He's not officially a member of the university community, although he's a longtime member of the Cougar Athletic Association, and his company—Weber Electric—does a lot of work for the university. Carl Davis told us Weber bids low, which Davis sees as a contribution to the university."

"Thank you, Detective," President Billingham said to me. He turned to Chief Murtaugh. "Am I permitted to ask if you have made any arrests in these three murders?"

The chief said, "We have not made any arrests. The autopsies of Lake Williams and Kendra Crimmons are complete, but the autopsy of Cory McDermott is not. The investigations are ongoing."

"But do you expect to make any arrests soon?"

"I don't know." The chief sighed. "I'm not trying to be evasive, Bob. The truth is, unless we can develop enough good evidence to establish probable cause, we won't be able to secure any arrest warrants."

"You do believe, however, that A.D. Freedlander or Coach Baxter—or both—are involved?"

"Let me put it this way, Bob. We have no evidence that any CMSU people are involved in the murders. However, we strongly suspect that Mr. Freedlander and Mr. Baxter are aware of the illegal activities that Mr. Weber has been carrying out for years. By the way, Mr. Weber has admitted supplying not only drugs but also cash and prostitutes to players and recruits."

President Billingham closed his eyes and bowed his head, the folds of his chin hanging over the open collar of his dress shirt. His eyes remained closed for a long moment.

Ryan spoke. "President Billingham, if I can speak for a moment. I've done a little research on A.D. Freedlander and Coach Baxter, both of whom have had successful careers at CMSU and in previous positions. When A.D. Freedlander was a football coach, his college incurred a number of NCAA violations—both major and minor—for impermissible practices. And before Coach Baxter came to CMSU, his college, too, incurred numerous major and minor NCAA violations. For both men, these violations included academic infractions, such as sham courses and grade-changing. One thing that Coach Baxter neglected to tell us, when we interviewed him, is that, when he was a freshman, his coach was John Freedlander.

"And one other thing you might not know. Mr. Weber is

what is called a bagman, a fixer. Although fixers are more common in the SEC, where football programs are a bigger business, they exist around the country. They are not officially affiliated with the team they support. They donate their own money and gather money from other fans to funnel to players, all of it in violation of NCAA regulations—money for food and other living expenses, but also for jewelry, tattoos, and cars. Even for prostitutes and drugs. And they use money to bribe recruits into signing with their programs. All of this is done in cash, off the books."

President Billingham sat silently, looking down at his hands folded in his lap.

"Bob," the chief said, "I'm sure this information comes as a shock and disappointment to you, and we wouldn't have presented it to you except as an explanation of why we suspect that Carl Davis, John Freedlander, and Andy Baxter might have some involvement in these crimes, through their connection with Ronald Weber. We believe it is possible that Lake Williams, who was suffering from CTE, somehow represented a threat to the football program and, by extension, to the university."

"What kind of threat?" President Billingham said.

"We don't know. But it's reasonable to assume that it was related to his serious CTE-related health problems, including cognitive deficit, memory problems, and psychological problems, including uncontrollable anger. He was living in a tent in a homeless camp in a public park. He might have threatened to speak out against a system that he saw as exploitive."

President Billingham nodded. "I'm aware of the CTE research. We have a very bright young faculty member who works in the field. She's won some lucrative grants." His tone was wistful, like he'd much rather be talking about faculty like her than his football guys.

"Liz Ouvrard," Ryan said. "Our medical examiner called on

her. She was the one who diagnosed Lake's CTE for us. She was very helpful."

"But as we said," Chief Murtaugh continued, "we have made no arrests and have not charged anyone with any crimes related to the three killings." The chief paused. Billingham's shoulders slumped forward again. Finally, he raised his head. "Bob," the chief said, "do you have any questions for us?"

President Billingham's eyes were glassy with tears. "No, Robert, I do not. I want to thank you for telling me this." He turned to me and Ryan. "Detectives, thank you both." He pushed down hard on the arms of his chair and slowly lifted himself to his feet.

The chief spoke. "Please let me know if you want to talk— anytime—about these cases. I know I can count on your discretion."

Bob Billingham nodded slightly. "Yes, you can. You've been very generous. I sincerely appreciate that."

"Let me escort you out," the chief said.

President Billingham had a giant personnel problem on his hands, but that didn't seem to be what was causing his pain. He seemed to be genuinely distressed by his people's behavior.

Ryan and I went back to the detectives' bullpen. "I got a real bad feeling about this case," I said, collapsing into my chair.

"What kind of bad feeling?" Ryan sat down, too.

"We're gonna go cold on all three murders."

"Because the football guys outplayed us?"

"That's what I think," I said.

"Well, if the game's over, at least we shouldn't have any more bodies turn up."

"Look at who died: two junkies and a dealer. Look at who survived: four guys with a combined annual income of, what, a couple of million?"

"The system is rigged," Ryan said. "It has been for decades.

The NCAA exploits the student-athletes and tosses them aside when they get hurt or can't help the team. A Division 1 football player brings in about one-hundred-and-fifty-thousand dollars in revenue to the school; a similar basketball player, almost three-hundred-thousand. But eighty percent of those athletes live below the poverty limit. The athletes have to remain amateur; the coaches get paid by equipment manufacturers to make the athletes wear their branded gear."

"And you volunteered for that world?"

"I didn't really know about it. For some of the guys on my team, it was their career. Some made it to the NFL; most didn't. I was never in that league. I'm just lucky I didn't get hit in the head that much." He knocked on the wooden arm of his desk chair.

"Well, we did what we could. Sometimes, it doesn't work out. We'll catch another case."

"I have no doubt," Ryan said. "I'm going to get back to the forms."

"You're gonna stick around?"

"Yeah, I told Cali I'd be done by mid-afternoon."

It was a little after two when a uniform, Ann Fredericks, came up to my desk. I stopped typing and looked up at her.

"Detective, there's a woman downstairs wants to see you. She seems real upset. You know, crying."

"You get a name?"

"Alicia Templeton."

"Oh, Jesus. Escort her up, please." Fredericks nodded and left. I said to Ryan, "Great. Now she's gonna blame me because her father got shitfaced and crashed his car."

But that wasn't why she was here.

# *Chapter 30*

Officer Fredericks led Alicia Templeton along the winding path through the desks, cabinets, and tables in the detectives' bullpen. I almost didn't recognize Alicia. It wasn't that she was wearing jeans and a hoodie instead of her realtor outfit. It was that her face was a wreck. She wore no lipstick, and her eyeliner was smudged beneath her bloodshot eyes.

"Hey, Ms. Templeton. Good to see you," I said. "Want to go somewhere to talk?"

She nodded, wiping at her eyes and her nose. "Please."

I stood and led her and Ryan to Interview 2. Ryan closed the door behind us. When we all were seated, I said, "Okay, Ms. Templeton, we're not recording anything. This is not a formal statement. But we can speak undisturbed in this room. Is that all right with you?"

"Thank you." Her voice was weak. "You'll have to excuse me. It's been a terrible day."

"We were sorry to hear about your father's car accident." She nodded. "How is he doing?"

"He's got some broken bones and everything, but the doctors said he'll live."

"That's good." I waited a few seconds but she looked like she was struggling to compose herself. "Is there something we can do to help?"

She didn't appear to hear my question.

"My mom and I thought there was some kind of problem the

last week or so. We were afraid he had started to drink again. He was keeping unusual hours, giving her evasive answers about where he had been. We were so scared it was going to be like it used to be."

"Yeah?" I could think of a few reasons he was keeping odd hours and giving evasive answers.

"It was the pressure of the police investigation. I'm sure of it. It was a nightmare, learning that he was injured so badly, and that he'd been drunk."

"I'm sure it was a nightmare." I didn't know where this was going—if she had come in to blame the cops for her father's decision, or if she needed to talk to someone. If that was it, I wondered why she wasn't with her husband or her mother. "I can certainly understand that. How can we help?"

"I came here because I wanted you to know that my father couldn't have killed Lake or that woman or the drug dealer. He couldn't have killed anyone. You have to believe me. That's not his nature. Since he became religious, he couldn't have done that."

"I hear what you're saying." I nodded. "Do you mind if I call you Alicia?"

She waved it off. "Of course."

"Alicia, our job is to follow the evidence. I'm sure you love your father and he's a great dad and all that, but we have to carry out an investigation—three murder investigations, in fact. We really can't consider that as we carry out the investigation."

"But he had nothing to do with those murders. He looked me in the eye and swore that he didn't. That's what he told me."

"Did he also tell you about his relationship with the university?"

"I know all about that: He does a lot of the electrical work for them. I know he bids low, but there's nothing illegal about that. What are you saying?"

"He's been supplying illegal drugs and prostitutes to the

football and basketball teams ever since Lake was on the team."

"No, that can't be true. I don't believe that. I know he gave players cash sometimes, you know, to help them with food and rent, but I can't believe drugs and prostitutes."

Ryan spoke. "Alicia, he told us that, on two occasions. He was very explicit about it. And you need to be prepared. Those are felonies, and if the prosecutor can bring charges against him, he will."

She looked upset but maintained her composure. "What does that have to do with the murders? You don't seriously believe he was involved in murder, do you?"

"The third victim was named Cory McDermott," I said. "Did your father mention that name? Does it ring a bell?"

"No, it doesn't." She looked confused. "Who is that?"

"Cory was a member of the football team when you were a cheerleader. When Lake was a player."

"It's a big team, more than eighty players. I didn't know all of them."

"Cory wouldn't have made much of an impression. He was dropped from the team, and then he flunked out. He became a drug dealer here in the city. He was your father's favorite source. Your father was the link between a drug dealer and the athletics programs."

She shook her head. "That doesn't mean he was a murderer."

"That's right, it doesn't. And we haven't filed charges against your father or anyone else. The investigations are ongoing. But Cory's body was recovered at the construction site at Eagle's Nest, where your father is doing a lot of work. Your father was seen there around the time of Cory's murder."

She shook her head vigorously. "You need more evidence than that."

"Yes, we do, and we're gathering evidence. But, Alicia, you have to understand that you saying your father couldn't have done it—and how he told you he didn't do it—that's not really the kind of evidence we can use."

She was silent a moment. "You don't understand what happened."

"Why don't you tell us what happened?"

"My father was trying to help Lake."

"Help him in what way?"

"He was going to get Lake into some kind of program. You know, for the mental problems and everything else."

"You can see why that's difficult to understand, right? Your father was going to help the guy who raped his daughter?"

"Not if you've seen the way my father has changed since then. I don't really understand what he's gone through with the religion, but I know he's not the man he used to be."

"You mean, an alcoholic? You realize he's in the hospital because he had twice the legal limit of alcohol in his blood?"

"I realize that, but this is the first time he's had a drink in over five years."

"Alicia, we're sorry your father was drinking again and he got hurt in that car crash, but unless you can give us something we can work with, we're gonna have to get back to work." I stood.

"Lake came to me."

I lowered myself back into my chair. "What do you mean 'he came to me'?"

"It was about ten days ago. He walked into my office. I was working in the back, in the little room. My receptionist buzzed me. She said a man was there to see me. I could tell she was scared out of her mind. I said, 'Who is it?' She said, 'He says his name is Lake. That you'll know who he is.' I couldn't believe it. I hadn't heard from him since he left school. Then, when I saw him, it broke my heart. He was so … it wasn't that he was all slumped over and skinny. It was his eyes. His eyes looked dead."

"What happened next, Alicia?"

"I brought him back to my office, and we talked."

"What about?"

"He told me he was having real problems. He couldn't think straight. He couldn't make sense when he talked. I knew that was true because I had a hard time making sense of what he was saying. And he said his anger was out of control. He said he needed help, and he didn't know where to turn."

"So he turned to you?"

"We were in love, in college."

"That isn't what you told us. You said you dated for a while."

"It was a time in my life I don't talk about. We were in love."

"Did he rape you, Ms. Templeton?"

She looked down at the metal table. "No, he didn't rape me. He hit me a few times. And he cheated all the time. But he never raped me. I was trying to get his attention. I needed him to realize how much I loved him." She shook her head, then looked up at me. "Did you ever do anything stupid like that?"

Not exactly that, I thought, but that stupid? Many times. "Why did you withdraw the rape allegation, Alicia? Did it have something to do with your father?"

"I know my dad loved me, and he still loves me. I don't doubt that."

"Were you embarrassed because of his outburst at the hearing? When he tried to attack Lake?"

Alicia Templeton smiled sadly. "No, that wasn't it. I loved him for that. That was the father I loved."

"What did he do, then?"

"It was a few days later. He came to me, and we talked about what to do. I was so mixed up, I didn't know what I wanted. I was so hurt by Lake, I just wanted to punish him. You know, for the way he treated me. But I wasn't thinking straight. My dad said he wanted me to think it through before I made a decision that would affect Lake and me for the rest of our lives. He said it was my decision but that he thought I should withdraw the allegation."

"What was his reasoning?"

"He said most people wouldn't believe the allegation. I mean, because we were hooked up already and everyone knew it. Then I'd be a girl who accused her boyfriend of raping her but there wouldn't be any evidence and I'd just look kind of pathetic. I hadn't really thought about that. And he asked me if I'd considered how the allegation would hurt Lake. He could be arrested and go to prison. He'd be kicked out of school. He wouldn't be able to play football, which was the one thing he was really good at. The thing he loved. He wouldn't be able to make it to the NFL—this was before he tore his ACL, when people were telling him he would be able to go pro. My dad asked me if that was what I wanted to do to Lake."

"Is that why you and your dad didn't speak for a while? Because you thought he cared more about how Lake could help the football team than about his daughter, who told him Lake raped her?"

"I tried not to think that about him. Then Carl Davis came over to the house."

"He did?"

"He and my dad were really close, almost like he was my dad's dad."

"Did Mr. Davis talk to you about what you should do?"

"He was really sweet. He never knew that the accusation was false. He told me it was a terrible thing that happened, but sometimes you need to get keep going to get past it. How sometimes if you make a fuss about things, it can create new problems. It can be smarter to just keep your mouth shut and move past it. And I think he was right."

"Do you think part of why he said that was because he wanted to protect Lake, so he could keep playing?"

"I think Mr. Davis loved me and wanted to help me get through a bad time."

Alicia wasn't ready to understand why her father and Carl Davis acted as they did. But I felt I had planted the idea, and if, sometime in the future, she thought about it, she might understand what had happened. "Okay, Alicia, let's get back to ten days ago. Lake told you he needed help. What did you say to him?"

"I asked him what he wanted me to do. He said, I want you to tell your father. I asked him why my father. He said my father would be able to help him."

"Did you understand what he meant by that?"

"No, I didn't. I thought he was just mixed up. I asked him if he'd gone to see the coach. He said he contacted the coach, but the coach told him to go away and never call him again. That Lake was a loser, a junkie loser, and he regretted he ever recruited him. I didn't know what to say about that. I never had much to do with the coach."

"Did Lake say he'd tried to contact anyone else?"

"He said he tried to reach out to John Freedlander, the athletic director."

"What happened?"

"Freedlander wouldn't talk to him."

"Then what happened?"

"That's when he asked me again to see if my father could help him. I told him I'd try. But to be honest with you, I was sure my father would say he didn't know what Lake was talking about."

"And you went to your father?"

"I did. I told him what Lake had told me. He said he'd try to help, see if he could get Lake into some kind of program or something."

"Did he say how he was going to do this?"

"It was a couple of days later that my dad called me. He said he had reached out to Carl Davis, and they were going to work on it. Like I told you before, Mr. Davis is my godfather."

"Here's my problem, Alicia. You've told me a very nice story. But the facts are that someone bought some really deadly heroin and paid another person to deliver it to Lake, and he died that night."

"All I can tell you is what my father told me. That he was working with Carl Davis to help Lake, then all of a sudden he finds out Lake is dead."

"Like I said, Alicia, we know someone wanted to kill Lake. We think it was because he was going to make some problems for the coach or the A.D. or the university. Someone decided to kill him. We haven't determined who it was. We need evidence. Unfortunately, all you've given us is a story about how nice your father and Carl Davis were for wanting to help Lake. But we can't do anything with your story. It's not evidence."

She reached into a pocket in her sweatshirt and pulled out a folded business envelope, which she slid across the table to me.

"What is this?" I opened up the envelope. There was a little plastic thing in it, no bigger than a fingernail.

"It's the SIM card from my phone. I need it back."

"What's on it?"

"I shot video of Lake telling me his story."

"Why did you do that?"

"I don't know. I just wanted to have it." She paused and looked down at the table. "Maybe just to … maybe to remember him."

I turned to Ryan. "Would you see if you can copy this?" He took the envelope and hurried out of the room.

"Do you have any video or audio or anything of your discussions with your father about Lake?"

She shook her head. "I wish I did."

"Did you tell anybody else about Lake coming to see you?

Other than your father? Or show them the video?"

"No, nobody. Well, I showed it to Max."

"Max Thomas?"

"Yeah, he used to be Lake's roommate. He's some kind of coach for the team now."

I tried to stay steady and not reveal anything. "Why'd you show it to Max?"

"I thought he might want to know about the problems Lake was having. I was hoping he might work with me to change the coach's mind about helping him. You know, if my father and Carl Davis were willing to help Lake, then Coach Baxter, too, they might be able to do more for him."

I nodded. "Have you stayed in touch with Max since you graduated?"

"Yeah, I have. Max is a sweetheart. We went out a few times, before I met Lake. In fact, Max was the one who introduced me to Lake." She shook her head sadly. "That was a long time ago. At least things have turned out well for Max."

"Yeah, they have."

Ryan came back into the room, handed Alicia the envelope, and took his seat. "Sorry," he said.

"No, that's fine," I said. "We were just wrapping up." I turned to Alicia Templeton. "All right, thanks for coming in, Alicia. I hope your father gets better fast."

"I'm sorry I didn't have something to convince you my father is innocent in all this. He was trying to help Lake. That's all it was. I wish I could have helped you more."

"It was very helpful, what you told us." I turned to Ryan. "Would you mind escorting Ms. Templeton out?"

A few minutes later, Ryan and I met up at our desks in the bullpen. "You want to take a look at that video of Lake?" Ryan said. "Got it right here." He held up a SIM card between his thumb and forefinger.

"Not at the moment. It's gonna show what she said it shows."

"You believe what she told us?"

"Every word."

"Why? She loves her father," Ryan said. "She thinks he's wonderful. But she didn't tell us anything that says he's innocent."

"When she told us how her father and Carl Davis got her to withdraw the rape allegation, she said they were looking out for her, right? Think for a moment, Ryan. Who were they looking out for?"

He did take a moment. "Themselves," he said. "They were protecting Lake Williams."

"That's right. She didn't realize it, but she just told us her father and Carl Davis were douchebags. She still doesn't realize it. She's a child. She's telling the truth."

"So her father spun the story for her. How does that make him innocent?"

"Her father is innocent. She told me who the killer is. Want to come with me and pick him up?"

He looked at me, slack-jawed.

"Sorry," I said. "You must've been out of the room when she told me."

# *Chapter 31*

"Go onto the DMV site," I said. "Find out what kind of vehicle Max Thomas owns."

"You want to tell me why?"

"Now, please."

Ten seconds later, he spoke. "A Hyundai Elantra. White. 2015."

"Shit," I said.

"What kind of vehicle would you like him to own?"

"A big goddamn dually pickup truck."

"He's the one who delivered the drugs to Kendra at Ten Mile Park?"

"There you go."

"Alicia told you that?"

"No, Alicia told me she told Max about Lake coming to see her. You know, the SIM card?"

"So we're chasing the football guys because we think they killed Lake and the two others, but you think Max Thomas did it?"

"That's what I think."

"Why did Max kill them?"

"Because he's in love with Alicia. Has been all those years. Plus, he's batshit crazy."

"You're kidding."

"No, I'm not kidding. It's a hunch. Cory's body at the construction site? That's a frame. Max framed Ronald Weber for selling out his daughter to keep Lake on the field. First he killed Lake for raping Alicia—"

"Which he didn't really do."

"Focus, Ryan. Then he killed Kendra, because she could identify him and he knew she was talking to us. Then he killed Cory, because he was the only one left who could identify him."

"Not to be disrespectful," Ryan said, "but do we have any evidence to support any of this?"

"Not yet, but if you'd stop asking dull questions and help me, maybe we could get the evidence."

"Okay, sorry. What do we need?"

"Explain how Max Thomas got Cory's body to the construction site in a Hyundai Elantra and drove it into the materials-storage area."

Ryan thought for a second, then pulled the skinny notebook out of his sweatshirt pocket. "Just a second." He started tapping some keys on his desktop. "Remember Max's father runs a tree service? It's Thomas Trees, out on Centennial Parkway. They might have a big goddamn dually pickup. Want me to call them?"

"No." I stood. "He might warn his son we're onto him. I want you to come with me in the cruiser." We rushed down to the parking area behind headquarters. "What's the address on Centennial?"

Ryan navigated me there, and thirteen minutes later we pulled into the parking lot behind a small cinder-block building that housed Thomas Trees, plus a pest-control service and a furniture-stripping place. We walked around to the back. There it was: a Ford 250 dually in dark green with the name of the tree service on the doors.

"Can you access the case file on your phone?"

"What do you need?"

"Robin's photos of the tire tracks at Ten Mile Park."

Ryan hit his screen a few times, then started swiping. "The

inside right rear tire was underinflated; it's worn down on the outsides." He got down on his back and took some shots of the tires, then stood up and showed me the screen. "Just like this one."

"Bingo."

"Shoot the license plate, too." I walked around to the bed. The plastic tarp was big enough to cover up a body. I lifted the tarp, and there it was: a three-foot length of electrical cord. I had my hand on one end when I heard a voice.

"Can I help you?" It was a black man, about fifty-five, wearing work clothes. He had the same beefy build as his son. He didn't look happy.

I dropped the cord. "You must be Mr. Thomas." I gave him a smile and walked toward him, my hand extended. "Danielle Hampton, State Farm." We shook hands, and I pointed to Ryan. "This is my partner, Leonard Santoro. Sorry for stopping by unannounced. We got a report that a truck with your plate was involved in a hit-and-run this morning. We get reports like that which, quite often, they turn out to be inaccurate. So we always check before proceeding. The report says the right front of the truck was smashed in. But I looked; your truck doesn't have any damage on it. I'm just gonna note that the plate number must be wrong. So that's good news. We'll be on our way."

Mr. Thomas nodded. "No problem."

Ryan and I got back in the Charger. I started driving us back toward headquarters.

"Shit, I was this close to getting the cord."

Ryan held up the electrical cord in his right hand. "This one?" Then he opened the palm of his left hand: it was filled with what looked like concrete dust.

"Very nice."

He pulled a couple of evidence bags out of his jacket pocket and placed the items in them. "Not so nice, really."

"Why, what's the matter?"

"They're inadmissible. No search warrant. The cord was not visible. Besides, we were on private property, uninvited."

"Well, Max Thomas might not know that. Anyway, it confirms my hunch."

"It's evidence for your hunch. Plenty of reasons a tree guy could have electrical cord and concrete dust in the bed of his pickup. And we'd have to do more work to confirm that the tire treads are a match."

He was right, so I gave him a nasty look. "Okay, if the electric cord is inadmissible—even though I bet it has Cory's DNA on it—we'll just get Max to confess."

"Darn, I should have thought of that."

"Yeah, you should've. Let's go visit Max. Any idea where he is?"

He glanced at his watch. "I know exactly where he is." He just looked at me.

"Well?" I looked at him. "You're not gonna tell me?"

"It's three o'clock on a balmy Saturday afternoon in the fall." He paused. "Just to be clear: That's a hint."

I kept looking at him. "What the hell does the weather have to do with anything?"

"Where might a college football coach be at three o'clock on a balmy Saturday afternoon in the fall?"

"Okay, glad I saved it up: You're an asshole."

Heading over to Cougar Stadium, we worked out our strategy.

The closest we could park was about a hundred yards from Entrance D. The lot was filled with hundreds of cars, pickups, and RVs of all shapes and sizes. Interspersed among the vehicles were portable picnic tables sitting under shade tents on four metal poles. People were cooking on grills, drinking beers from coolers, and watching TVs. Kids were tossing footballs. It was like the city was holding a giant cookout in a huge parking lot, and everyone came.

We shielded our way into the stadium at Entrance D. Ryan led me toward the field and out into the sun. The stadium was full, the noise deafening. The phony plastic grass under my feet was vibrating from twenty-eight thousand people shouting and stomping their feet. The marching bands in the stands played little bursts of music. Cheerleaders did their acrobatics and whipped up the crowd, which obediently cheered on cue. After each play, a booming baritone voice on the PA system announced what had just happened. Then, the big video displays in the two end zones showed the play, and the crowd cheered or booed a second time.

Shirtless college-age boys with their faces painted blue and gold shouted and whooped and high-fived each other. There were dozens of Darth Vaders, Spidermen, Batmen, and even a few Wonder Women. Foam fingers and plastic picket fences were everywhere. Guys shouted through long plastic horns; some fans blasted air horns. Everyone was eating something. There were nachos covered in cheese. Hot dogs, bags of peanuts, sodas. Tall plastic cups of beer. Thousands of cups of beer.

Ryan shouted in my ear. "Follow me." We walked along the edge of the field, where the artificial turf met the base of the concrete stands. The CMSU football staff were clustered around the forty-yard line. "There he is."

"Got it," I said. "Your phone's ready?"

Ryan retrieved his phone from a rear pocket in his jeans and slid it up the right sleeve of his sweatshirt. "Yep."

"Okay, let's go." We approached Max Thomas, who was talking with another staff member and a couple of hulking players. He jabbed at his tablet and yelled something to the players, who were leaning in. I tapped Max on the shoulder. He looked up and recognized us.

"Mr. Thomas, we need to talk to you." I kept it clipped and official.

"You gotta be kidding." He put his hands out in a gesture of exasperation. "This really isn't a good time."

"It'll take just a couple minutes."

"After the game?"

"No, now. Here or at headquarters."

"Let me tell the coach." He wove his way through the mass of players and staff, equipment boys and girls with water bottles with long straws, and a small cluster of VIPs with plastic visitor badges around their necks. I spotted A.D. Freedlander chatting with Carl Davis. Max Thomas sidled up to Coach Baxter and spoke into his ear. The coach turned and craned his head. When he spotted me and Ryan, he gave us a really nasty look. The two talked for a moment, then the coach waved his hand dismissively to tell Max to go with us.

Max made his way back to me and Ryan. "This way," I said, pointing to the tunnel that leads to the locker rooms. Max walked alongside me, with Ryan following.

The crowd let out a huge roar. Max stopped, looked up at the video screen, and waited for the replay. A Cougar linebacker had tackled the other team's runner for a big loss. The runner was lying on his back. When he finally moved his legs, the crowd applauded because he was apparently okay. Trainers trotted out from the sidelines. Max smiled.

We started walking again and made it a few yards into the empty tunnel. "You're busy, so I'll get right to it. We figured out who killed Lake, and we're gonna arrest him this afternoon. When we do that, the shit's gonna spray all over the football program. We know you're a good guy, so we wanted to give you a heads-up."

"My God."

"Yeah, it's pretty upsetting. There's some bad guys in the program and, unfortunately, it's gonna screw up some good guys like you."

"Who killed Lake?" Max Thomas said. The noise in the tunnel wasn't quite as loud as it was out on the field, but an annoying echo made it hard to understand him.

"First we thought it was Kendra Crimmons, but we determined she was just a courier. She needed money. That was all she cared about: money to buy dope. That's how she got into this. She actually liked Lake, used to sleep with him off and on. She didn't have a motive for killing him."

"Then someone killed her." Max leaned in to make it easier for me to hear him.

"Exactly. We thought it was Cory McDermott, your old teammate. We figured he killed Kendra and Lake. You know, so nobody could finger him for supplying the drugs. But that didn't set right, for the same reason: He didn't have a motive to kill Lake in the first place. He was a drug dealer. He didn't want to kill his customers; he wanted to keep them alive."

"Then someone killed Cory," Max Thomas said. "One guy killed all three, right?"

I smiled at him. "Yeah, one guy killed all three of them."

"Who was it?"

"Ronald Weber. You know, Alicia's father? He confessed to us that he's been the team's fixer for years—this is where you come in."

His expression darkened. "What do you mean?"

"I'm sorry. Didn't mean to suggest you're involved in that. I meant this is the part that's gonna mess you up. We've discovered that A.D. Freedlander and Coach Baxter have been working with Weber all these years. They know all about Weber supplying drugs and girls to the players. They're going down. It'll take a few days, but it's gonna break big. I don't mean Rawlings big; I mean nationally."

"Did he confess to killing Lake?"

"Not yet, but he will. Cory McDermott's body was discovered

out at this job site where Weber and his crew work. Plus, the construction manager saw Weber in the vicinity right at the time of the murder."

"What was his motive?"

"It was Lake raping his daughter. We know Weber threatened Lake in front of a bunch of people. The other two victims? That was just cleanup. Because, in my experience, it's very rare that a killer says, Yeah, I did it, and I'm willing to pay the price. Most killers are cowards, and they don't want to be caught."

"So you're going to arrest Weber this afternoon?"

"Yeah, that's the plan."

Ryan began to cough. "Excuse me," he said. He turned away from us, coughing into his fist. I didn't see him slide his phone down from his sleeve. Max didn't see it, either.

"Where were we?" I said.

"You said you're going to arrest Weber this afternoon."

My phone rang at just the right time. I pulled it out of my jacket pocket and looked at the screen. "Excuse me a second." I held up a finger. "I have to take this—it's the manager at the construction site where Cory's body was found." I half-turned away from Max but spoke loud enough for him to hear me in the tunnel. "Yes, Mr. Stoughton." I listened a bit. There was so much crowd noise I didn't worry that Max would realize I wasn't talking to anybody. It was enough that my phone was lit up. "Okay, Mr. Stoughton, that's great. Appreciate it." I ended the call.

I turned back to Max Thomas. "Could you just give me another second here? He said he sent me the CCTV video from when Cory was killed. It shows the pickup truck driving into the materials-storage area. It's only, like, ten seconds, he said, but it shows the license plate clearly."

Max stepped in toward me so fast I couldn't duck out of the way. The last thing I saw was a huge forearm coming at my face. I felt the impact and my head snapped back. It lifted me off my feet, and I felt myself flying. Then I felt another crack as my head hit the concrete tunnel wall. I slid down the wall and collapsed onto the floor. My head started to buzz.

I got onto my hands and knees. Ryan was calling out my name. "I'm okay," I said. "Go." I grabbed at the concrete wall and struggled to my feet. Max had already run out of the tunnel; Ryan was following him, maybe twenty yards behind. I grabbed my phone off the tunnel floor and ran out into the sun and the noise. It sounded like thunderclaps, real close to me, one right after the other. The light was a thousand suns piercing my eyes. I had double vision and both images were blurry, but I thought I made out Ryan pursuing Max Thomas up the concrete steps in the stands.

I felt like I was going to pass out. Waves of nausea rose in my throat, and my legs were rubbery, but I kept going, pulling myself up the concrete steps with the metal handrail down the center of the aisle. The steps kept changing height, or at least it seemed that way to me. I pushed past people on the steps. I knocked one guy hard, and when his beer cup went flying out of his hand, he screamed "Bitch" into my face.

Max was headed full speed toward the Cougar Skybox, a big grey metal structure sitting on top of the bleachers. The Skybox, which housed a restaurant and the luxury boxes, was where the rich fans sat, warm and out of the weather, as they dined and watched the game through the glass.

I followed, as fast as I could, pushing past the people on the steps, falling farther behind every second. A door opened, and Max disappeared into the Skybox; a few seconds later, Ryan made it into the Skybox. Finally, after what seemed like minutes, I heaved the heavy door open and staggered inside, to where the boxes were.

There were clusters of comfortable arm chairs with attached tables, the clusters separated from each other by thin walls. The people in the boxes were standing, their expressions confused and concerned. "Where did they go?" I shouted. They pointed to the passageway that led to the restaurant.

I rushed in. Nobody was seated at the tables. Four students dressed in crisp white shirts and black slacks were setting up the tables in preparation for the formal meal service after the game. When they saw me, they pointed to the far end of the restaurant. I rushed in that direction. A hallway led to the bathrooms. Off to the side, a neon sign read, "Emergency Exit." I pushed open the door. It was a metal staircase. I stood there a second on the metal steps, listening and trying to feel any vibrations in the metal handrail that would tell me whether they had gone up or down. Then I realized that Max was leading Ryan up onto the roof. He was going to kill Ryan up there.

I pulled myself up the long flight of stairs and burst through the door. The roof, covered in fine gravel, was cluttered with all kinds of vents and fans and AC condensers and other mechanical crap I couldn't identify. I scanned the roof but didn't see the two guys. I pulled my pistol, flicked off the safety, and got into a crouch.

It was ten seconds that felt like ten minutes before I spotted them, forty yards away, diagonally across the rooftop. I approached as quickly and quietly as I could, but they were moving around faster than I could keep up with them. I knew Ryan was expert at Krav Maga but had also studied karate. And I knew Max was a black belt in karate.

The two men were feeling each other out, about five yards apart, advancing and retreating together like fencers. I saw a lot of punches, most of them blocked. There was a flurry of front and side kicks, a few spin kicks. It didn't look like either of the two guys was hurt badly. They seemed evenly matched. Every few seconds they would vanish behind some metal equipment sticking out of the roof.

When Ryan eased into the Krav Maga fighting stance, with his left leg forward and his arms bent, hands open in front of his face, I knew he had decided to attack. He rushed at Max Thomas, who retreated. The sounds of flesh hitting flesh mixed with grunting and groaning as the punches and kicks landed. They were in tight now, like boxers, and moving so quickly I couldn't risk squeezing off a round. Ryan took a punch to the face, his head snapping back. I got into a boxer stance, left foot forward, the one they'd taught us in the academy, so I could take out Max if I had a clean shot.

The two men disappeared behind a big silver hunk of curved ductwork over near the edge of the roof. I couldn't see either of them. As I was rushing to get into position to take a shot at Max, I heard a long, high-pitched scream that trailed off, then silence. I spun around but didn't see anyone. I raced over to the raised edge of the roof, which was only about three feet tall, and leaned over.

Five stories below, on a ribbon of grass ringing the Skybox, a small crowd of people were gathered around a motionless body that had landed on top of a large nylon tailgate tent that had torn free of its support poles. I could barely make out "Cougar Athletic Association" written in large letters on the front of the tent. In the middle of the tent, partially covering the cougar logo, lay the victim, a circle of blood pooling under his head.

People were screaming, frantically pushing aside the picnic table, chairs, coolers, grills, and the generator that surrounded the tent. I grabbed my phone and dialed in the 911. My vision was still fuzzy. I couldn't make out who the victim was. "Ryan," I shouted. "Ryan." Nobody on the ground seemed to hear me over the crowd noise and the metallic roar from the stadium speakers.

"What is it, Karen?" It came from behind me. I recognized Ryan's voice immediately cutting through the din. I started to break down. I rushed over to him and hugged him. He groaned and pulled my arms off and pushed me away. "Think I've got a couple of fractured ribs." His face was covered in pink bruises and welts. His left eye was starting to close up.

"Where the fuck was your pistol?"

"I came in to talk to the university president. I wasn't planning to shoot him."

"Probably half the people in the stands are carrying." I slapped him as hard as I could on the arm. "Next time you leave the house without your pistol, I'll shoot you myself."

"Understood, Detective." Ryan smiled, then winced and touched his jaw. "Ow."

# Chapter 32

Ryan and I rushed down to the Cougar Athletic Association tent. We set it up like a windbreak so that Max Thomas's body was hidden from the dozens of fans streaming past. In a few minutes, the ambulance and a detail from the department arrived. We briefed the officers. They wanted to call in another ambulance to take us over to the hospital, but we decided it would be faster to walk the hundred yards back to the Charger and drive there ourselves.

Ryan insisted on driving in case I threw up or passed out or something. Now that the adrenaline had started to wear off, the pain settled in. I felt the cheekbone where Max Thomas slugged me; it was sore but not broken. I touched the golf-ball lump on the right side of my head, where I hit the tunnel wall. My head was pounding, the sunlight shining off car windows blinding. Ryan put on the lights but turned off the siren.

Any time a suspect hurts a cop in the line of duty, it's a big deal. For one thing, the department has to figure out what kind of charge to add on to the existing charges. Even if the suspect is dead, you write it up anyway because sometimes the dead guy's people will sue you for excessive force.

The other reason police departments take cop injuries seriously is that there can be issues about worker's compensation or limited duty. The department needs to get all the medical facts out on the table in case there's a question about whether the cop can return to work and, if so, when and in what capacity.

For those reasons, I didn't fight it when Ryan told the attending ER doc what had happened to me and asked them to do a concussion workup. While a nurse led me off, I heard the doc ask Ryan what happened to him.

They put me in a wheelchair and rolled me over to get a CT scan and some kind of vision test. It involved watching a video through a machine while they looked at my eye movements through another machine to see if my two eyes were working together. Apparently, if your eyes don't point in the same direction, that's strong evidence of a concussion. I knew my eyes were screwed up because I still had double vision. Turns out I did have a concussion. They put me on some pain meds and gave me a few brochures telling me what to do about it.

While I sat around between procedures, I thought about Max Thomas. I'm not the kind of cop who gets all weepy when a killer goes down. I did wish we'd had a chance to talk with him about why he killed Lake, but I thought I understood the main outlines. Part of it, I'm sure, was that he believed he was protecting Alicia's honor: If Lake's video went public, it would hurt her. Part of it might have been jealousy. He had envied and hated Lake for more than seven years. Now Lake was back—and back in Alicia's life. Maybe he thought he was losing Alicia to Lake a second time.

So he decided to kill Lake. He knew Cory McDermott from their days on the team. He must have approached Cory and lied to him about how Ronald Weber needed to get some uncut heroin to Lake in the homeless camp. Cory knew the perfect courier: Kendra Crimmons, a hopeless junkie without an ounce of curiosity or imagination. So Cory slipped some loser a few bucks to make the deal with Kendra under the overpass out at the skate park. She signed on, and Max delivered the heroin to her that night out at Ten Mile Park.

Then, when Max found out that Kendra hadn't OD'ed with Lake and was talking to us, he realized he had to kill her. She was

easy to find, and easy to lure into a truck. Then there was only
one person left who could identify Max: Cory McDermott. At
first, Max thought all he needed to do to keep Cory quiet was beat
the crap out of him. But then Max learned that Coach Baxter,
A.D. Freedlander, and even Carl Davis were getting all agitated
about the cops talking to Cory. That was when Max decided he
had to kill Cory right away.

I didn't know when Max came up with the idea of framing
Ronald Weber for Cory's murder. Max knew that Weber was the
team's fixer, and that Cory was his main connection. And Max
probably assumed a clueless woman cop like me would fall for the
frame. Besides, framing Ronald Weber would be appropriate
revenge. After all, instead of being a good father to Alicia seven
years ago, Weber had decided to be the good team player in
making sure Lake didn't get in trouble and miss any games.

Sitting in the wheelchair in the hospital, my head pounding, I
tried to figure out how I got everything so wrong about the case. I
was pretty sure the football guys had killed Lake because he was
going to do something that would hurt them. The theory made
sense. After all, if Lake had dragged himself to one of the local
TV stations and told his story on camera, there was no telling
how badly that would have damaged the football program. There
were thousands of local fans who remembered Lake when he
could play. If they saw him in his present state, all busted up and
incoherent, that would have been trouble. No, the football guys
couldn't take that risk. Lake would have to die a junkie, not a guy
with CTE.

But that wasn't what happened. The football guys—from Carl
Davis to John Freedlander to Andy Baxter—were bad guys. Ryan
and I were right about that. They broke every rule in the NCAA
book, and they turned their backs on Lake, just as they turned
their backs on any player who couldn't help them anymore. But
they were cold and calculating. Toss some cash at the players? No

problem. Buy them recreational drugs? Of course. Arrange for
some hookers when the high-school seniors came to town?
Absolutely. Just do it quietly, and don't write anything down.
Cash is king. In plain envelopes, please. But kill someone? That
wasn't their style. They played the odds, weighed the risks. Better
to slam the door in Lake's face. He'd probably be dead in a few
days, anyway.

No, killing Lake, and then Kendra and Cory, called for a
passion the football guys didn't have. They exploited passion, but
they didn't feel it themselves. Max Thomas felt it. Max Thomas—
well-behaved, dependable Max—was still in love with Alicia and
still hated Lake Williams. And he was still crazy. He was the killer.

My head was hurting pretty bad at this point, and I threw up a
few times. A nurse saw I wasn't doing too well and got me some
kind of sedative and something to calm my stomach down. In a
little while I drifted off into a restless sleep. The doctor admitted
me, and I tried to settle in for the night.

A few hours later, Ryan called and we talked for a few
minutes. He had been released earlier and had already briefed
Chief Murtaugh. The department issued a statement saying that
Max Thomas, a graduate student and a member of the Central
Montana State University football staff, had died in a fall after
assaulting two detectives and resisting arrest in connection with
the murders of LaKadrian Williams, Kendra Crimmons, and Cory
McDermott. The statement did not get into motive.

The doctor discharged me the next morning. Ryan and I were
both cleared to return to work full time on Wednesday. That day,
we met with the chief and Larry Klein, the prosecutor, to discuss
how to wrap up the case. We had already told President
Billingham that his guys were dirty, but that was before we got
our hands on Alicia's cellphone video of Lake's meeting with her,
and before Max Thomas died.

Larry wanted us to ask Alicia's permission before we did

anything with the video. We all agreed that was the right thing to do. I couldn't quite follow the discussion about who actually had the legal right to use the video, but, as far as I was concerned, it was her property because she took the video on her phone.

I met with Alicia privately later in the week. It didn't take any arm-twisting to get her to give us permission to hand the video to President Billingham. She knew that the football program was dirty—not dirty because it violated NCAA regulations or conference rules or anything like that. It was dirty in that it exploited the players. She told me to do whatever I wanted with the video; she trusted me on that. I told her that if President Billingham chose to make it public, it might upset her family. She thought about it for a moment. "If it does, it does," she said.

The next day, the chief, Ryan, and I met with President Billingham, who sat there silently, his eyes wet with tears, as he watched the video of Lake stumbling through his story. We handed him the video and told him Alicia said he could do whatever he wanted with it. When the chief asked him if he had any questions, the president said no in a quiet voice, thanked us for stopping by, and shook our hands.

A couple of days later, the university announced some personnel changes. Carl Davis was stepping down as president of the Cougar Athletic Association. Athletic Director John Freedlander was retiring, effective immediately. And Coach Andy Baxter had resigned. When the press questioned the coach in a news conference that aired that night, he said he wanted to pursue other opportunities, and he had decided not to take his salary for the remaining three and a half years of his five-year contract. The sports reporter said a lot of people were caught off guard when Coach Baxter announced he would resign in the middle of a successful season. But, the reporter said with a broad smile, nobody was surprised that a man of Andy Baxter's character would give up his salary for the good of the university.

I never did find out how President Billingham got Coach Baxter to walk away from his remaining salary, but I assume that was the price the president exacted for not releasing the video of Lake.

I asked the chief if he was going to work with Larry Klein to bring any charges against Ronald Weber for distributing dangerous drugs and promoting prostitution. He said he made the offer, but Larry didn't think there was much he could do unless Weber wanted to come in and give him a list of particulars of his crimes.

About a week later, Alicia Templeton called to invite me to go for coffee with her. I didn't know exactly what she wanted, but I said yes. We met at a place near her office. She asked me about my injury and about Ryan.

"We're fine." The hissing from one of the fancy coffee machines drowned out the light jazz coming out of the speakers on the ceiling. "I've still got some headaches and sensitivity to light, but I'll be okay. And my partner has some bruises and busted ribs. Hardest thing for him was not coming in to work for a few days."

A couple of businesswomen my age came in and ordered some cappuccinos to go. They were talking loudly. A young guy working at his laptop looked up, annoyed.

"Your dad doing better?"

Alicia took a deep breath and exhaled slowly. "He's still in the hospital. I go over there every day. We've had some good talks. But it's hard. He's still crying all the time about what he did—you know, when I accused Lake of rape. I try to assure him that I understand he was under a lot of pressure at the time, and how I don't blame him."

"That's a good attitude you've got."

She took a long moment. "I want him to get better," she said. "His apology was heartfelt, and I want him to get better."

She hadn't quite worked out the language, but I think she did realize that he had let her down badly. I decided to change the subject. "When you told Max that Lake had come to see you, how did he respond?"

"He said it was terrible what had happened to Lake, and that he would do anything he could to help him."

"And you thought he was going to help you convince the coach to get Lake into some kind of program?"

She shook her head, like she was a fool for not knowing Max's real intentions. "I had no reason to think Max would want to hurt Lake."

"Max never told you how he felt about you?"

"Never. He never said anything like that." She paused. "But you know how sometimes you can tell from how a guy looks at you? For just a second, I thought I saw it in his eyes. I remember thinking that if he had feelings for me maybe he would try to help Lake." She shook her head. "I really screwed up."

"That's ridiculous," I said. "I'm sure you've had guys coming on to you since you were fourteen. There's no way you could tell which ones were crazy."

"Nice of you to say that."

"So Coach Baxter and the A.D. were telling the truth that they had nothing to do with killing Lake or the two others," I said.

"Yeah, that's true. And Carl Davis, too. But the only thing I really care about is that my dad had nothing to do with it. I knew that about him. I knew that all along. He couldn't have hurt anyone."

"That's really good," I said to her.

She was looking down at her cup of coffee. "I wanted to ask you something." She raised her gaze.

"Sure."

"Couple of nights ago I had a talk with my husband."

"Yeah?"

"I'd never told him anything about my relationship with Lake. I laid it all out—the pregnancy, the adoption, everything." The tears came now.

"What happened?"

"He moved out yesterday."

"I'm sorry to hear that." I took a second. "It could be the shock of learning all that stuff at once. When he has a chance to let it sink in and think about it …"

"Are you married, Karen?"

"Used to be."

"What do you think I should do?"

I half-smiled. "I'm the last person you want to come to for marriage advice. I screwed up my marriage—and every other relationship I've ever had with a man."

"What should I do?"

"Tell me what you've been doing this week."

"Nothing. I've spent a lot of time at the hospital. I showed some houses. Took my daughter to a birthday party."

I raised my eyebrows. "That's what I would do."

She looked disappointed, like she was hoping for a plan. "My husband knows that I love him. But I told him I used to love Lake. If he can't deal with that … well, he'll have to decide what he wants to do. If he wants to come back, then I'll have to decide if I want him back." She took a deep breath and brushed a strand of hair back behind her ear. "One way or another," she said, trying to smile, "I guess I'll have to let it work itself out."

Which was smarter than anything I could have told her. "It will work itself out. It'll take some time. But you're gonna be okay, Alicia."

###

# *About the Author*

Mike Markel is the author of the Detectives Seagate and Miner Mystery series:

*Big Sick Heart* (Book 1)
*Deviations* (Book 2)
*The Broken Saint* (Book 3)
*Three-Ways* (Book 4)
*Fractures* (Book 5)
*The Reveal* (Book 6)
*Players* (Book 7)

He lives in Boise, Idaho, with his wife.

Thank you for taking time to read *Players: A Detectives Seagate and Miner Mystery*. If you enjoyed it, please consider telling your friends or posting a short review. Word of mouth is an author's best friend.

MikeMarkel.com

# The Detectives Seagate and Miner Mystery Series

To sample or buy any of these titles, visit Mike Markel's author page on Amazon.

Visit MikeMarkel.com.

### BIG SICK HEART (Book 1)

Bad decisions have finally caught up with police detective Karen Seagate. Her drinking has destroyed her marriage and hurt her job performance, and the chief is looking for any excuse to fire her. Still, she and her new partner, a young Mormon guy who seems to have arrived from another century or another planet, intend to track down whoever killed Arlen Hagerty, the corrupt leader of Soul Savers. Clawing his way to the top, Hagerty created plenty of enemies, including his wife, his mistress, his debate partner, the organization's founder, and the politician he was blackmailing. When Seagate causes a car crash that sends a young girl to Intensive Care, the chief thinks he finally has his opportunity. But even the chief can't believe what Seagate does when she finally catches the killer.

### DEVIATIONS (Book 2)

Former police detective Karen Seagate is drinking herself to oblivion and having dangerous sex with losers from the bar when the new police chief tracks her down. The brutal rape and murder of a state senator by a lone-wolf extremist gives Seagate a chance to return to the department, but the new chief has set down some rules, and Seagate is not good with rules. At this point, she is just trying to stay alive. With nothing left to lose and nobody left to trust—not even her partner, Ryan—Seagate goes off the grid to find the killer. She doesn't care that she will be fired again. She has much bigger problems, now that she has been captured inside the neo-Nazi compound.

## THE BROKEN SAINT (Book 3)

Seagate and Miner investigate the murder of Maricel Salizar, a young Filipino exchange student at Central Montana State. The most obvious suspect is her boyfriend, who happens to have gang connections. And then there's Amber, a fellow student who's obviously incensed at Maricel for a sexual indiscretion involving Amber's boyfriend. But the evidence keeps leading Seagate and Miner back to the professor, an LDS bishop who hosted her in his dysfunctional home. Seagate takes it in stride that the professor can't seem to tell the truth about his relationship with the victim, but her devout partner, Ryan Miner, believes that a high-ranking fellow Mormon who violates a sacred trust deserves special punishment.

## THREE-WAYS (Book 4)

When grad student Austin Sulenka is found strangled, nude on his bed, the first question for Seagate and Miner is whether it was an auto-asphyxiation episode gone bad. Evidence strewn around his small apartment suggests that he spent his last night with three or four women, each of whom had a motive to kill him. Later, when one of the women is pulled from the reservoir with a bullet in her brain, Seagate and Miner wonder which victim was the prime target—and whether there will be more. As Seagate and her partner try to unravel the complicated couplings, she finds herself in a three-way relationship that threatens to destroy her own fragile sobriety.

## FRACTURES (Book 5)

The fracking boom in eastern Montana has minted a handful of new millionaires and one billionaire: Lee Rossman, the president of Rossman Mining and the leading philanthropist in the small city of Rawlings. Rossman is the last person Detectives Seagate and Miner expected to discover dead in the alley next to a strip club. Later, when Lee's son is found out at the rigs, with significant internal injuries, numerous broken bones, and a belly full of fracking liquid, the detectives know the two crimes are related but can't figure out how. Seagate and Miner must try to solve a mystery awash in enormous fortunes, thwarted ambitions, and grudges both old and new.

## THE REVEAL (Book 6)

Many citizens in the small college town of Rawlings, Montana, were unsurprised to learn that Virginia Rinaldi, the world-famous sociologist, was murdered. A few were secretly pleased. Her political enemies knew her as an ideologue who used insults, threats, and blackmail to promote her unpopular social views. When Detectives Seagate and Miner begin their investigation, they discover that a local prostitute had recently moved into the professor's house, angering Rinaldi's college-age son. And when the community learns that the prostitute made a lesbian porn video with one of Rinaldi's students, tensions on campus erupt, leading to more bloodshed. Drawn into a horrifying world of sexual violence and exploitation, Seagate devises a plan to flush out the killer. The plan appears to be on track—until Seagate unwittingly jeopardizes the life of her partner, Ryan Miner.

### PLAYERS (Book 7)

The death of Lake Williams, a former football player at Central Montana State, in his squalid tent in a homeless camp looks to Seagate and Miner like a routine heroin overdose. Soon, however, they discover that someone hired a courier to deliver the uncut heroin, knowing that Lake would shoot up and die instantly. When a second body turns up, and then a third, the evidence points to the head coach and the other leaders of the football program, who appear to be covering up a secret that would destroy the program. When a man comes forward, claiming to have committed numerous felonies on behalf of the program over many years, the detectives don't know whether he is the killer or merely a decoy in an elaborate misdirection play. In a heart-pounding final confrontation, Seagate and Miner confront the killer—and realize they have walked right into the trap.

###

70852902R00166

Made in the USA
Middletown, DE
18 April 2018